UKULELE OF DEATH

UKULELE OF DEATH

E.J. Copperman

**SEVERN
HOUSE**

First world edition published in Great Britain and the USA in 2023
by Severn House, an imprint of Canongate Books Ltd,
14 High Street, Edinburgh EH1 1TE.

Trade paperback edition first published in Great Britain and the USA in 2023
by Severn House, an imprint of Canongate Books Ltd.

severnhouse.com

British Library Cataloguing-in-Publication Data
A CIP catalogue record for this title is available from the British Library.

ISBN-13: 978-1-4483-0970-2 (cased)
ISBN-13: 978-1-4483-1233-7 (trade paper)
ISBN-13: 978-1-4483-1049-4 (e-book)

Typeset by Palimpsest Book Production Ltd.,
Falkirk, Stirlingshire, Scotland.

For everyone who ever felt . . . different.

And with apologies to Mary Wollstonecraft Shelley.

AUTHOR'S NOTES

This is – get ready – my 30th published novel. That wipes me out every time I consider it. Your mileage may vary. It's been a long and twisty road. From the first three Aaron Tucker books from Bancroft Press through Elliot Freed and his movie theater, the Haunted Guesthouse series, the detours of Duffy Madison and Rachel Goldman (with her menagerie) to our own Sandy Moss and entourage, I've never known what was next and I still don't. I sort of like it that way.

But given that this is a chance to look back, let's go all the way back. Thank you to Bruce Bortz for making me a published author 21 years ago. Thanks of course to Shannon Jamieson Vazquez for reading NIGHT OF THE LIVING DEED and telling Berkley it should be a series (and for teaching me how to really write a novel). Thank you to Christina Hogrebe for getting that book to Shannon.

Thank you to Crooked Lane for picking up the Guesthouse series for two extra novels and for launching Duffy, even if he didn't get very far. And to Marsha Markham for listening to a one-sentence pitch for the Agent to the Paws series and saying, "Sold."

But let's get back to the present. Sandy Moss exists and continues because of the fine people at Severn House, chiefly Rachel Slatter and Kate Lyall Grant. Sandy had been waiting a while to tell her story, but they loved it and decided you might enjoy it too.

And Rachel also liked meeting Fran and Ken Stein, and that's why you're reading this book. Sure it's weirder than usual, but Rachel saw the humanity in these almost-humans and laughed, turned pages and got this story to you. I hope it's everything she thought it might be.

The hero of the story, as ever, is Josh Getzler and all at HG Literary. Josh brings me down off the ledge when I'm sure I'll never sell a book ever again and encourages my personal strangeness that led to Fran and Ken.

The people who most keep this author sane (if you use that word in a flexible manner) are Jessica, Josh and Eve. They are invaluable, which given the odd language we use, means really valuable. They are my real world. The one in my head has people like Fran and Ken, and they're lovely, but high-maintenance.

The most heartfelt thanks are for all the booksellers, librarians and (especially) readers. Without you I'm some bizarre human ranting about imaginary people. Never feel like you're not valued.

It's been a crazy first 30 books, but I think I'm starting to get good at this.

E.J. Copperman
Deepest New Jersey
November, 2022

ONE

When Evelyn Bannister first asked me to find her ukulele, I thought she was kidding.

I realize that our economic times are not fabulous, and a working private investigator should probably take any job that's offered, but it was hard to believe that Evelyn, who was tall, tailored, and trim, would need a detective to find a small Hawaiian stringed instrument.

'You want us to find what?' I asked. Clearly I'd misheard her and now she would make her request more clear.

'A ukulele, Ms Stein,' Evelyn insisted, looking me straight in the eye, which was possible only because we were both seated. Evelyn was tall; I was *really* tall. There's a difference. 'It's very rare and quite valuable, but that's not why I'm interested in finding it.'

'You realize that our specialty is helping people find their birth parents,' I reminded her. It's not the only thing we do, but it is what we do most often.

Evelyn nodded. 'And that's why I came here. I think the uke might be the key to finding my father.'

Ooooookaaaay . . . Actually, I'd heard weirder stories before. I couldn't think of one at the moment (aside from my own), but I was sure I had. 'How's that?' I asked in my best business voice.

My brother Ken and I had opened K&F Stein Investigations after I'd received my master's degree in criminal justice from Fordham University. It wasn't that I couldn't find a job with a city, state, or federal agency – I'd had offers – it was more that I wanted to help people like us who had never met their birth parents. Ken and I technically never would, but I'll get to that shortly.

Ken had been working on the docks at Port Elizabeth in New Jersey, exercising his absurdly strong body and putting his mind on hold. My brother is a wildly handsome, brawny man, and at the age of twenty-six, was more interested in letting women discover that than planning a serious career for himself, so I took it upon myself to create one for him.

'I'm opening a detective agency, and I need someone who can back me up if things get physical,' I'd told him one night at the apartment he was sharing with two other guys and one very open-minded girl near the South Street Seaport.

Ken looked me up and down and let out a sound like *pfff*. 'Dude,' he said, despite the fact that I'm not one, 'I'm pretty sure you can take care of yourself.'

I couldn't really argue that point; besides being unusually tall and a little muscular for a woman, I was also trained in three martial arts, and was a black belt in two. I'd never been in a situation in which I'd felt the slightest bit physically threatened, at least not since the fifth grade, when a high-school kid tried to take my friend Patty's bike and I'd left him panting on the sidewalk saying something like – no, on second thought, saying something *exactly* like – 'Please just don't hurt me. Please.'

'I can, but there's only one of me,' I said to Ken now. 'Besides, do you want to unload ships for the rest of your life? Here's a chance to be partners in a business. You get half the profits.'

'Or half the losses when the place goes belly up,' Ken said, opening a beer from the third-hand refrigerator. 'You've never run a detective agency. What do you know about it?'

'I know how to do research, I understand the legal system, and I'm tied into some government databases through friends I met during the program,' I told him. 'I know how it feels to be left on your own and not know who your family is. I know the nagging questions that come with parents who aren't there when you're growing up. And I know about office space I can get really cheap on 25th Street over a Jewish deli.'

Ken plopped himself down on a sofa that, once he'd landed on it, looked like a child's armchair. He took a long pull on his beer, so long in fact that it was empty before he spoke again. 'I wouldn't mind coming home at night and not smelling like Port Elizabeth,' he said. Ken's also a deep thinker. It's not that he's unintelligent – he's actually very smart – but he's, let's say, intellectually lazy. If there's a game, any game, on TV or a certain type of woman (breathing) nearby, he can be a little distracted.

'Right. You'd be here in Manhattan, you'd be a full partner, and you'd be doing work that will help people like us.'

His eyes focused sharply on me. 'There are no people like us,' he reminded me.

I tilted my head to the right to concede the point. 'People who have concerns similar to ours,' I corrected. Ken nodded, allowing me the distinction. 'And it'll only cost you a few thousand dollars to buy in.' I stood up, reaching out my hand for him to shake in agreement.

But I hadn't slipped that last point in sneakily enough; Ken sputtered and sat up with a jolt. 'A few thousand to *what*?' he asked. 'I've got to put up money for this wacky idea of yours?'

'I'm doing it too,' I pointed out. 'But I'm a little short on operating capital, and it's just while we get started.'

'Frannie,' my brother said, 'you have a way of only telling me the part of the story you think I want to hear.' His eyes narrowed. 'How much?'

There was no point in being coy. 'About eleven thousand. That's the security deposit on the office space, some furniture and a receptionist for a month.'

'Eleven grand!' Ken huffed. 'What are *you* putting in?'

'I'm still paying off student loans, Ken. I haven't been working for three years like you.'

He cocked his left eyebrow. 'So you're putting in nothing.'

I'll admit it – I avoided his glance. 'I wouldn't call it nothing,' I said. 'I'm paying for the first shipment of office supplies and having the place painted.' The landlord was having the place painted for nothing, but Ken didn't need to know that.

'So you need me for muscle and money,' Ken said, grinning. 'Not to mention negotiating advice, because the landlord should be paying to have the space painted.' Touché.

I put my hand on my hip. 'Are you in, or not?'

His grin got broader. 'What do you think?' he asked.

Evelyn Bannister nodded her understanding at my confusion. 'The ukulele in question is a Gibson Poinsettia, with hand-painted flowers and fret markers. It's quite rare and sought after by collectors.'

'How much is it worth?' I asked.

Evelyn seemed surprised by the question. 'I haven't the faintest idea,' she said.

'But you think somehow it can lead to your birth father?' I asked, trying to get some idea of the relevance of a small Hawaiian guitar to my job. 'You are adopted?'

She nodded. 'Bannister is the name of my adoptive parents, and they're the ones I've always known. It's really a question of curiosity for me.'

I was taking notes on my laptop. 'Why just your father?' I asked. 'Do you have some knowledge of your birth mother?'

'Yes,' Evelyn answered, her hand lightly grazing her forehead. It wasn't hot in the office, but Evelyn appeared to be a little damp around the hairline. I reached over and turned on a small electric fan positioned on a file cabinet. It's a classy operation I run. 'I met her last year, after I contacted the agency through which I was adopted. Her name is Melinda Cantone, and she lives in Bethesda, Maryland. She agreed to meet with me, but only in public, so I don't have her address.' Evelyn slid a file, which she dug out of a Louis Vuitton tote bag, across the desk to me. The vacillating fan made the cover of the file flutter a bit, and then vacillated out of position, and the cover lay down again.

'But your father was not willing to allow contact, is that it?' It's not unusual for birth parents to move on and not want to reconsider their choice to part with a child. Most of them are very young when they put the baby up for adoption. It's never an easy decision.

'That's right,' Evelyn answered. 'But I have questions I need answered, and he's the only one who can tell me. Will you help?'

'At this point, I need to find out if we *can* help before I can say if we will,' I told her. It's best to keep expectations realistic, especially when you don't know what you're talking about. 'Now, what do you know about your biological father?'

Evelyn seemed like she was concentrating very hard on her answer; her eyes narrowed to slits and her lips pursed just a little as she thought. 'The adoption agency wouldn't tell me much. You know, you can't even get a name when the parent doesn't consent. But my birth mother told me they never married. They were just a high-school thing.'

'And she wouldn't tell you his name, either,' I guessed.

'No. She said it was his choice. But she did tell me that he had moved out of Nashua, New Hampshire and made a lot of money here in New York on the stock exchange. Not like a billionaire or anything, but he's apparently quite wealthy.' Her long, elegant fingers seemed nervous; she had folded her hands but her fingers were fluttering.

'What's this ukulele thing all about?' I asked. 'Why is that a clue to your birth father's whereabouts?'

'Apparently he is a collector of rare stringed instruments. He has a guitar that once belonged to George Harrison and a harp that was played in a movie called *Duck Soup* by Harpo Marx.' Evelyn said 'Harpo Marx' like you'd say an unpronounceable name in another language. 'This ukulele, being so rare, was once in his possession. If you find it, perhaps you can trace it to its previous owners. Find the one who used to live in Nashua, and you'll find my birth father.' (For the record, there would be virtually no way to trace previous owners of an instrument, but there were other ways to track down where it might have been, starting with where it was right now. Whoever sold it this time would know where *they* had acquired the uke, and so on. It wasn't much, but it was something.)

I've worked on cases that were bigger leaps of logic, but not many. How many George Harrison guitars or Harpo Marx harps could there be? (Probably a decent number, actually.) Now was the time in the client intake interview where I perform a ritual: I take off my glasses (which are mostly for show, anyway — I see just fine, but people think you're smarter if you wear glasses), put down my pen, and look into the potential client's eyes with great meaning.

'Are you sure you want to meet a parent who has chosen not to meet you?' I asked Evelyn. 'You could be setting yourself up for a painful rejection.'

'I've thought about it a long time, Ms Stein,' she answered in a voice that had no waver to it. I pay attention to that. 'There are too many things I don't know. Medical histories, geographical origins, personality traits that might have been passed down. I don't need to jump into his lap and call him "Daddy." I have a father, and he's terrific. He just happens to not be my biological parent. That's OK. But I do want to look my birth father in the face and have a conversation. That's all.'

That was clearer and more reasonable than a lot of the arguments I get in this office. I picked up the pen again, but this time I handed it to Evelyn, along with a clipboard that had a form to be filled out. 'Well,' I told her, 'I don't know if we can help you, but we're certainly going to try.'

Evelyn, visibly relieved, thanked me profusely and set about filling out the form, which is four pages long and very thorough. I excused myself to give her a little privacy and myself a break, and walked to the inner office door, which I opened.

Inside, I closed the door quickly. Ken was sitting in a tattered armchair we'd actually found on the street. An electrical cord was plugged into an outlet a few feet from where he sat, and he had attached the other end to a small USB port that was implanted in his left side just under the armpit. He was reading a copy of *Maxim* with a picture of Kesha on the cover. A yellow light on the module plugged into the port indicated that he was charging.

'You took the case?' he asked without looking up.

'Yeah. How much longer are you on?' I pointed at the outlet.

'Another ten minutes, maybe. Why, do you need to plug in?'

'No. I did that yesterday.'

Maybe I should tell you a little more about us.

TWO

The first thing you need to know is: We're not robots. Ken and I have no mechanical parts; we're totally organic and human from head to toe. We started as babies and developed at the same rate as everybody else, I'm told. We're just not your general off-the-rack people like everyone else you meet in the street.

We were – how do I explain this – sort of put together rather than born. And there isn't that much more I know about it.

I first found out about our . . . unusual origins when I was nine years old and Ken was ten. We were being raised by the woman we call Aunt Margie in a three-bedroom up-and-down townhouse in Queens, and had settled into the idea, which I especially had believed all my life, that our parents had died in a car crash when I was less than two years old. I really had no memory of either of them, although Ken told me many times that he remembered our mother holding him when there was a thunderstorm and he was afraid (he still hates thunderstorms). Our father, he said, was a smallish man, which we thought was hilarious since we're both well above average in height.

Nine is an age when girls start becoming seriously aware of their own bodies, and in the shower one morning, I noticed a scar just over my left thigh that seemed to go all the way around my leg. It was very faint (and is barely visible now), but definitely there, so I asked Aunt Margie about it at breakfast that morning.

She was frying bacon at the stove, and didn't hear me the first time I asked because she had the exhaust fan on. 'What's that, Frannie?' she asked.

'I have a scar that goes all the way around my leg,' I repeated. 'Did I hurt myself when I was little?'

Aunt Margie's back was to me, but I saw it stiffen up. Immediately, I figured I had some rare form of cancer that manifested itself in a faint scar around the upper thigh, and that she'd been too heartbroken to tell me. How she would have received such information when I couldn't remember visiting a doctor in my life was not something I considered at nine.

It turned out there were a lot of things I hadn't considered at nine.

'You had a little *accident* when you were . . . three,' Aunt Margie answered. Even at that age, I could tell when she was lying. She's a terrible liar; she can't ever get the sentence out in one breath, and she stumbles over certain words, usually the key ones. Here, it was *accident*.

I took a chance, although I hadn't actually thought to check. 'I have one on each arm, too,' I said. 'Was it a bad accident?'

Aunt Margie, you have to understand, is a dear lady who was a radio news reporter in her youth, and at fifty-six was still doing five-minute updates for WOR-AM on weekend overnights, when almost no one was listening. If you live in the tri-state area you've probably heard her and didn't even know it. She said she just liked to keep her hand in it, and money never seemed to be a problem around our house, so I guessed she meant it.

'Oh, no,' she lied now. 'It was nothing, really. You fell off your tricycle. I'm surprised you don't remember.'

I looked closely at her; her pupils were slightly dilated, there were beads of sweat just at her hairline, and her mouth was slightly open, indicating that she was breathing through it, rather than through her nose.

'You're not telling the truth,' I said. 'Now, what *really* happened?'

Aunt Margie – it was never really clear whose sister she was supposed to be – was about to deny she was lying, but Ken, leaning in the doorway, cut her off. 'She's right,' he told Aunt Margie. 'All your vital signs indicate that you're telling her a lie. What's going on?'

I told him about the scar I'd discovered. 'Oh, I have scars all over,' he said casually. 'I figured we were in the car when our parents had the accident and the doctors had to stitch us back together.' Ken, at twelve, was cavalier about our parents and matters of danger or tragedy. He never considered anything to be serious.

We could both see the wheels turning in Aunt Margie's brain, although she took only a split second to turn toward him and point like a teacher whose pupil has hit upon the correct answer. 'Yes, that's it exactly,' she said, her voice less convincing than when she would read radio ad copy promising that discounted Lasik eye surgery was 'one hundred percent proven foolproof.' 'I didn't want to mention it because I thought you'd be upset.'

'You thought we'd be upset?' I echoed. 'Aunt Margie, you're a very bad liar. Why don't you sit down here and tell us whatever it is you're holding back.' I pointed to an open kitchen chair.

'I can't,' she protested. 'I'm making breakfast.'

'I've seen you read news copy that someone had actually set on fire,' Ken said, walking all the way into the kitchen and sitting backwards on one of the chairs because he thought it made him look cool. Boys. 'You're saying you can't talk and scramble eggs at the same time?'

It took another eight minutes and seven seconds of arguing, but finally Aunt Margie, having whipped up two perfectly lovely plates of scrambled eggs and bacon, sat down at the table and agreed to 'fess up' on the condition that we eat. Neither Ken nor I had expressed any reluctance to chow down, so it was a very small concession on our parts.

Aunt Margie took a deep breath and looked around the kitchen as if she were trying to find a hidden exit she hadn't noticed before so she could avoid the coming conversation. There wasn't one, so she nodded once, having made her decision, and looked me straight in the eye. *Me*, not Ken.

'This is gonna be tough,' she said. 'For all three of us. But you're right. It's time you knew.'

Ken took on the goofiest grin I can ever remember seeing. 'Knew what?' he asked, with a tone that suggested he was about to get the real lowdown on James Bond's personal harem and how to get them into his room in an orderly fashion.

But Aunt Margie's face was serious, and even though my pre-adolescent brother didn't pick up on that, I did. 'You two aren't like other people,' she began. 'I'm guessing you noticed that.'

'We're big,' Ken said, his expression now one of confusion. Not only wasn't he getting Pussy Galore's personal mobile number, but he was being told he was weird. Maybe this wasn't going to be such a terrific surprise after all.

'Yes.' Aunt Margie nodded. 'But that's only a part of it.'

'You mean the ports,' I suggested, referring to the way we would plug ourselves into an electrical outlet for energy every few days. The truly bizarre thing was, it had never occurred to me before that moment that everybody didn't have one of those. 'We plug in.'

Aunt Margie pointed a finger like a gun barrel at me, indicating I was right. 'That's a big part. It's about the way you guys were . . . born.'

The way she said that rang an alarm in my nine-year-old head. There are times I think I am a natural detective. 'What does that mean?' I asked. 'Weren't we born like everybody else?'

'No,' Aunt Margie admitted. Ken looked like he had a foot of water over his head, but his looks can be deceiving; he was understanding what he heard and not liking it. 'You weren't. In fact, you weren't really born at all.'

That quieted down the room. Ken and I stared at each other. What did she *mean* we weren't born – we were right here! 'We were born,' Ken told Aunt Margie, addressing her like you would a person who had recently suffered a severe blow to the head. 'This is us.' And he gestured at himself and me, just to make sure she knew who we were.

'You're here and you're alive, but you weren't *born*, at least not in the literal sense,' Aunt Margie insisted. She shook her head. 'I'm being cryptic.' Before Ken could ask what that meant, she added. 'You guys were put together, created, rather than born like other babies.'

My mind was racing. *Put together?* 'We're not real people? We're robots?' I asked.

But I still wasn't understanding, apparently. Aunt Margie shook her head. 'No. There's nothing mechanical about you. You're human, all right, believe me. I changed a few of your diapers, and I can say it without hesitation.' There was an image I really didn't need.

'Look,' she continued. 'Don't ask questions for a while. Let me explain what happened.' And explain she did.

Our parents, whom we had always identified as George and Emily Stein, were neither George and Emily Stein nor our parents, at least in the biological sense, she said. They were a pair of scientists – a professor of genetics and biology at Rutgers

University and her husband, a physician specializing in neurology and thoracic surgery (he apparently was a genius and a showoff at the same time) who had exhibited an extraordinary talent for cosmetic surgery during a rotation at a hospital during his residency.

Aunt Margie said when she knew them, they were calling themselves Olivia Grey and Brandon Wilder, but she had discovered later those were aliases to help our parents (that's what I'm going to continue to call them, because that's how I think of them) elude people who were dogging their trail, with the implicit purpose of taking our parents – and Aunt Margie insisted, us – to an undisclosed location for 'further study.'

'I never found out who was coming after them, but Livvie and Brad were absolutely terrified of whoever it was,' she said. 'They were especially scared that you two would get found out and taken away.'

'How did you meet them?' I asked. I knew instinctively that you can get more and better information from someone if you ask them about themselves.

'I was working full-time as a street reporter for WINS in those days,' she answered, referring to an all-news radio station in New York City. 'A friend of mine who worked for Johnson & Johnson over in Jersey told me about this professor he knew who was working on a drug that would decrease healing time for wounds and surgical patients by about a factor of seventeen. Small cuts would heal before your eyes. Sounded like a story.'

She smiled at me. 'Turned out to be your mom. But she didn't want any word of her work to get out. At first she denied it existed at all, said she had no idea what I was talking about. Wouldn't talk to a reporter, not even one who pretty much staked out her office for three days. It wasn't until I did some digging and found out she had two little babies' – she gave us both significant looks – 'who needed constant attention that I could convince her I was a friend. And when I found out what really was going on, months later after I'd met your dad and gotten close to both of them, of course I never ran with the story. It would have been dangerous to them and more dangerous to you.'

'I don't get it,' Ken said. 'What does fast healing have to do with us being . . . put together?'

'I'm getting to that.' Aunt Margie was trying not to get testy, but we were interrogating her and not letting her tell the story her way. She hadn't been planning on telling it this morning at all, and it was clearly stressful for her. That didn't make me even a little less anxious to hear it. 'The fact was, Livvie and Brad didn't tell me much about you two except that you were a few years apart in age and their children, and they were worried about you. I started out – and I'm not proud of this – getting to know them because I thought they'd be good news sources, but after a while, we really did become friends, all three of us.'

'So you're not really our aunt.' Ken sometimes lets people think he's not as smart as he really is. This was not one of those times. We were having our world upended all at once, and realizing there were things we'd always taken for granted because they'd been told to us when we were very small children and we'd never questioned them.

Aunt Margie looked at him sadly for a moment. 'No, not by blood,' she said. 'But when Livvie and Brad had to leave, they were very specific about me taking care of you two.'

Well, that made . . . wait. What? 'When they had to leave? Our parents weren't killed in a car crash?' I sputtered. Nothing I'd known for certain was true. I'd go out later and take a good look at the sky to make sure it was in fact blue. Did I really know what 'blue' was?

'Oh, no, honey,' Aunt Margie said with a frown. 'I thought I'd made that clear. About a year after I met them, something happened; they wouldn't tell me what. But they were terrified they'd be found out – about you guys, I think. And they told me they had to leave you behind, because you'd get found if they were found. They . . . they asked me to watch you until they got back.'

'But they never got back,' I said, my mind reeling.

'Not yet,' Aunt Margie responded.

THREE

After consulting with Ken, who was almost done charging himself, I walked back into the outer office and sat behind my desk until Evelyn Bannister finished filling out her intake form. I took it from her, made it a point not to look it over (clients don't want to see your reaction when you read their personal information), and got into the uncomfortable part of the interview – asking for a retainer of three thousand dollars.

Evelyn didn't blink, but wrote out a check with her name and address – you'd be amazed how often people come into a detective agency using false names and forget to have bogus checks printed – and handed it to me. I stood to accept it and thanked her. But I did make a mental note again to have a credit card reader installed.

'We'll do our best, Ms Bannister,' I said. 'You should be hearing from us with an update in a few days. Your contact information on here is all current?' I nodded toward the form.

'Yes,' she answered. 'But please call my cell phone first. I'm in and out of the apartment a lot – I work in the hospitality industry planning events, and I'm out all kinds of crazy hours.'

'Not a problem,' I told her. 'You'll hear something the minute there's something to hear, I promise.'

Evelyn stood, adjusted her skirt, and shook my hand. 'Thank you so much, Ms Stein,' she said. 'I'm starting to feel better already.'

I almost warned her not to get too confident, but decided that would be bad business. Besides, Evelyn was already almost out the door.

Ken ambled in at almost that exact moment, his shirt tucked back into his pants so nothing suspicious could be seen in case our client was still in the room. 'She left?' he said.

I nodded. 'And she wants us to find a rare ukulele.'

'Was any of what she said true?' he asked.

'Some,' I told him. 'But not much, I don't think. What gave it away for you?'

'Her respiration was up when you asked her for contact information and her temperature was much too high for the room,' Ken answered. Either she was lying and nervous or she had malaria. 'You?'

'*Duck Soup* is the only Marx Brothers movie where Harpo *doesn't* play the harp,' I said.

'What happens now?' Ken asked. He walked to his own desk and sat down. 'Do we look for Evelyn's dad and hope he knows what she's trying to put over on us?'

I shook my head. 'Not the dad,' I said. 'The ukulele.'

Ken cracked his knuckles and stretched a little. 'Be easier to get the dad to talk.'

'But easier to find the uke,' I told him. 'Tell you what: You try to track down this Melinda Cantone, see if she's a real person, and I'll look for a rare Hawaiian instrument.'

'Stop talking dirty in front of your brother,' Ken said.

FOUR

As I recall, we did not go to school the day Aunt Margie came clean.

Her story was, at best, sketchy from there, but our pre-adolescent worlds were so rocked by this flood of information that following our regular routine would have been out of the question. Aunt Margie – she insisted we continue to call her that – knew it, and simply wrote us notes saying we had both been ill and sent them with us when we returned to school. The following Monday.

We spent our time getting what few details there were left from Aunt Margie, who swore us to secrecy on each and every one roughly every three minutes. Which is why I'm telling you now. Make sure you don't let on.

What was left were the details of our . . . assembly. Aunt Margie said our mother, who had developed this quick-healing process that could regenerate tissue that had been damaged or destroyed, was about to bring the secret to her department head at Rutgers when our father sat her down and talked her out of it, saying she should be careful about who she told because the process she'd developed could potentially be turned into something much darker. Aunt Margie wasn't there for the conversation (it happening about three years before she met our mother), but she understood that our father had used a hypothetical example of a prisoner who could be tortured, badly injured, and then healed with Mom's solution, only to have the interrogation start again.

Instead, Brad (as Aunt Margie called him) suggested something that could be a much larger purpose: With his surgical knowledge and her miraculous breakthrough, they could literally create their own life.

This touched a nerve for my mother. She and Dad had very much wanted to have children, but were unable to conceive. They were still fairly young, in their thirties, and had not yet considered adoption. Surely some sort of in vitro procedure could have helped them, but with this new idea, the merging of their own two specialties and their knowledge creating children for them seemed perfect.

Mom hadn't told Aunt Margie much about the science involved in creating Ken and me. But it had involved an electrical charge, one that we needed to in some way replicate on a regular basis to keep our systems active. We don't have any metal in our bodies except for the ports, but our hearts need periodic jumpstarts. I know I can feel it – if I don't plug in every three days or so for about an hour and a half, I get sluggish and my head starts to swim a little. (Ken was now working on ways to reduce the charging time, and swears he will eventually get it down to forty-five minutes or less.)

I'd just never considered the fact that Aunt Margie always made me plug in the day before I'd go to a sleepover, or that none of the other girls needed to connect themselves to a wall socket while we were watching scary movies and eating popcorn. I just figured they'd plugged in a day or so before in anticipation like I had.

Sometimes the depth of my own naiveté can amaze even me.

Aunt Margie said she'd never heard directly from my parents since they'd fled our apartment late one night. Occasionally, she'd receive an envelope in the mail with no return address and carrying various postmarks. The envelopes contained cash but no note.

In the ensuing years, I did a good amount of research. Ken, for the first few years, refused to help; he felt abandoned by our parents, believed that they had left us either because they considered us too much trouble or worse, because they were repulsed by 'the monsters they'd made.' After about three years of coaxing from Aunt Margie and me, he had come around to the point that he'd keep an eye out on the internet for what we considered to be suspicious behavior in the science realm that might point to our parents' whereabouts.

He also made sure to hack into some government agency sites, just to make sure there wouldn't be an unexpected knock on the door one night looking for people with USB ports and a need for fresh current every now and again.

I discovered the odd article here or there about a scientist doing something unusual with hormones to promote healing, but it was never a woman of the right age. We did, after a while, get a sense of our parents from what Aunt Margie could tell us and from some journals she had been keeping safe for them, which she showed to us.

A lot of it was scientific data I didn't entirely understand. You'd think given the scientific genius of both my parents, I'd have inherited something, but then one has to remember that my DNA and that of the people who made me might or might not have intersected; we were never clear on that. Ken, however, did understand science, although hardly at the genius level, and was beginning to make some sense out of what they'd done, but it was taking (in my opinion) forever.

Even if we weren't unlocking the secrets of creating life, through the journals we got to know our parents. Mom was earnest but kind and caring, and Dad, whose entries were much more infrequent, seemed just a little arrogant, but with the sense of mischief and fun that a ten-year-old boy would bring to a new chemistry set. He probably blew up a lot of stuff.

But neither Ken nor I had found a decent trail to our parents, whom Aunt Margie insisted would be back 'as soon as it's safe for you.'

Eventually, it was time to move on with our admittedly bizarre lives. Ken went to college, then I went to college, then Ken got out and started working on the docks. I went to grad school, decided to open an agency for people who couldn't find their parents (if I couldn't find mine, maybe I could find *theirs*), talked Ken into being my partner and moving into my apartment one floor up from Aunt Margie (who had moved us out of Queens and into Manhattan years before), to share expenses, and here we were.

Trying to find Evelyn Bannister's ukulele.

FIVE

The block of West 48th Street in Manhattan between Sixth and Seventh Avenues was once known as 'Music Row.' Small specialty shops that catered to working musicians like Manny's and Rudy's Music Shop were side by side so players could browse, shoot the breeze, and occasionally jam while looking over instruments almost nobody else could appreciate or afford.

Now the block is just another row of office buildings, the real estate under them far too valuable to have been left to a bunch of crazy musicians anymore. There is a gigantic Sam Ash music superstore there, and some of the employees are actually knowledgeable about guitars, basses, keyboards and drums. If you can corral one long enough to ask a question. The word 'ukulele' had gotten me a point to a rack that had exactly two specimens on it (in addition to a couple of mandolins) and a suggestion that maybe I should look for something in a nearby souvenir shop or go to the nearest Target store, which was on 117th Street in East Harlem.

Luckily, there was one holdout from the good old days. Pedro's Music Emporium, almost literally a hole in the wall now that it was surrounded by enough granite to provide countertop for every home on the planet, had guitars, trombones, sheet music, and triangles (!) hanging in its front window, proudly flouting the trend that had wiped out its neighbors.

The day after Evelyn Bannister told us her probably bogus story, I had spent two hours online researching the Gibson Poinsettia and then gave Pedro's a visit. I prefer talking to real people. No jokes, please.

Asking for Pedro inside would be stupid – the awning held a banner reading 'Est. 1925' – so I walked to the counter, noticed the two tattooed, mohawked, acned boys trying out a bass guitar in the back of the store, and nodded to the guy behind the counter. He was about fifty, bald (not shaved – natural bald), and gawking at me because I was roughly six inches taller than he was.

Besides, I looked really good. Even the mohawked guys in the back were watching. Like they had a chance.

'How can I help you?' said the counter guy after he was finished craning his neck. I leaned over on to the counter to give him a break. He unconsciously started looking down my shirt, and I stood up again.

'I'm wondering about a ukulele,' I said.

'Your hands are too big,' he said without hesitation. 'You'd never be able to get the chords right.'

Yeah, thanks a lot, buddy. 'It's not for me,' I said. I pulled the PI license out of my purse and showed it to him; he did not so much as raise an eyebrow. That was what I'd expected, but it's so much faster than telling the guy you're a detective, having him be skeptical, and *then* having to produce the license as proof. 'I'm trying to find a guy who might have owned a rare ukulele.'

That startled him. 'A rare . . . ukulele?' he asked, the concept being something new and alien to him. 'What kind of rare uke are we talking about?'

My cell phone vibrated, and I checked. The call was from a number I didn't recognize, so I figured it was a robocall and ignored it. 'A Gibson Poinsettia, I'm not sure what year. But they don't make them anymore, and I'm told it's something of a collector's item.'

The guy scratched the top of his bald head, then looked me up and down again, and this time I got the impression it wasn't for fun. 'They're sort of rare,' he told me. 'But it's not like it's worth millions or anything. Sure, there might be a few collectors, maybe one or two here in the city, who would be interested, but I don't think I've ever seen one in my life, and I doubt the excitement would be too intense.'

I nodded; that was fine. 'I don't actually care if I find the ukulele,' I told him, noticing that the word 'ukulele' became more ridiculous every time I said it. 'I'm trying to track down a guy who'd own one. Do you know any collectors of that sort of thing? It doesn't just have to be ukes.' (I tried that one out to see if it was any better, but it wasn't.) 'Any stringed instrument. As long as it's rare.'

'Wouldn't want anything well done,' snarked one of the

mohawked kids, and the other laughed and high-fived him. I was more than ten feet away, and could smell pot smoke on them, but then, my sense of smell is a little more developed than most. I ignored them because I'm an adult. And because putting them in the hospital would have been time-consuming. All that paperwork.

The bald guy chewed on his lower lip for a while, which I took to be a sign he was thinking. 'I don't have any regulars who are into that sort of thing,' he said. 'The collectors in this city, they have real money. Go around picking up a vintage Les Paul from 1951 for like thirty grand or more. A thing like this, I think you're lookin' at eBay, to tell you the truth.'

'I thought this thing was kind of the Holy Grail of ukuleles,' I said. 'People aren't running around looking for them?'

Just so you don't think I'm stupid: My research into the Gibson Poinsettia had indicated it wasn't exactly the Maltese Falcon. There were varying reports as to the worth of such an instrument, but none of them was exactly eye-popping. I thought maybe someone at Pedro's would have an idea as to why Evelyn might be on the trail of one because I was pretty sure that whole story about her long-lost birth father was nonsense.

He shrugged. 'In Hawaii, maybe. Nobody plays the uke anymore. Nobody cares.'

This was turning out to be the deadest of ends. 'Just out of curiosity, what's something like this worth?' I asked the guy.

He made a 'who knows?' face and said, 'Outer limits, absolutely the most you'll ever get for it? Maybe ten grand. But it would have to be practically untouched and sealed up since the day it was made. Maybe autographed by Don Ho.'

That was about what I'd expected, and ten thousand dollars wasn't exactly life-changing money for anyone but the completely indigent. 'Nice, but not worth traipsing all over searching for it,' I thought aloud.

'Unless you're a collector,' the guy said. 'Real aficionados will go to any lengths to get a rare item they want. I had a guy once flew in from Amsterdam to get a Rickenbacker violin bass that he was sure Paul McCartney played on "A Hard Day's Night." He didn't – Paul – but you couldn't convince the guy of that. Paid forty thousand for it.'

'You charged the guy forty grand and you knew it wasn't McCartney's?' one of the tattooed boys in the back asked.

The counter guy shrugged again. 'Not my fault he wanted to spend all that money. If it was autographed, he'd probably have paid a hundred.'

'You should have signed it,' one of the kids said. The other hooted at his rapier wit. I felt a growl in the back of my throat, but didn't voice it.

This wasn't getting me anywhere, but now I felt bad that I'd wasted the counter guy's time. I looked around the store. There must be something I could buy that wouldn't be so cheap as to be insulting (guitar picks were out of the question) but not so expensive that I couldn't make the rent the following month.

I don't actually play an instrument, which was something of an impediment. But Ken does.

'Do you have violin strings?' I asked. I wasn't sure how often he had to restring his Cremona, but hey, the date we called his birthday was coming up. I knew it was a Cremona because it said so on the case.

'Sure,' the counter guy said, but the two wise guys in the back were snickering anew.

'Violin strings?' the taller one, who was probably fifteen minutes closer than his buddy to getting a girlfriend, but that still put him at ten years off, sneered. 'Are we playing at the symphony tonight?' he asked in a bad upper-crust accent.

The counter guy ignored them. 'What kind do you want?' he asked me.

'Kind? There are kinds?' I should have just gotten a piece of sheet music and been done with it. This would teach me to try and do something for my brother.

'Sure,' counter guy answered as the two skinny dweebs in the back dissolved into hysterics. 'Depends on what kind of violin you play, is it classical or bluegrass fiddle? Do you want gut strings or steel-centered? You've got a bunch of gauges . . . There's a lot of different choices with strings.'

'Maybe she should play some Beethoven for you and you can figure it out,' the shorter little pain in the butt said. 'Violin!'

I smiled politely at the counter guy. 'Excuse me a moment, please,' I said. He had a suspicious look on his face, but nodded.

I walked to the back of the store, where the two tattooed fans of Anthrax (according to one's T-shirt, which his mother had probably ironed) were still laughing loudly.

There was no point in trying to reason with them. I grabbed each by the front of the black faded T-shirt, lifted them up one on each arm and watched their legs dangle a foot off the ground. Both their respiration and heart rates skyrocketed.

'Don't disrespect classical music,' I said calmly, and without any exertion in my voice. 'You know, Slash is a big fan of Mozart.' I had no idea if that was true, but it certainly could be. 'Are you going to buy anything from this nice man?'

The taller one, whom I could feel trembling in my hand, said, 'No, we're just here looking.'

'Go look outside and don't waste his time,' I said. 'He's trying to make a living.'

The two boys looked suitably impressed, and said nothing. I let them down to the floor again, did not wait to hear their responses. As soon as their feet hit the ground and my hands left their shirts, they were out the front door. I walked back to the counter and put down one of my business cards. 'In case you hear anything,' I said.

The guy stared at me. 'Sure.'

'Maybe I should just make it a gift card,' I said.

SIX

'I think I've got something,' Ken said even before I could get my jacket off when I returned to the apartment. He was sitting at what we laughingly called the 'dining room table,' which was simply a door we'd put up on cinderblocks in the middle of the space next to the kitchen.

'What kind of something?' I asked, kicking off my boots and flopping into the armchair we'd hauled over from his old apartment.

'Something about the way we were put together,' he said, pointing at the screen of his laptop like I could see it from where I was sitting.

I sat up; we didn't get breakthroughs often. 'What?' I asked.

'It's not about where Mom and Dad might be; it's too old for that.' We knew that our parents tended to move around a lot. 'It's a clip from over three years ago. But it refers to a pair of scientists who managed to grow a human ear on the back of a lab rat.'

I stood up and walked to him so I could peruse the screen, but I wasn't excited. 'That's not new,' I said. 'That's been going on for years. They're hoping to grow a liver. Organs for transplants that wouldn't be rejected. That sort of thing.'

'Yeah, but this is different. After they talk about how some people are up in arms about the ear, they refer in passing to an experiment some unnamed scientists did. And in that one, they grew a whole arm, and they did it with nothing but DNA from a sample of saliva.'

OK, that *was* different. Before, any time we'd heard of experiments in which some organ was generated artificially, it had been done beginning with something from a donor, like a piece of a liver or a kidney someone didn't need. This report, if it was true, could point to a breakthrough we'd never heard of before.

'But that's not what happened with us,' I pointed out.

'We don't know that. Maybe we've been going in the wrong

direction.' Ken gave me a significant look. If our parents were able to create organs from something as small as a cheek swab, our creation could have been considerably simpler than we'd assumed.

'You mean maybe we were grown rather than stitched together?'

He tilted his head: *Sort of.* 'I mean, what if our organs, at least, were grown from tiny bits of DNA? We might not be as different as we think.'

'Other people don't have to plug in,' I reminded him.

'I'm not saying we're normal,' he scoffed. He closed his laptop and shook his head. 'OK. What did *you* find out?'

Ugh. I went back and slouched into the chair again. 'A grand total of not much. This ukulele is valuable compared to the cheap ones with plastic strings you can buy at Walmart, but it's not exactly what you'd call the holy grail. The guy at the music store didn't know anybody who collects them. I don't see how it's going to lead us to Evelyn Bannister's father.'

Ken rubbed his eyes, which he thinks makes him look thoughtful, when in fact it makes him look like he has red eyes. 'Let's forget the ukulele,' he said. 'What do we know about the father?'

'What have you found out about the mother?' I asked in retaliation.

'I'll get to it later.'

I waved a hand. 'We, meaning I, know he grew up in Nashua, New Hampshire and then moved here to work on Wall Street, made himself some money and didn't check in on his daughter.'

'They put her up for adoption,' Ken said, as he had many times before. 'In most cases, the whole idea is that the parents aren't ready to raise a child.'

'Like ours?'

He forced eye contact. 'Never use us as examples of *anything.*'

That made me angry, but seeing as how it made sense, I didn't respond. I just sat in the chair – which really needed to be sprayed for bedbugs, I'd guess – and stewed. Neither of us said anything for a while. Ken opened up his laptop again and started . . . doing something.

'I almost beat up two kids in the music store today,' I blurted out.

Ken, who was drinking a soda, very nearly sprayed it over his keyboard. 'What?' he laughed. 'You went after a couple of children?'

'No. I mean kids, like late teens, early twenties. They were being snarky about Beethoven, so I levitated them a few inches off the floor.' I mimed the move so he would know what I was talking about.

Ken put his head back and roared. And when I say 'roared' . . . My brother has a big voice. When he could control himself again, he looked at me beaming. 'You're a pistol, Frannie.'

'They were making fun of the violin,' I defended myself.

He stood up and walked over to where I was sitting, looked down at me. 'You weren't that mad about the violin. What's the problem?'

I frowned. This wasn't something I was really prepared to discuss, but Ken is really good at never giving me a break. 'It's the Evelyn Bannister thing,' I told him honestly. 'I took it on because I understand how it feels to want some information about the people who . . . made you . . .'

'I'm aware,' Ken cut me off. 'That's why you take most of the cases we do. So what's different about this one?'

My head felt heavy; I started to rotate it around on my neck to loosen up the tension I hadn't been aware I had. 'I don't know,' I answered. 'Usually we have more to go on. And there's something else.'

I didn't go on, so Ken stared at me. He's not happy to feed me the straight lines. And his stare is intense. He never so much as moves a facial muscle.

'OK,' I said. 'I'll tell you. I got a weird vibe off of Evelyn. I felt like maybe she didn't really want to find her father.'

Ken shrugged. 'We both thought that. She was lying. We've had clients lie to us before.'

'This was different. I got the sense that she might have a purpose. I thought maybe she was angry at her father and wanted to find him so she could . . .'

He waited again, then rolled his eyes. 'So she could what? Kill him?'

I never got the chance to answer. I stopped rolling my head, although that still felt good, and looked into his eyes. But my phone started ringing in my pocket, and I pulled it out, still looking Ken in the face.

'Mrs Fran?' It was Igavda, the Romanian woman Ken had hired to be our office's receptionist. The fact that Igavda spoke at best broken English had not struck him as a problem. She was six feet tall, which took some of the heat off me, and as Ken put it, 'built like a brick gulag,' which had been qualification enough for him. I had foolishly put him in charge of the task on a day I was in Washington DC looking through some adoption records from 1957.

'It's just "Fran," Igavda.' We'd had this conversation roughly fourteen million times before, but I persevered, assuming that someday I would get the only full-time employee of K&F Stein Investigations besides the two partners to call me by my first name. 'What's going on?'

'Called the police.'

Ken had turned away to walk back to the laptop on our 'table,' but I snapped my fingers to get his attention, and he turned to look at me. 'The police!' I said. 'Why did you call the police?'

Igavda was not breathing heavily or shouting, but I could hear the edge in her voice. 'No, not call police. Called police.' Oh, of course. How silly of me.

'What happened, Igavda?'

Ken, who would normally be amused by this type of conversation, looked concerned. He considered himself Igavda's protector in America. She was convinced that some secret police organization from her home country was after her for reasons she'd never been able to communicate, and had impressed upon my brother her damsel-in-distress qualities. The fact that she was strong enough to take out a bull ox with one punch belied the act, but Ken lived in the hope that someday Igavda would impress something more than her damsel-in-distress qualities on him, and he always rose to the bait when she sounded worried.

'Give me the phone,' he said, but I didn't.

Igavda answered me, 'Called police, few minutes ago. You go to station for questions.'

OK, maybe I had a handle on this. 'So you didn't call the police? The police called our office?' I asked.

'Da,' Igavda said. 'Called police. Sergeant Bendix.' Inwardly,

I groaned just a little. I knew Sergeant Bendix, and he didn't like me much.

'Why do they want me to come to the station?' I said.

'Is dead.'

'Sergeant Bendix is dead?' One could hope. OK, that was mean; I didn't want Bendix to die. But his extended leave of absence for, say, hemorrhoid surgery wouldn't be the worst thing that could happen.

'No, not Sergeant,' Igavda said. 'Sergeant call. Somebody dead. Go to station.'

'Who's dead?'

'Go to station.'

That was the most I was going to get from her. I tossed the phone to Ken, who luckily has good reflexes. He put the phone to his ear and purred into it as if he were trying to soothe a puppy through a thunderstorm. 'It's OK, Igavda,' he cooed. 'I'll be right there. Don't be afraid.'

I didn't hear what Igavda said, but she obviously imparted the information that she was in no need of rescue at the moment.

I reached for my jacket and headed for the door. After getting my phone back from my brother, who looked disappointed.

Sergeant Emil Bendix was a cop from another time. There were moments when I thought that was a literal statement, like Bendix had discovered a time-travel device and brought himself here from the 1940s. He talked like someone from a Warner Brothers tough-guy movie sent to give Edward G. Robinson a hard time before he or Robinson ended up dying in a bloodless hail of bullets. It was killing him – Bendix – that the NYPD no longer allowed smoking in precinct houses. I'm sure he thought a cheap cigar would have cemented his image and solved the vast majority of his problems.

'I didn't tell your "receptionist" that anybody had been murdered,' he was telling me now, drinking a cup of Starbucks coffee – which I could guess he'd insisted be 'just coffee, none of that fancy stuff' when he was ordering it – instead of the famous tepid police department industrial strength brews of the past, which had come on hot plates or through a Mr Coffee device. The poor guy probably even missed that stuff. 'I told her that I'd found out someone was dead. I would have told her who, if you'd had the brains to hire an American for the job. Should I call ICE, Gargantua?' Bendix likes to remind me that I'm taller than most women he knows. OK, *all* the women he knows. Assuming he knows women.

'You don't have to call Immigration on my receptionist,' I told him. 'She has perfectly legal papers and she's studying for her citizenship exam.' That was mostly true; actually *Ken* was studying for Igavda's exam, with the hope that she'd let him come over at night to help her 'cram.' I love my brother, but he can be a real pig sometimes.

'I'll bet,' was all Bendix could give back. The man was a wit worthy of comparison to, say, Tarzan. No, that's not fair. Tarzan's probably a riot if you speak Elephant.

'So who's dead?' I asked.

He consulted a clipboard he'd left on his desk, which was in the bullpen of the precinct, not exactly the most private area on the planet. 'Dr Aziz Mansoor,' he read. 'By his driver's license, fifty-seven years old, five foot ten, with brown eyes.' Bendix looked up from the file and lifted an eyebrow in a fashion I'm sure he considered wry. 'Imagine that.'

'And he wasn't murdered,' I said, ignoring his racial biases and trying to get back on topic.

'Nope. Drove his Infiniti G37 sedan smack into a tree on West 48th Street.'

'Wow,' I said.

'I know,' Bendix commiserated. 'I didn't know they had trees up there, either.'

'I was wondering why you have the case,' I said in an effort not to respond to anything Bendix said directly. 'That's the 18th Precinct. This is the 13th. How'd you get it?'

'They called down to me asking about you,' he said, barely hiding the grin from what I was now sure would be unpleasant tidings he'd be pleased to deliver.

'Me?' I asked. 'I don't know Dr Mansoor. He's not a client, I'm not his patient and he's not a friend. The guy had a car accident and he died. That's too bad. But what does this have to do with me?'

'That's the interesting thing,' Bendix answered. 'Dr Mansoor appears to have known you.' The grin was almost ear-to-ear now.

'How do you figure?' In order to get the moment to end, sometimes you have to perform idiotic rituals to accelerate its arrival.

'He had three of your business cards in his car. Wallet, glove compartment, front seat. How do you explain that, Gargantua?'

'I don't. Anybody can take a business card. Maybe the doctor was *thinking* of calling me. I can't account for every business card I give out, or somebody gives out for me. Why'd you call me down here, Sergeant?'

'I'll tell you why.' Bendix's desk was right next to that of Detective Richard Mankiewicz, and the diminutive cop gave me a wink as he took his seat, then made a face behind Bendix's back. When I laughed, caught off guard, Bendix turned to look, but Mankiewicz immediately turned toward his computer. Bendix, nonplussed, looked back toward me. 'The midtown cops went over his cell phone, which amazingly was still in one piece after the crash, and the last call he made was to you.'

OK, that was odd, but hardly amazing. 'So he called my office,' I told Bendix, who still looked like he had swallowed a canary. 'I'll call Igavda and find out whether he said anything important.' It was a car crash; why were the cops treating it like a homicide?

Bendix shook his head. 'Not your office phone. Your cell phone.'

Instinctively, I pulled my phone out of my purse. Sure enough, the call I'd ignored when I was at the music store was there, and it was from a number the phone didn't recognize from my contacts. I showed it to Bendix. 'Is this his number?' I asked.

He checked it against the file on his clipboard. 'Yep,' he said. 'That's our good doctor. So he calls you, and he's dead maybe an hour, hour and a half later.'

'Is there something you're not telling me, Sergeant?' I asked.

Bendix ignored the question. 'Did you speak to Dr Mansoor?' he asked.

I felt my eyes narrow. 'No. You want me to see if he left me a voicemail?'

'Please,' Bendix said, overemphasizing the word. I sat down

on the edge of his desk, and saw Mankiewicz watching me from his desk. Mank had asked me out more than once, I'd declined for a number of reasons (not the least of which was that I thought dating a cop would be a distraction for me and a possible conflict of interest for him), and now the attention was a little overripe. Mankiewicz, who's about five foot eight, would look bizarre next to me. There would be laughter. It would be embarrassing for both of us. The rough part was that Mank was a nice guy, really.

I punched up my voicemail and put in the password. The computer-generated voice at the other end informed me that I had only one new message, and I pushed the button that would play it back. I looked at Bendix, who made a rotating motion with his hand to indicate I should open the phone up to speaker so he could hear the message. I didn't want to, but I couldn't think of a good reason to refuse.

'This is Dr Aziz Mansoor,' said a fairly deep and unaccented voice over definite background noise that could have been traffic from inside a car or just walking down Seventh Avenue. 'It is very important that I speak to you within the next forty-eight hours.' He left a phone number and there was silence but for the background noise.

I was about to turn off the voicemail when the doctor added, 'This is a personal matter. I was a close friend of your parents, and I think they might be trying to contact me.'

SEVEN

I tap-danced around the message, telling Bendix the standard story, that my parents had been killed in a car crash when I was very young, and implying therefore that the doctor must have been either mistaken or crazy. Surely there were other Frances Steins (my legal name actually is Fran, but I tell people otherwise because they tend to believe that more easily) in the world. He looked skeptical, but he always looks skeptical, so that might not have been important.

After about fifteen minutes, he had ascertained that he wasn't going to get much more than that out of me, and waved me away like a pesky housefly on a summer day. I picked up my bag and headed for the stairs, but Mankiewicz intercepted me at the stairwell door. I smiled at him, because he really is a nice guy, but I had to look down to smile so he could see that I thought so.

'What's going on, Mank?' I asked. 'Some reason you need a private detective?' Maybe I could keep this on a professional level.

'Heard about this new Thai place on Bleecker,' he said. OK, so maybe I *couldn't* keep it on a professional level. 'I'm not working Saturday night. Why don't we go check it out?'

I looked down at him, staring up at me without a hint of irony. 'I really don't think it's a great idea, Mank,' I said as gently as I could.

'You don't like Thai?' Not a glimmer. 'Because there's an Italian place I've been to a couple of times . . .'

'I'm fine with Thai,' I said.

Before I could continue that the cuisine wasn't the problem, Mankiewicz blazed on. 'Great! Should I pick you up at your office or your apartment?'

I looked around at the cops in the squad room, some of whom were looking at us. Bendix wasn't one of them, thank goodness, but a couple had amused expressions on their faces. 'Come with me,' I said, and opened the door. He appeared puzzled, but followed me through the door and into the stairwell.

'What's the problem, Fran?' he asked me as soon as the door was closed. 'You don't like to date cops?'

'I'm about six inches taller than you,' I estimated. 'You're currently staring directly into my neck.'

'You say that like it's a bad thing,' Mankiewicz replied, and I noticed he was staring a little bit lower than my neck.

'Hey. I'm up here.' He adjusted his gaze toward my face, still smiling. 'Mank. You're a nice guy. Really. I like you. But . . .'

'You're a heightist,' he said. 'You discriminate on the basis of height.' And he looked me right in the face, daring me to contradict him.

So I did. 'I'm not a . . . *heightist*,' I argued. 'It's natural for a girl to want to look a guy in the eyes when she's dating him.'

'You can sit down a lot. The restaurant has chairs, I'm pretty sure.'

'You're impossible,' I told him.

'No, *you're* impossible. I'm not even improbable. Come on, Fran. You like me; you said so. Guess what? I like you, too. What's wrong with two people who like each other going out to have dinner together?'

'You're going to want to kiss me,' I warned him. 'I can tell.'

'I'll stand on a box. What do you say?'

The fact is I'm not terribly skilled in matters of dating. Being the tallest girl – and usually the tallest person – in every classroom I ever entered was a real obstacle for most guys. And the fact that there was an electrical outlet just under my left armpit had made me, let's say, a little leery about going too far with a guy. I hadn't had a lot of practice in the romance area. It's not that I *can't*, you understand. Our parents made sure everything works. But I'm, let's say, *reluctant*.

'I say, you're buying dinner, and if people stare at us . . .'

'It'll be because they envy me,' he said, grinning. 'I'll pick you up at seven thirty. How's that?'

'You're a lunatic,' I told him as he opened the door.

'So you're going out on a date with a lunatic,' he answered. 'Saturday. I'll wear something that makes me look taller.'

'Stilts?' But he was already through the door and back into

the squad room. I started walking back downstairs, shaking my head. This whole day hadn't gone the way I'd planned it. I did notice, however, that I was smiling when I hit the street.

'A date!' Aunt Margie crowed. 'That's wonderful, Frannie! I was starting to give up hope!' Aunt Margie and Tact have met, but they've never really gotten serious about each other.

She makes dinner for Ken and me once a week, usually on Tuesday. This week it was on Thursday, just so Aunt Margie could say that it wasn't a set thing every time. She likes to pretend that we have a choice in the matter.

Ken, sitting at the kitchen table inhaling spaghetti (one of the few dinner things Aunt Margie can actually cook to an edible state, although she's great at breakfast), waved his hand until he could chew and swallow. There would be no talking with his mouth full at Aunt Margie's table. 'The date isn't the interesting part.'

'Thanks a heap,' I answered.

'No, this dead doctor and his message – that's what I'm trying to figure out,' Ken said.

Aunt Margie looked . . . not dour, but certainly concerned. 'I don't see how what he said is possible,' she told us. 'If your parents were going to get in touch with *anybody*, it would be me.' She looked up from her dinner and saw our expressions. 'Well, after you two, of course,' she added. 'I think this guy was lying, or mistaken.'

'We'll never know,' I said. 'He's dead. I saw the pictures of his car, and it's amazing that even his cell phone managed to survive. I wonder if he had it in his pocket, or somewhere it could bounce around without breaking.'

Ken stood up to begin pacing. He's always said he can't think sitting down. I always tell him that's because after he stands, the blood flow to his brain is normalized. You can't expect to think when you're sitting on it like that.

I'm funny.

'We need to find out more about Dr Mansoor,' Ken said. 'I'm going to run some searches on him. We need to talk to his family, his friends, see if anyone else knew about this connection to our parents.'

'Slow down, Sherlock,' I told him. 'We don't even know what names Mom and Dad are using these days. The fact is, we don't really know if they're still alive. Aunt Margie, when's the last time you heard from them?'

Aunt Margie, sprinkling Parmesan cheese on her meatballs, stopped to think. 'I haven't gotten a package of cash from them in years,' she said. 'I think you were still in college the last time, Frannie.' She shook her head. 'There hasn't been anything else. There never was.' She always seems just a little insulted that our parents haven't checked in with her. Ken and I, of course, are a tiny bit miffed that they don't seem to have looked in on our progress, either. Just build 'em and leave 'em seems to have been the philosophy.

I manage by reminding myself that there are always at least two sides to every story, and I don't know the other side yet.

'I'm saying, this Dr Mansoor is our best lead in years,' Ken protested. 'We can't just ignore it.'

'We're not going to ignore anything. I want you to do the online checks you were talking about. And I'll make a few phone calls. But we're not bothering the family of a man who just died so unexpectedly when they haven't even gotten him buried yet.' I stood up and put my hands on Ken's shoulders. 'I want to find them just as much as you do,' I said. 'We have to do it right.'

'Do you really want to find them?' Ken asked quietly. He didn't wait for an answer, gave me a disapproving look, and walked out the apartment door, no doubt to head back up to our place. I looked at Aunt Margie.

She walked over and gave me a hug. 'He's just anxious,' she said. 'He doesn't want to see an opportunity go by. You know Ken. Stomp first and ask questions later.'

I laughed in spite of myself. 'You've got him down, all right. But he has no reason to be mad at me.'

'He's *not* mad at you. But you're the only family he has here.'

'Sort of,' I said.

Aunt Margie let go, and I sat back down at the table, but I didn't feel like eating anymore. 'Why haven't they ever gotten in touch, Aunt Margie?' I asked. 'Why haven't they ever checked in to see how we're doing?'

She raised an eyebrow. 'How do you know they haven't?'

That got me. 'You think they're watching us and not getting in touch?'

Aunt Margie shrugged as she stood up and started to clear the table. 'All I know is that when they left, they were scared to death that someone would find out about you guys,' she said. She lowered the dishes into the sink; no dishwasher for Aunt Margie. 'I can't imagine they're not keeping tabs on you somehow.'

'I guess I always thought *you* were the way they were keeping tabs on us,' I told her. I walked to the sink so I could at least dry the dishes she washed.

'I thought so too, at first,' she admitted. 'But they never got in touch. I kept journals about you two, how you grew, what you were doing, the . . . differences you had. But nobody ever came and asked. After a while, I stopped keeping track. I figured if your mom and dad showed up, you and Kenny could tell them anything they needed to know.'

The door flew open and Ken, as if on cue, came charging in, carrying his MacBook Pro. 'Something's up,' he said.

'Nice to see you, too,' I responded. 'Remember how you ran out on me in a huff a few minutes ago?'

He waved a hand to declare it irrelevant. 'I just saw something online that you need to see.' He opened the laptop and started hitting keys.

Ken's manner had me intrigued, and I actually did forget that he'd stormed out of the apartment only minutes before. 'Something about Mom and Dad?' I asked.

'No. Look here.' He pointed to the screen.

'Meet hot singles in your area?' Aunt Margie was looking under my shoulder.

'Not the ad – there!' Ken insisted.

The headline at which he was pointing was from a Reuters article two days earlier with a London dateline: 'Rare Ukulele Sells at Auction for $1.2 million.'

EIGHT

'It was a Gibson Poinsettia, but it was kind of a unique one,' I reminded Ken in the subway. We were taking the #6 train up to Evelyn Bannister's 72nd Street apartment to discuss the developments in her case, which admittedly weren't much. But I had promised Evelyn regular reports, and she had said she would show me the letter from her birth mother in which the few details she had about her biological father were disclosed. 'It was the first one made, signed by the maker on the inside, and it had . . . what did the article say?'

I'll admit it: I didn't want the $1.2 million ukulele to be the one Evelyn asked us to find. For one thing, it had been in London only days before, which might have necessitated an expensive trip for at least one of us (that Evelyn would be billed for, I'll grant you), but also because I suspected Evelyn's story was an extended lie and this seemed close to being a deliberately placed red herring. I didn't say any of this to Ken because he'd immediately hop on a plane to the UK and not be seen for who knows how long. Just to prove me wrong. And to see how the women in London might react to him.

'Gold fret bars and special ivory inlays,' Ken recited. 'But it went for over a million bucks, probably even before we were asked to find it. In reality it shouldn't have gone over ten thousand no matter when it sold. Don't you find that the least bit suspicious?'

I was holding on to one of the steel bars that replaced the leather straps they had in these trains in, like, 1948. But we still call them 'straps' and the people who use them 'straphangers.' New York traditions never die; they're like Shea Stadium or the Brooklyn Dodgers. Maybe those weren't great examples.

'I'm not sure I can say it makes me suspicious,' I answered Ken. We were getting looks from a couple of tourists – you can spot them a mile away, with backpacks on their backs so anybody can snatch them and belly packs they think will safely hold their wallets – because neither of us had to reach very far to hold the straps. 'I think it's a coincidence. They do happen.'

'Not this big, they don't,' Ken said. Ken has a flair for the dramatic, and would have been an actor if he'd had, you know, ambition or training or talent. 'This is something bigger than a woman looking for her birth father, Frannie.'

'Don't call me "Frannie" in front of the client, OK?' I reminded him. 'It makes me sound frivolous.'

Ken made a show of looking me up and down. 'On your best day, you couldn't do frivolous,' he said.

I chose to overlook that remark. 'All I'm saying is that I don't see a scenario in which Evelyn Bannister asking us to look for a rare ukulele leads to this one being sold for tons of money in London,' I said. 'What's the benefit to her? She clearly didn't have the uke and didn't know it was up for auction, or she wouldn't have asked us to find it.'

We stopped at 42nd Street/Grand Central, which meant that about sixteen thousand people were about to get on an already crowded train. Instinctively, Ken and I inhaled deeply, anticipating the crush of humanity about to press itself against us.

And press they did. The guy to my left, who was wearing shorts and a T-shirt that read, 'Bubba Gump Shrimp Company,' smiled from ear to ear and tried to put his arms around me to reach a pole for support. I gave him the look I usually reserve for Sergeant Bendix or a pit bull without a leash. He looked disappointed and grabbed the pole next to the one he'd originally targeted.

'Obviously she didn't know it had surfaced in London,' Ken suggested as the doors closed and the usual groan went around the car. The engineer was clearly new to the job, and the train jolted a couple of times before finding its groove, which made nobody happy. I was almost launched into a family of Swedes, and I'm used to the subway. 'Maybe she thought she could get her hands on this incredibly valuable instrument and not have to cut us in on it by giving us a sob story about wanting to meet her dad.'

'That's my point,' I answered. 'She didn't *need* a sob story. We're a detective agency. If she wants something found, she can ask us to find it.'

'But if it's something worth 1.2 million bucks, we'd ask for a finder's fee,' Ken retorted. 'Evelyn doesn't want to share.'

I considered that, but shook my head. 'Why that whole elaborate story about finding her father?' I asked. 'She could have just said she'd lost this ukulele that was a family heirloom or something.'

'We're the agency that finds birth parents,' Ken reminded me. 'She played to our specialty.'

'Exactly. Why do that? Why choose us? There are hundreds of detectives in Manhattan. Why come to the one that finds biological parents if that's not what you want us to do?'

That shut him up for a while, and he didn't answer until we'd gotten out at 68th Street and were climbing the stairs to the street. 'Maybe the guy isn't her father, but she thinks he has the uke, and she doesn't know where he is, so she sends us to find him.' Ken, in addition to being dramatic, is also an ace conspiracy theorist.

'Now you're really stretching,' I told him.

He sighed. 'Yeah. I am.'

We passed three Starbucks on the four-block walk to 72nd Street, and with all the willpower of Pavlov's dog, I decided I needed coffee. But I was perverse enough to get it from a bodega just to spite those Seattle wise guys. Ken looked simultaneously annoyed at the delay (even though we were ten minutes early) and amused at my behavior.

We stood outside the bodega while I took my first couple of sips. No sense in bringing hot coffee up to Evelyn's apartment, especially since I wasn't bringing one for her.

'What do you think about this Dr Mansoor thing?' Ken asked me after an appropriate pause.

'I think the guy got unlucky, or fell asleep, or had a heart attack or something, and ended up crashing his car,' I said.

'You're evading the question,' my brother told me.

'I know.'

So we stood for a very long moment. Like I said, Ken can stare me down without half trying. 'I don't know,' I blurted out. 'I don't see how this guy could be a friend of Mom and Dad's and Aunt Margie's never heard of him. I don't know what it means that he said he thought he had heard from them. I have no idea how three of our business cards got into the doctor's car. And for the life of me, I haven't a clue how this is going to help us find our parents. OK?'

'We could ask his friends and family at his funeral . . .' Ken sing-songed.

'No. We couldn't.'

'Yes, we could.' Nobody can get you to act like a four-year-old faster than someone who was there when you were. A four-year-old.

'I don't want to play this game, Ken. Let's go see our client.' And without waiting for a response, I dropped the cup of coffee, about a third full, into a garbage can and headed across the street toward Evelyn Bannister's building. I didn't have to look to know Ken would be right behind me.

The doorman let us in after checking a list of approved visitors, to which Evelyn had clearly added our names. The lobby into which he ushered us was ritzy, but not at the multimillionaire level of excess. It was mostly marble, clearly vintage, and one of those spaces in which you are naturally silent. I think it's a primal fear we each carry after the first time a librarian shushes us.

Evelyn's apartment number was 7C, and we were the only ones using the elevator at the moment, so there was no stopping until we reached the seventh floor. The doors opened and Ken said, 'I'm just saying, there's more to this case than we know yet.'

'I agree with that, but I don't think it's the ukulele from Sotheby's in London.'

'Yes you do. You just don't *want* it to be. That's different.'

We reached Evelyn's door and buzzed. Then we waited what is, for a New Yorker, an appropriate period of time. We're an impatient lot, but we've all been in the bathroom when the door buzzer has gone off, so this situation is an exception to our usual insistence on being admitted quickly.

Still, this went on too long. Ken buzzed again, and again, nothing.

We exchanged a look, and I called Evelyn's cell phone with my own. Through the door, we could hear hers ringing.

It continued to ring. For a long time. This was no bathroom break.

'What do you think?' I asked my brother. I was whispering. I didn't know why.

His face took on that closed, efficient, cold-blooded quality it gets when he thinks something is wrong. He didn't answer, but he turned the doorknob, and it turned. The door opened.

Again, Ken and I passed a look between us – we didn't want to speak in case there was someone nearby who didn't necessarily need to know what we would have been saying. And we knew each other well enough to communicate through signals.

Except that we didn't have any.

Ken reached into his pocket and pulled out a snub nosed .38 I didn't know he had with him. But I didn't mind. He went in first.

I'm tall, but Ken is taller and broader. I couldn't see around him, so I relied on him to take in the living room, which he did with the gun drawn. There was no one there, but Evelyn's cell phone was on a side table.

I followed Ken through the living room, which was very tastefully furnished, taking in the period of the building but not looking like a museum. I took notice in case I ever had an apartment that would have furniture not made of doors.

The place had that feeling of being empty. It was so quiet that it was impossible to imagine someone there. Still, we were both very careful not to set a foot wrong or to call out. We were technically breaking and entering, but that was probably not going to be an issue. I, for one, was careful not to touch anything. If we left and had not handled the knickknacks, it was possible no one would ever know we were there.

That became a moot point when we reached the bedroom. There, we found Evelyn Bannister, sprawled on the floor with an instrument case lying next to her, open and empty. But the loss of the ukulele-sized instrument that had clearly been here was the least of her problems.

Her head had been bashed in with a very lovely brass candlestick, lying on the floor next to her. She was dead. A lot.

NINE

'Aukulele?' Detective Bernard Miller scratched his head with the wrong end of the pen he was using to take notes. You'd think these days cops would record all conversations with an iPad or something.

'Yeah,' Ken told him. 'She hired us to find it for her, said she thought it would lead to her birth father.'

We'd called 911 immediately on finding Evelyn's body, and it had taken the first two uniformed cops maybe seven minutes to get to her apartment. Including the elevator ride. That was fairly impressive. They'd called in for detectives, and we'd gotten Miller and his partner, whose name was Harris, a tall, thin man with a tired look.

'Why did she think that?' Miller asked. Harris was in the entrance hall of the apartment, interrogating the super, a little guy named Gus who had already said he had only met Evelyn Bannister once, when she'd complained of a leak under her kitchen sink. He'd been meaning to get to it any day now. You wouldn't have heard him say that from this distance, but Ken and I certainly could.

'I couldn't say,' I answered. Which was a way of telling him that I *wouldn't* say. I don't like to give client information to the police unless I have to, even if the client is lying with a severely cracked skull on the floor of the room. If word gets out that you broadcast your client's personal data to the authorities, it can ruin your reputation.

Letting the client be bashed to death with a candlestick wasn't going to be a tremendous help, either.

Miller nodded. If he'd been chewing a stick of gum and wearing a non-ironic fedora, the image would have been perfect. 'Why couldn't you say?' he asked.

'Huh?'

'Why couldn't you say? Did Ms Bannister not tell you why she thought finding the ukulele would lead to her father, or do you mean you couldn't say because your vocal cords are ruptured and you're having trouble speaking?' Funny cops are a scourge on society, and should be avoided at all costs.

'She had a theory with nothing to back it up,' I answered. 'I don't want to send you off in the wrong direction.'

'You just tell me what you know and let me worry about the direction,' Miller said. He held up his notebook and pen and managed not to draw blue lines on his scalp again. 'Why did she think the uke was a lead to her father? Did she have a bad relationship with her father?'

'As far as we know, they never met,' Ken answered. 'She hired us to find him so they could meet for the first time.'

'Right.' Miller was a detective out of Central Casting. You'd think the NYPD would have at least updated the model by now. So slow to upgrade. 'The ukulele.'

'What about it?'

Miller let out a breath that wished it had smoke in it. 'I'm going to ask, and this time you're going to answer: What was it about the ukulele that was going to help find her dad?'

'All she knew about him was that he was a Wall Street big wheel who collected rare stringed instruments. She believed he had once owned a rare ukulele, and that if we could find it and trace its ownership, we'd be able to figure out who her father was. And I wasn't kidding when I said I wanted to keep you off the wrong path. I'm not sure the uke was a lead to her father at all.'

'And yet, unless she was playing the world's smallest guitar, that appears to be a ukulele case lying next to Mrs Bannister's body,' Miller pointed out. 'Right now, it's looking like a decent clue.'

'Except she hired us two days ago to find the uke,' I answered. 'If she'd found it, why didn't she call us?'

Miller took another glance at the figure of Evelyn on the floor. Her legs were twisted in a grotesque position and her face, still buried in the rug, was being digitally recorded by a police videographer. It occurred to me that our conversation would be duly recorded as well, and that was one reason Miller needed only the notebook. The videographer had kept shooting the scene even after he'd probably gotten every angle. Clever.

'Doesn't look to me like she had a lot of time to make phone calls,' Miller said.

'None of it makes sense,' I told him. I noticed Ken had been backing off, slowly blending into the background as well as someone his size can do. He leaned against the tall seven-drawer dresser, his hands casually behind him. I wondered what he thought he could lift out of Evelyn Bannister's dresser drawers, and hoped it was not my brother being a frat boy idiot. 'If the ukulele was here, why wouldn't Evelyn call us off? I'm told it was only worth a few thousand dollars. Why would someone kill her to get it?'

'Good questions,' Miller said. 'If we answer them, I'll be sure to give you a call and let you know how it came out. Or you can read it in the *Daily News*. Online.'

'But for now we're free to go?' I asked.

Ken stood up straight but kept his hands behind him for a moment. The very picture of ease and innocence. He walked to my side.

'For now,' Miller said. 'And for good, probably. Thanks for your help in the case. I imagine we won't see you again.'

'Why not?' Ken said. You can always count on my brother to deliver the set up for a pithy line, and never know exactly that he did so.

Miller pointed to the floor. 'Because your work is done. You don't have a client anymore.'

'He had a point,' Ken said, legs up on the door/table. 'Nobody's paying us. We get no fee for finding out who killed Evelyn Bannister.'

Ken had already scoured Google in an attempt to track down Melinda Cantone, Evelyn Bannister's birth mother, given that the information Evelyn had given me about her had proven to be useless, an address that currently housed a car wash. So far he had come across only one match for the name, but it was from an obituary printed in 1978, so that wasn't terribly helpful.

'No, but it's bothering me and I want it to stop bothering me,' I said. 'Evelyn asked us to do something and gave us a retainer to do it. Just because we can't report back to her doesn't mean we can just stop. We made an agreement.'

'That's pretty thin reasoning.' Aunt Margie, who had walked up from her apartment but wasn't, thankfully, cooking dinner tonight, liked to stand aside and watch Ken and me argue. She didn't really appreciate the conflict, but she thought we revealed things about our personalities in the way we went about making a case. Now, however, she was pacing the room and scratching her nose, which was a sign she was thinking hard. I figured Aunt Margie was missing her days as a crime reporter. 'You're not helping anybody. You can't make Evelyn Bannister come back to life by finding out who killed her.'

It occurred to me that considering how Ken and I had been brought to life I couldn't guarantee that anything was impossible, but that would have been a stretch at best. 'That's not the point,' I said. 'Evelyn hired us and now the result of what she asked us to do is that she got killed. It had to have something to do with the ukulele. So that obligation is left hanging.'

There was a Melinda Cantone who was currently living, Google told Ken and Ken told me, but she was eighty-seven years old and lived in Tuscany. It seemed unlikely. I told him to keep searching.

My brother is most dangerous when he looks relaxed, and the feet up on the table were putting me on edge. Sure enough, he felt the need at that moment to offer up a bit of psychoanalysis. 'You just want to do this because you feel guilty,' he said to me. 'But you know perfectly well that nothing we did got Evelyn killed. So what you're doing is postponing the search for our parents by concentrating on her murder.'

Ken can be unbearable, especially when he's right. I'd be damned if I would give him the satisfaction. I *was* reluctant to get back into the Mom-and-Dad search because it had frustrated us so many times before. The best defense, in this case, was deflection. 'What did you pick up in Evelyn's apartment that you didn't give to the cops?' I asked Ken.

Aunt Margie turned and regarded him with some concern on her face.

'What are you talking about?' Ken's face was so passive I thought it might fall off his head out of sheer indifference.

'You know.' But Ken sat there staring at me with fake incredu-lity. 'You had your hands behind you when you were leaning against Evelyn's dresser. You had the drawer just a little open; I could see. So tell me whether you were collecting evidence on a case *you* don't think we have to pursue, or if you were just being unbelievably creepy. And remember that Aunt Margie is in the room.'

That last bit got to him; Ken reflexively looked at Aunt Margie, who was doing her best not to laugh at how easy he was to manipulate. 'Well?' she said, drawing the word out a bit. Aunt Margie was not the most subtle of actresses.

'OK, fine.' Ken took his feet off the table and stood next to his chair. Even I had to look up at him. He reached into the back pocket of his jeans, where he had obviously stashed whatever he'd lifted from Evelyn's dresser. 'I found this.'

He extended his right hand, which was holding a small packet wrapped in clear plastic. 'I thought it was interesting.'

Inside the thin plastic package were four flat packets wrapped in paper. The legend on the first one, which I could see, was the logo of a company called D'Addario. 'They're guitar strings,' I said. 'But there's only four of them instead of six.'

'They're ukulele strings,' Ken corrected me. 'New ones.'

Aunt Margie's eyes narrowed. 'How'd you find those?'

'And why didn't you give them to Detective Miller?' I piled on.

'Take it easy.' Ken spread his hands out, palms flat as if he were doing a push-up on the air in front of him. 'I was just running my hands in there, see if I could find anything that would explain what happened, and I came across those. I didn't know what they were exactly, because they were behind me. No sense showing it to Miller if it was, say, a package of handkerchiefs or something.'

I sat between Ken and his laptop so I could do the research myself, if he wasn't going to. Melinda Cantone might very well have married and changed her last name, which was not really going to be a huge help if I didn't know what it was, but I started searching through marriage records, which are public, in Bethesda, Maryland. If she'd moved out of Bethesda or gotten married elsewhere I'd be completely out of luck. So far this tactic wasn't turning up much, but I didn't know which year I should be watching, either.

'So you just idly ran your hands through a dead woman's, you

should pardon the expression, drawers, in the hope that you'd
find something, and when you found something you withheld it
from the investigating officer?' Aunt Margie's arms were folded.
That wasn't a positive sign. For Ken.

'It's something you do.' Wow. That was the best he could
come up with? If I'd been in Aunt Margie's sightline I'd have
moved just to avoid being hit by a stray heat beam.

'No it's not,' she said. 'And you damn well know it. I want
you to call Detective Miller immediately and tell him what you
found. And don't you touch that packet without gloves on
anymore. In fact, put it down this second and don't touch it again,
gloves or not.'

Ken obediently put the packet down on the door. He didn't
reach for his phone to call Miller, and I doubt he even had the
detective's number in his phone. But he didn't touch the packet
again.

Instead, I did. I did put on a pair of latex gloves I keep for
cleaning up our kitchen, which I do religiously every couple of
months or whenever I can't stand it anymore. I'm not exactly
what you call the domestic type. Then I sat down at the door
and examined the packet of ukulele strings.

'No price tag,' I said.

'Why?' Ken was being petulant. 'You want to buy them?'
Aunt Margie and I were stomping all over his boyish prank and
not giving him credit. It was hardly worth getting up in the
morning from my brother's point of view. He sat back down and
folded his arms. If he had shaved more recently he would have
looked exactly like he did at the age of eight.

I didn't answer him, but continued my scrutiny of the strings.
'I'm not going to open it and take them apart,' I said, mostly to
placate Aunt Margie, who was looking itchy to call the cops.
'There are four of them, each wrapped separately in paper with
an indication of the pitch to which they should be tuned: G, C,
E and A.'

'Speak to me in Swahili,' Aunt Margie said. 'I'll understand
more. What difference does it make what notes the strings are
supposed to sound like?'

'It speaks to the kind of ukulele it would fit,' Ken grumbled.
Even in this mood he couldn't resist being the Music Authority.

'A baritone or even some tenor ukes would have strings like the highest four strings of a guitar at D, G, B and E.'

'I take it this one was pretty standard,' I said.

'Yeah.' Ken was warming to our renewed admiration for his genius. He didn't get up, but he uncrossed his arms and smiled a tiny smug grin. 'I don't know anything in particular about the Gibson Poinsettia but I don't think it was a baritone uke. It's possible she was going to restring the instrument after she got her hands on it, which it appeared she did.'

This wasn't adding up for me and I wasn't able to find any marriage records for Melinda Cantone. It would take weeks just to look through all the records of women named Melinda who had been married in Maryland the past year, never mind the past ten. Or twenty. I closed Ken's laptop and focused on the strings at hand.

'If the ukulele was a special collectible, wouldn't changing *anything*, including the strings, make it less valuable?' I asked. 'Why would she want to make that kind of move if she didn't have to?'

Ken mused on that for a moment and twisted his mouth around like he was chewing my words over. 'Maybe it wasn't the Gibson,' he said. 'Maybe it was just a normal uke and she was stringing it for whoever was going to play it.'

I sat back because I was too tired to get up. I was going to need to plug in this evening. 'I don't get any of this,' I said. 'She wanted to find her dad, or at least that's what she said. So she sent us to look for a ukulele because it might lead her to her dad.'

'Or at least that's what she said,' Ken chimed in. Helpful.

'Yeah. So when she ends up with her head bashed in and an empty ukulele case on the floor, what are we supposed to think?'

'We're supposed to think I should go to Dr Mansoor's funeral and talk to his family about how he knew our parents,' Ken said. Now I was *really* tired. Especially of Ken. My brother is a sweet guy – no, I mean it – but he can get on my last nerve like nobody else.

'Well, we don't think that,' I said. I stood up. 'We think I should go into my room and plug in.'

'That is true,' Ken said. 'That is what we think.'

I turned, worried. 'Are you trying to get rid of me?'

Ken walked over and put his hands on my shoulders lightly. 'Frannie, you are paranoid. I'm concerned about the way you look like you feel. I know what that's like. I'm the *only* one who knows what that's like. You're running really low and you shouldn't ever let that happen. So go inside and plug in and we'll talk about all this stuff when your brain is clear, OK?'

I didn't argue with him. I probably should have, but I didn't. I went into my room and opened the closet door. Inside was a box on the second shelf. The box was marked *DVDs* because I figured no one would ever look at that. Who watches DVDs anymore?

I took off my shirt while I was walking to the bed and put it on my bedside chair. Then I lay down and reached across to the far side. There was an electrical outlet on that wall easily accessible to my hand. I was practiced at this well enough that I barely had to look when I plugged the unit – a small metal box with two prongs sticking out the back – into the wall. I let the unit hang but held on to the wire that stuck out of it.

The end of the wire held a USB coupling, which I plugged into the port that was embedded in my left armpit. I always like to consider that it's the female end and chuckle thinking about that being in Ken as well. I was sure he didn't think about it in those terms.

Immediately I felt the surge. It's not an electrical tingle, which you might have expected. There's nothing especially electricity-based about the feeling. Mom and Dad (probably Dad) had been careful about making us sustainable and not uncomfortable in the process we knew we'd have to go through for our entire lives.

The feeling is actually more like a weird internal massage. It rejuvenates as it empowers. I like it. But it takes more than an hour to complete and the placement of the port (thanks, Mom and Dad!) makes it difficult to do much else while you're charging.

So I thought. The Evelyn Bannister case was making my temples ache (although that too could have been my batteries running dangerously low) so I concentrated – for the moment – on Dr Mansoor's voicemail.

He'd said it was important for me to get back to him within

forty-eight hours, and that had been about three hours before I heard the voicemail. What could have been so urgent? Why would someone who believed our parents were trying to contact him insist he only had two days to impart whatever information he had tragically taken to his grave?

It was imperative that we talk, and now we couldn't. I knew Ken would be working his magic on the web, so there was no point in running the same searches. But when I saw Mankiewicz on our 'date' (I couldn't possibly think of that in serious terms) I could see if he'd run a background check on the doctor and see what came up. It was the least the guy could do in exchange for me getting tall-girl stares all night.

Better, I could ask him now to run the report, or at least to see what the detectives in the eighteenth precinct had dug up, so he could tell me about it at the restaurant. That would cut down on his cute little mooning glances at my face.

Wait. Did I just say *cute* in regards to Rich Mankiewicz? My batteries were more drained than I'd thought.

The exercise in my brain was making me tired. I checked the meter on the charging unit, and I was only at sixteen percent. That was really low. I lay back and closed my eyes.

Naturally, there was a knock on the door.

'Go away,' I said. 'You can tell me in the morning. Or in an hour. Whichever comes first.'

'I'm not trying to sell you something,' Aunt Margie said from the hallway. 'Can I just come in and check on you?'

My mind screamed *no!* But it was Aunt Margie and she deserved better. She always deserved better. 'Sure, come on in.'

The door opened slowly as if Aunt Margie was afraid of what she'd see. But she had actually been the one who taught me how to plug myself in, so I knew she wasn't shocked at the sight of me drawing life force from ConEdison.

I sat up, but she motioned me back on to the pillow. 'I know you're tired. I just wanted to see if you were OK.'

'Of course I am.' Although I did close my eyes just then because it felt so good to do so. 'I do this every few days. You know that.'

'I didn't mean the plug,' she said. 'I meant hearing that your parents might be alive and trying to get in touch with someone who isn't you, right at the same time your client ends up murdered.'

'I've had better days.' My voice sounded weak. I was about to wonder why when I remembered that I was at sixteen percent.

'I know. But this Dr Mansoor thing. I need to tell you about it.'

That made my eyes open. 'Huh? I thought you had never heard of Dr Mansoor.'

She pointed to the edge of the bed. 'May I sit down?' I gestured and she sat. I lay back on my pillow; only up to eighteen percent so far and that wasn't going to be good enough for a while no matter how fascinating Aunt Margie's story might be. 'I haven't ever heard of Dr Mansoor, at least not before tonight,' she said. 'But I knew there was someone out there who had a line on your parents.'

'Had a line? What does that mean?' I was simultaneously excited by the prospect of a possible new lead on our parents' whereabouts and worried that I might sleep through part of the explanation. It's hard to describe, or hadn't you noticed that yet?

'Brad and Livvie didn't work alone entirely,' Aunt Margie explained. 'I mean, they did the bulk of the work and certainly they had figured out all the science necessary to make you two, but they had some people in their lab who knew only parts of what they were doing. Nobody knew the whole picture except your mom and dad.'

'What'd they do?' I mumbled. 'Dig up the corpses of those recently dead and bring back pieces to stitch us together?'

'You've read Mary Shelley too many times,' Aunt Margie admonished. 'You know nothing like that happened with you two. Your body parts were grown, not transplanted.'

I closed my eyes again just because I didn't need to see anything. I could hear and that was enough. 'You're dodging. Come out with it. Who was Dr Mansoor and what did he know about my parents?'

'Again,' Aunt Margie's voice said from the comfortable darkness, 'I never actually knew of Aziz Mansoor before tonight. I'm just guessing that he had a hand in the experiments that created you. But Livvie did tell me that a couple of the lab assistants were under the supervision of a colleague, not a medical doctor but a Ph.D. in biology, and that I might need to find him if something went seriously wrong with your health or Ken's. She didn't give me a name, just a phone number.'

'Did you call it?' My voice was sounding a bit stronger, although I was still pretty weary. I guessed I was hovering around twenty percent.

'Once. Nothing was wrong with either of you, but my curiosity got the best of me. The number had been disconnected. I imagine the scientist had given up his landline and gone to a cellular phone.'

'And you think he was Dr Mansoor.'

'Maybe. Ken will find out more about him and see if he was in New Brunswick, New Jersey around the time Brad and Livvie were working. But I wanted to ask you about the message he left.'

I was getting stronger, but I still felt like sleeping. 'What?' I sort of, well, moaned.

'He said you had to get back to him within two days?' I looked at her. Aunt Margie's brows were down so low I was afraid her nose would have to get out of their way.

'He said forty-eight hours, yes.' It was what I'd been thinking about, but I didn't get why Aunt Margie was so obviously concerned. 'Why? Does that make sense to you?'

'Only under very specific and unlikely circumstances,' she said, not looking at me. She seemed to be talking almost completely to herself.

'Such as what?'

'Such as . . . maybe your parents are in town. Right now.'

TEN

Normally it would have been hard to sleep after a statement like that, but I was run down enough that sleep was the only thing I could do. Aunt Margie saw my face, told me not to worry (ha!) and left, quietly closing the door behind her. Like the sound of the door closing was the real obstacle here.

I fell asleep in record time for me, I'm sure. I don't actually remember anything after Aunt Margie dropped her bombshell and left the room. That is, I don't remember anything until two the next morning, when I was wide awake for no discernible reason. I panicked slightly when I realized I was lying on my left side, but the charging plug was no longer attached. Its meter, I could see, read one hundred percent. Aunt Margie must have snuck back in to disconnect me while I was sleeping, like she used to when I was too little to handle the apparatus myself.

It was impossible to stop rehashing the combined torments of the Evelyn Bannister case and what had happened to Dr Mansoor. So I did that for about twenty minutes before remembering that I'd intended to ask Mankiewicz about the good doctor's (I assumed he was a good doctor) demise. It was the middle of the night so I didn't expect that he'd be sitting by his phone, so I sent Mankiewicz a text message designed to reach him when he awoke.

So it was something of a surprise when my phone buzzed seconds later with a response from Mank: *Why do you need to know?*

I figured a good way to evade the question was by asking one of my own: *What are you doing up at this hour?*

What are you?

That was a question I'd pondered about myself almost all my life, but I didn't think Mank meant it that way. *I asked you first*, I sent back, largely because at two thirty in the morning my brain believes itself to still be in a nine-year-old.

Can I call you?

It did seem quicker and more direct. I turned off the ringer on my phone so Ken wouldn't hear the ring (he can hear through multiple walls, even when he's asleep but better when he's concentrating) and told Mank it was OK to call. Yes, I could have just called him, but he'd asked.

The phone rang in a moment and I immediately answered it, keeping my voice very low. 'Am I catching you in the middle of a case?' I asked. I knew why *I* was awake at this ungodly hour but I would gladly have bet everything I owned it wasn't the same reason Mankiewicz had.

'No,' he answered. 'I'm doing some research on something and it wouldn't let me sleep. I have tomorrow off anyway, so it doesn't matter how late I stay up.'

'How come you have tomorrow off?'

'Even cops have to take two days a week. Mine's tomorrow. Or later today, if you want to get technical. What's your excuse?'

'A client of mine got herself killed today,' I said. 'I couldn't sleep.' That was approaching true. It was true-adjacent.

'Killed? Like a homicide?' Cops are always cops. They're never just some guy. I could practically hear Mankiewicz's ears prick up.

'Yeah. You probably saw the alert. She got hit over the head with a blunt instrument in her apartment.'

Mank took a moment, no doubt looking up the NYPD post on the subject. 'Evelyn Bannister?' he asked shortly.

'That's the one.'

'The brass candlestick.' Mank was reading. Great. I'd come looking for a line on Dr Mansoor, preferably just to leave a message and have him call me back the next day, and now he was reliving one of the worst moments of my career, which had started not terribly long ago. Did I have more wonderful memories like Evelyn Bannister's bloody head on the rug coming in the future?

You think a lot of weird thoughts at two thirty in the morning.

'Yeah.' I wasn't interested in rehashing the scene of the crime, having hashed it quite thoroughly the previous afternoon with Detective Miller.

'It says here you and your brother discovered the body.' And yet, here was Mankiewicz determined to replay every last unpleasant detail. 'Are you OK?'

See? Just when you're starting to give up on Mank he decides to be a really sweet guy and that just screws things up. 'I'm OK,' I told him. 'It wasn't a close friend or anything. I just met her a couple of days ago.'

'You're lying,' he said. 'It's bothering you or you wouldn't be up at this time of the morning.'

'You're lying too,' I shot back. 'Research doesn't get you to stay up this late. You're probably still planning this dinner you and I are supposed to be going on.'

'Supposed to be?'

I decided to give up the mutual teasing and return to my original reason for texting Mankiewicz. 'I wanted to ask you a favor.'

'Wait. I'm still trying to figure out what "supposed to be" means. Are we having dinner or not?'

'Yes, we're having dinner. As friends.'

'If it's as friends you can pay for yourself. What's the favor?'

'You heard why Bendix called me in, right?' Unplugged now, I could move about the room freely if I wanted to, but I didn't want to. I lay in my bed and actually even closed my eyes. I wasn't tired, but not seeing things helped me focus. Does that make sense?

'Something about a doctor who died in a car accident.' Mankiewicz sounded a little puzzled.

'Well, Bendix probably heard the message and didn't understand what he heard, because it certainly doesn't have anything to do with the way he died, but in his voicemail Dr Mansoor told me he had been a friend of my parents.' Yes. Keeping my eyes closed was definitely the way to go here.

'I thought your parents were dead,' Mankiewicz said. Cops are so tactful.

'They are. He said he had been a friend of theirs.' I had to be careful about what story I told Mank because he was a cop, after all, and if I lied too blatantly he'd know it. The last thing I wanted on this was a suspicious cop. Why had I called him, again? 'But I don't know much about them because I was really little when they died. And now Dr Mansoor got into a car crash and died right after he called me to try and connect.'

There was a pause. Mankiewicz wasn't trying to determine if I was telling him a tale or not, though; I could see his face in my head and he was thinking his cop thoughts. 'You think there's some connection? That your parents were murdered?'

That would be far too much. 'No,' I said. 'I think it's just a coincidence. After all, it's decades apart. But it's so tantalizing to have been that close to more information on my parents and then not get it. I'd like to know more about Mansoor and Google isn't going to be enough. Can you do a little digging for me?'

'I'm not the detective on the case. It's not even my precinct. Bendix is the one who took the call. Why not ask him?'

This time I allowed the pause to happen. 'Seriously?' I said after a moment.

'OK, I withdraw the question. But it's early in the morning and you felt like you had to text me tonight instead of waiting for our date – yeah, I called it a date – tomorrow evening. What's so urgent?' Mank was a good cop. He knew how to think in a way that can lead to information, and what he wanted to know now was more about me than I'd allowed him before. I think I've made my reasons for that fairly clear.

'It's not urgent,' I sort of lied. The strategy here was that if I could get some decent information from Mank, maybe I could dissuade my crazy brother from attending a memorial service for poor Dr Mansoor, whose family needed anything but the Incredible Hulk hanging out at his funeral and asking them questions. Granted, I had no idea if Mansoor was even from the area, if his funeral would be in Houston or Zagreb rather than New York, or if Mankiewicz could find out anything that I couldn't myself, but it was worth the effort. I guessed. 'It's just that having heard about someone who knew them and wanted to tell me something kind of stirred it up in me.' That was at least largely true.

Mankiewicz, from the sound of his sigh, wasn't entirely buying it, but he wanted to go out on a date with me and therefore some concessions would have to be made. 'What do you want to know?' he asked.

'First of all, where is Dr Mansoor from? Could he have worked with my parents somewhere nearby? What's his background? Was he a medical doctor or some kind of research scientist? Had he been traveling recently, and if so, to where?' I'd given this some thought before calling Mank.

'What difference does that make?' he asked. 'Who cares if he was traveling? Your parents have been gone for thirty years.' He had no idea.

'Yes, but he chose to get in touch with me today. Yesterday. Whenever. That might mean he'd come across some new information and wanted to tell me about it. If he'd been out of the country, or even just out of state, that might lead me to other people who could tell me what it was he wanted to pass along.' OK, so it was a stretch, but not that much of one.

Mank exhaled again. 'Is that it?' he asked. 'You don't want a DNA sample, too?'

I gave it some thought; DNA might show if Mansoor had been created like Ken and me, which was after all a really unlikely possibility. 'No, I think that'll do it. But I will need to know how old he was and where he was born.'

'Uh-huh.' Mankiewicz was definitely trying to decide how badly he wanted to kiss me, and it must have been pretty bad because he didn't ask any follow-ups. 'You realize that Google would get you most of this, but I'll look into it without telling Bendix and I'll let you know what I found out when I see you for dinner. Now if you don't mind I need to get some sleep. I have a *date* tonight.'

I did not contradict him.

ELEVEN

'We don't have a client,' I reminded my brother.

'We *had* a client,' he corrected me. I mean, it wasn't relevant, but it was true. 'She gave us a retainer and now she's dead. I think it's incumbent upon us to find out who killed her, don't you? Wasn't that what you were saying? What made you change your mind?'

We were sitting in our office, me at my desk and Ken on the client chair, which was big enough for him and cushier than the more utilitarian piece of furniture I was sitting on. I was trying to get some files cleaned up from previous cases and he was . . . bothering me.

'Incumbent upon?' I asked. 'What classy woman you're dating or hoping to date is making you upgrade your vocabulary?'

'What makes you think . . . OK. I've been talking a little to an English professor from NYU and so I'm trying to up my game a little bit. Is that a bad thing? And don't change the subject. Evelyn Bannister asked us to find her dad. She ended up dead. We didn't find her dad and we don't know who killed her. I think we owe it to her to do at least one of those things.'

'This case is giving me bad feelings,' I said. 'Nothing adds up right.'

The sun was still just reveling in its ascent over Manhattan, glad to be out for the morning but nowhere near peaking yet and in no hurry to do so. In other words, it was nine in the morning. Usually you can't get Ken out of bed that early without a cold bucket of water, but he'd decided to come to the office and annoy me while I tried to run the agency and make him money. That meant he had an agenda, and as long as it didn't include seeing Dr Mansoor's remains committed to the earth, I was willing to listen.

'OK, I get it,' I told him. 'I feel like we failed Evelyn Bannister too. But I don't see the merits of doing something that she'll never know we did. It's to make ourselves feel better, not to try and make it right for Evelyn. Evelyn's dead.'

'That wasn't what you said before.'

'That was yesterday. I was a whole different person.'

Ken's eyes were half-closed as he was no doubt ruing his decision to get up at the same time as the rest of America. It gave him the air of someone who really didn't care when I knew that he did. Probably not the image he was trying to project. My brother is a number of wonderful things, but he is not subtle. Ever.

'So what do you suggest?' he asked. 'Forget the whole thing and move on to paying jobs?'

'You say that like it's a bad thing.' The Forsyth account was not going to bill itself, after all. I'd have left this work for Igavda, but she had the disadvantage of not speaking really good English, so her invoices tended to have misspellings and incorrect addresses, which was not the kind of thing a going enterprise should permit. In addition she was not at the office yet. Ken lets her come in at ten. Ken sometimes thinks with an organ other than his brain.

'Very amusing. I'm suggesting that we either keep trying to find Evelyn's dad, whoever he is, or figure out who killed her.'

He was being serious and I always realize that too late. 'OK,' I said, 'let's look at it logically. The police are already investigating Evelyn's murder and they have access to more information and resources than we do. So if we're going to do anything else – and I'm still not sure it's a great idea – we should concentrate on identifying and locating her father.'

Ken smiled. He loves it on those rare occasions when I agree with him, or at least when he thinks I do. He stood up to pace because he thinks it makes him look thoughtful. I should be nicer when I talk about my brother, but it's so much fun to not.

'So what do we know so far?' he asked. Now, that was largely because he had barely been paying attention when we were working on Evelyn's case until now. She wasn't his type and he figured I had it well in hand. It turned out I didn't, since Evelyn was dead, but I was still ahead of Ken in the information department.

'Have you looked at her file?' I asked my brother. I already knew the answer to that question but I wanted him to understand what a mistake he'd made in trying to prove he was as much an investigator as I am. Siblings. Never get between them.

Ken didn't make eye contact, a sure sign. 'I saw her client intake form,' he said. I knew what that meant: He's *seen* it, when it was sitting on my desk, but he hadn't *read* it. 'What else should I know?'

I resisted the urge to gloat. 'You should know that Evelyn's adoptive parents, the Bannisters, don't really know anything about who her dad might have been. Her birth mother, Melinda Cantone, knows but won't say because that was the father's wish. He is from Nashua, New Hampshire but made his money here in New York and collects stringed instruments for reasons I can't begin to explain. That's the bare bones. The rest is in her file.' I pointed at my computer screen in case Ken had forgotten where client files could be found.

'You're really getting after me today,' he said. He sounded so much like the twelve-year-old version of himself that . . . actually, that made me want to get on his case some more. But I didn't.

'I know. Maybe a little more than I should, but you need to start taking this agency thing a little more seriously. I feel like I've been doing most of the work and you come along in case somebody needs beating up.' OK, so that was a little harsh but not entirely inaccurate.

Ken actually looked surprised. 'Is that what you think?' He stopped pacing. He wasn't thinking about how he looked. This was serious.

'I don't know if it's what I think, but it's how I feel. Prove me wrong.' I sat back in my swivel chair and looked at him, trying not to seem confrontational. I wondered if Aunt Margie would say I was succeeding in that or not.

'I've done some digging on our parents virtually every day for at least two years,' Ken said.

'That's personal, not agency related. I know you want to find out about Mom and Dad. I'm pretty sure I want the same thing. But that's got nothing to do with our business, the way we can afford to pay the rent and the electric bill so we can plug into the wall. What are you doing for *that*?'

My brother seemed to have something caught between his teeth. His lips moved back and forth and his cheeks bulged out a little here and there. It took some seconds before he answered,

'Maybe it's because I'm not being asked to do anything but stand behind you and look intimidating.'

'So it's my fault you're not contributing?' I swear, it slipped out before I could think about what I was saying.

Ken stared at me for a moment, then turned and walked out of the office. I called after him a couple of times, but he wasn't about to come back in and let me apologize. So I texted him *I'm sorry* and waited for him to walk back through the door.

He didn't.

I worried about Ken for the rest of the day, which probably would have made him happy, I decided. So I was nervous while I sent invoices. I was nervous while I checked on active cases and found little that was urgent. I was nervous while I went down to the pizza place and got three slices for lunch. Usually I get four.

I'm a big person.

After a while being nervous just got tiresome and besides, I had to get nervous later about the date with Mankiewicz. So I decided to put the jitters aside for the time being and concentrate on Evelyn Bannister's father.

Yes, I *know* that's what Ken wanted me to do. I'm not saying he didn't make any sense at all.

Putting my thoughts about my absent, petulant, stubborn, annoying brother aside, I started looking seriously into what had already been determined about the as-yet-unnamed birth father of Evelyn Bannister. The file I'd compiled – with virtually no help from Ken, but I wasn't thinking about that now – had the most rudimentary information possible. I still had no idea who this man was, why he'd decided to stay anonymous from his daughter (although that's not terribly unusual, even after decades) or what, if any, connection his shadowy presence might have had in Evelyn Bannister's murder.

The only real leads I had among living people were Evelyn's adoptive parents, Howard and Cicely Bannister, and her birth mother, Melinda Cantone. Since the Bannisters were undoubtedly dealing with the loss of their daughter at the moment and probably didn't know anything about the birth father anyway, the obvious move was to contact Melinda, but we'd tried that and come up short, which was not typical for me. It was possible she was unaware of her daughter's death. That made me pause a moment.

There was, therefore, a long moment before I picked up the landline phone on my desk, which I use for business calls because you never actually lose a connection on a landline and besides, that way I don't have to give clients and business associates my cell number. I dialed the number Evelyn had given me for Melinda.

And was treated to an automated message indicating that the number I'd dialed was not in service. OK, so that wasn't exactly a surprise, but it was getting to be a pattern. Evelyn had given me the number only a few days before. The idea that Melinda had somehow gotten wind of the investigation and changed her phone number wasn't impossible, but it was pretty unlikely. I tried the number twice more and got the same result. The only conclusion was that Evelyn had been lying. But I kept trying.

Usually it's easy to locate someone on the internet; I should have had a location on Melinda by now. But this was different because there simply weren't any listings – at all – regarding anyone with that name in that city. That's pretty rare. Usually when I'm searching for a birth parent trying not to be found the biggest problem is sorting through the myriad options that assault my eyes. In this case, there were none.

The only reasonable conclusion to reach was that there was no such person as Melinda Cantone, and certainly none in Bethesda, Maryland.

I'd figured Evelyn Bannister was lying. I just hadn't realized how much.

Given that information, I immediately began searching for Howard and Cicely Bannister at the address Evelyn had given me for them.

I'm assuming you know what I found there, too.

Now my problem was not simply finding out who Evelyn Bannister's father had been. It was discovering who Evelyn Bannister really was.

TWELVE

'So this woman you were working for turns out not to be the woman you were working for?' Rich Mankiewicz squinted a little bit at me, as if I were far away. I *wasn't* far away. I was on the other side of a relatively small table at Pasta Perfect, which was specifically not a Thai restaurant, given that the place Mank had heard about had closed a month after opening. Welcome to New York.

'She gave me a false name and told me a false story,' I said. Mank was a cop and I was a private investigator. Even on what he insisted was a date, there was no chance we'd be able to converse without a level of shop talk. Besides, Ken was still being a brat and wouldn't answer my texts, even when I'd told him about Evelyn Bannister's deception. Fine. Let him act like a five-year-old. I was the grownup. I'd already told on him to Aunt Margie, who agreed I was the grownup. 'Now I have to figure out who she was, and I'm hoping the cops who are investigating her death took fingerprints and dental records.'

Mank smiled his little smile, which I'd decided wasn't nearly as charming as he seemed to believe. OK, maybe a little charming. 'It seems like a lot of your business relies on having police officers find things out for you,' he said.

'Wow,' I said. 'If this is you trying to get on my good side you'll be lucky to get a good-night handshake.'

'I'm relying on your innate ability to see what a good guy I am at my core.'

'I have no intention of seeing your core, Mank. But since you brought it up, what did you find out about my late lamented pal Dr Mansoor?' I dug into my spaghetti primavera, which was a way of convincing myself I was eating mostly vegetables. I wasn't, but it was close enough.

Mankiewicz finished his bit of veal piccata and wiped his mouth, which was a good move. 'So you do want to know what the police can do for you,' he said.

'I called you for that very reason,' I said. It was a little mean, but not a lot.

He nodded, acknowledging (in my mind) my wit and letting it go rather than trying to top me. 'Dr Aziz Mansoor was a pathologist, born in Milwaukee, who moved to New Brunswick, New Jersey thirty-two years ago when he was a medical student at Rutgers University. He worked in a lab with a Dr Olivia Grey for a while there, then went on to be a resident at a hospital in St. Paul, Minnesota and decided he liked it there when he met a woman named Maria Gonzalez, whom he married. They had two kids, both of whom are now in their late twenties.' He told me all that without referring to notes or even checking his phone. Either he had a very impressive memory for facts or he was making it all up, which seemed especially unlikely given that he'd mentioned the name my mother was using when she was at Rutgers.

Olivia Grey! So Dr Mansoor wasn't lying, and now he was dead and couldn't give me the message he'd tried so hard to deliver. I looked at Mank and tried – probably unsuccessfully – to mask the excitement my mother's name had stirred in me. 'What was he doing in New York?' I asked, and I think my voice stayed steady.

Mank, just into another bite of dinner, once again took his time before answering, which I appreciated. Nothing turns me off faster than someone who talks and lets you see what they're eating. Then he took a sip of wine (which I did not drink because I don't drink because . . . it's a phobia; I feel like I don't know what alcohol would do to me. Ken does not share this particular worry) and nodded.

'He and his wife moved back here about six months ago,' he answered. 'Dr Mansoor wasn't retired, exactly, but he'd stopped working at the hospital in St. Paul and was consulting, mostly as a medical examiner for a small town in Minnesota. He apparently gave that up too and came to New York, where he was working two days a week at New York Presbyterian Hospital.'

'As a medical examiner?' There were ways that might have had some connection to work Mansoor might have done with my parents all those years ago.

But Mank shook his head. 'Reading MRIs and PET scans,' he said. 'Seemed like very routine work from what I could tell.'

Maybe there was another way he could lead me to my parents. 'Was he traveling recently?'

Mankiewicz chuckled. 'I'm a cop, not his personal secretary. As far as I can tell Dr Mansoor had not been out of the country in the past four years, since a trip to India with his wife. Lately he might have traveled for business or gone on a long weekend but there's no evidence he's done any extensive traveling.'

Well, that was disappointing. 'Well thanks, Mank,' I said. 'I appreciate you looking into it for me.'

Mankiewicz had a subtle smile on his face. I'm not sure if it was calculated to be appealing to me or if he just thought something was amusing. 'Two things,' he said.

'What?'

'First, stop calling me "Mank" on a date. You can call me Rich.'

I shook my head involuntarily, not in a negative way but just because I didn't believe this was what we were discussing. 'We're doing this? Really?' I asked.

'Oh, hell yes. I've even figured where I can stand one step up to kiss you when I drop you off.'

'Two steps up.'

'Do you want to hear what the other thing is? Because it's about your Dr Mansoor and I think you'll be interested.'

Well, he had me there. 'OK, *Rich*,' I said. 'What's the other thing?'

'The FBI had a file on Aziz Mansoor.'

Whoa. That stopped me. I felt my eyes narrow as I tried to grasp what Mankiewicz had said. 'Why?' I managed.

He looked surprised. Not as surprised as I must have, but still. 'You think the FBI tells me anything?'

'Then how do you know they had a file on Mansoor?'

Mank – sorry, Rich – sat back and assayed his piccata, which was only about half eaten. My primavera, on the other hand, was no longer a viable reality. He – Rich, not the primavera – looked me in the eye and the smirk just barely snuck back onto his face. 'I do know a couple of feds, but nobody who can open a buried file.'

He was playing innocent but I had known the man for a while now and I could spot an act when I saw it. 'You wouldn't be telling me about this if it didn't have something good in it,' I told him. 'Let's hear it.'

Mankiewicz leaned forward with so much enthusiasm I thought he'd knock the piccata off the table; he'd been holding back as long as he could stand. 'Turns out our friend Dr Mansoor had a certain interest in eugenics.'

I must have blinked a couple of times because the room went dark then light then dark then light really fast, but I hadn't done so with any conscious effort. 'Eugenics? Like genetic engineering to create people with . . .'

'Certain characteristics considered superior, yes,' Mank (in my head I was back to that) said. 'It seems he picked up the bug from Dr Olivia Grey back at Rutgers. Now *there* was a mysterious figure.'

It occurred to me at that moment – and to my shame not a second before – that asking Mank for help on anything involving my parents might have been a really big mistake. But it was too late to turn back on it now. 'Mysterious how?' I croaked out. I don't think Mankiewicz noticed my tone because he was so excited about telling me his amazing findings.

'About three years after Mansoor left for Minnesota, our pal Dr Grey and her husband . . .' Mank stopped to think of the name and I almost blurted it out but stopped myself at the last possible nanosecond. 'Wilder, I think his name was. Brandon Wilder. Yeah. Anyway, they left New Jersey and there are abso lutely no records of them anywhere since then. In fact, there are no records of Wilder and Grey *before* she came to Rutgers.'

'So they were ghosts?' Maybe I could joke Mankiewicz off the topic.

No such luck. 'Far from it. They, or more to the point, *she* was a prominent scientist working on . . . wait for it . . . genetics when Mansoor happened into her lab. He wrote a paper on the possibilities of eliminating such things as birth defects and genetic predispositions to dangerous childhood diseases *before* the child was born, in fact at the cellular stage.'

This was more science than I could handle, which made me ashamed to call myself – privately – Olivia Grey's daughter.

Forget the research. 'So what happened to these two scientists after they left Rutgers?'

'I told you, nobody knows. Obviously they changed their names for some reason, maybe split up, I don't know. I haven't had the chance to look into research in that area that took place after their disappearance but I'll bet they were still out there, at least for a while, and the FBI wanted to know about it so they opened a file on Mansoor.'

'Are there FBI files on Grey and Wilder?' I asked, giving my mother top billing. If there were such documents it would be possible, if difficult, to get my hands on them and that would be invaluable.

But Mankiewicz shrugged. 'How would you even know where to look? If Grey and Wilder are listed as aliases on some other FBI file it would take a really deep dive to find them, and my source doesn't have that kind of access.'

The conversation drifted after that but I found myself thinking about how to research the possible research federal law enforcement might have done on my parents. Was the FBI the reason they'd had to leave and put Aunt Margie in charge? Could the FBI have files on Ken and me?

When I could focus again Mank was talking about Bendix and his search for coffee that was worse than what he could get near the precinct house. 'He won't be happy until he finds something that would take paint off his car,' he said, looking at me to see if I was amused.

I forced myself to focus on the person in front of me rather than the two who had been absent since I was very young, and found that Mankiewicz was actually a pretty likable dinner companion. He listened when I talked, which was a fairly unusual experience, and didn't let his eyes wander too far from my face, which I appreciated. When he talked, he was pretty sharp and had an eye for detail you find in good detectives, so he knew how to tell a story. By the time we'd sworn off dessert and I'd had an espresso to his decaf latte (caffeine doesn't bother me at all), I found myself feeling glad I'd accepted his invitation after all.

Mank paid the check despite my offer to split the bill with him. 'Next time,' he said and I did not question the possibility of another such evening. I decided to take it on a case-by-case basis and worry when he asked me out again, which I was certain he would do.

When we stood up to leave I noticed the stares from the crowd. After all, I was more than a little taller than my date and people still think that's strange or funny. I did hear a few chuckles in the room.

Apparently, so did Mankiewicz. 'The hell with the two steps,' he said quietly halfway to the door. Then in one swift motion he turned, dipped me down so he could reach me easily and kissed me like men do in the movies. And the man knew how to kiss.

Startled as I was, I actually enjoyed the moment. Then Mank let me back up and we walked to the restaurant exit.

The crowd applauded as we left.

THIRTEEN

I had trouble sleeping that night, not least because my stupid brother never came home.

He'd answered only one text with the words, 'I'm OK,' and answered no other questions. So I wasn't really worried about him so much as pissed off. But there were more issues to consider.

For one thing, was I dating Mankiewicz now? We'd kissed a little bit more when I dropped him off at his apartment. Kissing is like potato chips: It's really hard to stop after one. But Mank didn't want to be seen by other cops from his precinct, a number of whom lived in the neighborhood, and I didn't want to go upstairs to his apartment because I was queasy about what might happen if I did. We said goodnight and I went home to lie in bed and not sleep.

When I woke up (and checked Ken's bedroom, confirming he hadn't used it) I was determined to find the man who might have been the birth father of the woman who was probably not Evelyn Bannister. Because of course it would be a snap to find someone you weren't even sure existed.

I started once I got to my office (having assiduously avoided trying to find Ken) by calling The Association of Stringed Instrument Artisans, a real organization that consists largely of people who make guitars and other such musical devices by hand. I figured they would know about collectors of unusual instruments, and after some serious explaining about who I was and what I did, I got on the phone with Bryan Foster, the Association's vice president (they didn't have a publicist or promotions director), who said he'd been making guitars himself for more than seventeen years. And that was quite impressive. I tried to assemble a table from Ikea once and that was why we ate on an old door propped up on sawhorses.

'There are some groups of collectors. We actually make most of the instruments and they're mostly guitars we deal with, that's our focus, so we don't work with rare or antique pieces that much,' Foster said when I'd explained my interest in an obscure and – to everyone but a bidder in the UK – not terribly valuable ukulele.

'Are you in touch with any other groups that might have a better idea?' I asked.

'Well, hang on.' Foster sounded like he was rifling through some papers. I got the impression the Association worked largely from its officers' homes but I didn't know that for certain. I pictured Foster as a man in his fifties with a mustache behind a cluttered desk in a home office. But for all I knew he might very well have been a hipster with ironic facial hair picking a steel string guitar in a recording studio and taking a moment out to talk to some crazy lady about a Hawaiian instrument because he found it amusing. Phones are inexact instruments. If I'd cared enough about what he looked like I could have FaceTimed him, I suppose. 'I'm not saying we don't keep our eyes on things. I saw the story about that uke selling for all that money in England.'

Aha. So Foster was being cagey. 'What did you think?' It's good to let the subject think he is leading the conversation.

'I thought that was an awful lot of money to spend on a uke, any uke. There's no such instrument that's so rare it would get that high a bid. I know people who could hand-make a custom ukulele that would be state of the art and one-of-a-kind, and it would fetch maybe fifteen hundred bucks. That thing went for over a million. That's crazy.'

So nothing I didn't already know. 'Any idea why someone might be that crazy?' I asked.

I could hear Foster shrug. 'I dunno. They're smuggling drugs in it?' Funny guy.

'A million dollars' worth of any drug would take up more space than a ukulele and weigh more than one, too,' I pointed out. Sometimes you have to let the other person know you're actually not an idiot.

'Actually, there are baritone ukuleles that are about the size of an acoustic guitar,' Foster said, proving once again that idiots never *think* they're idiots. 'But I take your point: Even if you filled one with cocaine, it probably wouldn't be worth a million and any customs agent would notice the weight his first day on the job.'

There wasn't much point in continuing the conversation. 'Well, thanks,' I told Foster. 'I hope I didn't take up too much of your time.'

'Hang on,' he said, sounding disappointed. 'Don't you want to hear about the ukulele collectors I know?'

I was pretty sure I'd asked him about that already, but if he had names . . . 'I sure do,' I said. 'I just don't want to be a bother.' A *bother*? Who talks like that? Was my battery running low again so soon?

'No bother at all.' Foster was playing along with my conversation from a British movie of the 1930s. 'There are twenty-three people I know who actively collect ukes.'

Before he listed all of them I figured I'd cull the herd a bit. 'Do any of them collect stringed instruments of all kinds? I know the guy I'm looking for has at least one guitar and a harp that Harpo Marx probably didn't play in a movie.' That assumed, of course, that the woman I knew as Evelyn Bannister had told me anything at all that was true, which was a long shot at best.

'Oh. OK. That eliminates a lot of this list.' Foster was probably staring at a phone or computer screen. 'Give me a minute.'

'Take two,' I said.

He took me literally. 'Oh, it won't take *that* long.' You'd think with a musician you could riff, but no.

I thought it was best to stay silent. Sure enough, after about twenty seconds Foster let out a breath. 'I have three names for you,' he said.

'What are they?'

'The first is probably not who you're looking for because her name is Listrata Gingold and she's a ninety-year-old woman living in Pisa.'

'I agree. That's probably not my man.' I couldn't help it.

Foster likely blinked, trying to figure out if this human was indeed being sincere. But trouper that he was he pressed on. 'The second is a man from Syosset, New York named Augustus Bennett. I've dealt with August a couple of times and he's really a little obsessed with whatever instrument he's tracking at a particular time. I once helped him find a stand-up double bass that had been used in Josephine Baker's touring band and he flew all the way to Tanzania to obtain it. August is a serious collector.'

Would he have killed for the right instrument? It was a legitimate question, but one that I was certain Foster couldn't answer definitively. I didn't ask it. 'Who's the third person?' I said instead.

'A man named Robert Van Houten,' he answered. 'I've never dealt with him myself, but from what I can read and things I've heard from other luthiers, he doesn't even play an instrument. He just collects them as investments. He's based in Seattle, but he has agents everywhere. If he decides an instrument is worth his attention, you can bet it'll end up in his hands.'

'Sounds like a pretty wealthy guy,' I said. Had he amassed his fortune on Wall Street?

'He is,' Foster assured me. 'From what I can tell he put some money into Starbucks even before it was a publicly traded company and he's gotten very rich as the company has grown. I gather it was just an impulse; he knew the owners and asked if they needed a little extra cash. Before you know it, he's got millions.'

'If not billions,' I said more or less to myself.

'I wouldn't be surprised,' Foster said. 'But you never know.' You have to be careful what you say to serious people.

'Thank you for all your help,' I told him, but he still wasn't about to let me off the hook. Or off the phone.

'Why are you looking for this man?' he asked. People are always somewhat curious about it when a private investigator calls them with questions. They want to be able to tell their spouses, their friends, and possibly the local TV news what a huge part they played in the capture of a serial killer, of which there are far fewer than movies and TV shows would like you to believe.

'His daughter asked me to find him,' I said, and as far as I was aware that was true, although I still had no idea who Evelyn Bannister really was. And I doubted Melinda Cantone would confirm the identity of the birth father even if I had the correct name to suggest. And even if there was a Melinda Cantone.

'Well, good luck to her,' Foster said.

'You have no idea,' I told him.

FOURTEEN

I checked out Listrata Gingold just because I like to be thorough and she would be the easiest to eliminate from my search. Not only was she definitely not Evelyn Bannister's father, she was also at this moment completely dead, and not as a result of foul play. She had died of congestive heart failure in Florence, Italy at the age of ninety-two.

Augustus Bennett proved more elusive. He had indeed lived in Syosset for thirty years but had then moved away five years ago and left no forwarding address that the internet could provide. There was no point calling his former neighbors (who could be identified on the right kind of map available when you know where to look) because the one relative I did find, a sister named Sylvia who lived in Sherman Oaks, California, said she hadn't heard from her brother in more than ten years. She said he never really made 'human connections.' OK. I might have interviewed Bennett's cat but I've had very little success trying that tactic. Contrary to what some might believe, I am not a witch.

It was weird that there didn't appear to be any record of Bennett after he left Syosset (assuming he left: Maybe he was there in a different house). People generally want to be at least a little traceable so friends and family can locate them. In the social media age it's practically unheard of for a person to have no footprint whatsoever. It led me to wonder if Bennett had done that intentionally, and if so what he was trying to conceal from the rest of humanity. Maybe it was his inability to make human connections.

Since he appeared to be a dead end for the time being (there's always another way to search) I decided to shift my focus to Robert Van Houten. He wasn't trying at all to be anonymous on the internet so it was considerably easier to put together a profile of the man.

Van Houten had not simply invested in Starbucks when it was a local coffee company in Seattle, as Foster had suggested. He was a venture capitalist who had started at the age of fifteen and had a knack for finding companies about to become huge and getting just a tiny piece of them, which eventually became worth huge amounts of money. Besides the coffee business he'd bought himself a little slice of Microsoft back in his youth and had taken an interest in an alternative transportation company called Lyft (presumably because Uber sounded too German or something). So Van Houten was a very well-heeled individual.

In short, he was filthy rich.

Still he acted as a man of the people. Van Houten had open office days in a storefront in Seattle where aspiring investors could come by and gather the wisdom of the oracle, as it were. He also had a phone number that was easily findable on the web, although admittedly it did not go directly to Van Houten's own personal cell phone. It rang through to one of his seven assistants, who would answer personally, listen to your pitch, and determine if the Great Man should be next on your call list or you on his. Or, as I imagined happened often, neither.

I called the number to see what I could get and was immediately received by someone who identified himself as Steve. The simplest Google search told me he was most likely Stephen Ackridge, Van Houten's third most senior assistant. Not bad for a first try; this guy really was trying to appear to be trying to be transparent.

I told Steve I was a private investigator, which did not seem to worry him at all, and he asked what sort of matter I was inquiring about. 'Actually, I'm interested in Mr Van Houten's collection of rare stringed instruments,' I said. 'In particular, if he owns or is looking for any unusual specimens of ukuleles.'

You'd expect that to take at least a second to sink in, if for no reason other than that *ukulele* is a funny word, but Steve didn't miss a beat. 'I don't believe Mr Van Houten is in the market for any ukuleles, but I can certainly inquire with him and get back to you, Ms Stein,' he said. 'Can you give me any details?'

'I'd prefer to speak to Mr Van Houten directly, if possible,' I told him. 'It's not that I don't trust you, but I find it's better to hear the person's tone of voice and how he chooses to answer when I ask the question.' What the hell; if Van Houten was going to be transparent, I could be blunt. It's almost the same thing.

This time Steve did take a moment to consider. 'I'm not sure if that's going to be possible, but I will pass the request along,' he answered. 'In any case, is this number the one to call back? Or would you prefer an email?' I told him to go ahead and call my cell, which I'd used to contact him, since he already had the number. Apparently that whole thing about hearing the person's actual voice hadn't really landed for Steve. It happens.

I hung up with Steve and sat back. It was the first time in a while I'd had a moment to wonder where the hell my brother was, so I picked up my phone and texted him: *Where the hell are you?* Brothers and sisters have unique ways of saying how much they love and respect each other.

There was no answer and I didn't have anyone left to call about Evelyn's ukulele or her dad. And I realized at that moment that I was more interested in her murder than either of those things. That was a problem, since there was an ongoing police investigation to which I had no access. My only friend on the NYPD was Mankiewicz, who might have been inching his way out of the Friend Zone, but wasn't getting out of his own precinct and therefore didn't have any inside information on the case.

I do have a friend at the medical examiner's office named Karl, but the odds that he was working on Evelyn's case – or that he could tell me anything other than that she'd been bludgeoned to death with a brass candlestick – were not great.

My phone buzzed and – huzzah! – there was a text from Ken. *Be back for supper.*

Good lord was that man eloquent. He probably even expected me to cook. I'd show him and order in Chinese food. That would . . . not teach him a thing, but I'd be damned if I was cooking. Besides, that was six hours from now. I might even change my mind and order in from the barbecue place.

I did not need a charge but I found myself getting weary. Not finding out things takes a good deal out of me. Having no good ideas I decided to call Detective Miller, the lead cop on Evelyn Bannister's murder. He wouldn't tell me anything, but asking him would kill a few minutes.

It took a couple of explanations before I got on the phone with Miller himself. Obviously Midtown North was a larger precinct than the one where Mankiewicz and Bendix worked, and that meant more layers of administration between the public (me) and the detective (Miller). But when I mentioned my private investigator's license and the fact that Miller had questioned me at the scene of the Bannister murder, I managed to get through to the man in all his cop glory.

'You think of something else that can help?' Miller's telephone manners were impeccable. You'd think he'd start with 'hello' or something but no, the man was all business, and business meant me helping him. To protect and to serve.

'I don't have anything new,' I answered in what I hoped was a friendly tone. 'I was wondering what you've determined from the crime scene. I have Ms Bannister's family asking me for updates and I don't know what to tell them.'

You know how they always say lawyers shouldn't ask a question in court when they don't know the answer? It's basically the same for a private investigator hoping to get more information out of a cop. Technically I hadn't asked Miller a question, but I had nonetheless fallen into that very trap.

'That's funny,' he said. From the sound of his voice I didn't think he considered it the least bit humorous. 'I haven't been able to find one living relative and I'm pretty sure Evelyn Bannister wasn't even the victim's real name, so maybe you can enlighten me as to how you have her relatives on your back. And while you're at it, tell me their names, addresses and phone numbers.'

Miller, alas, wasn't a stupid cop. He had called me out on my lie and I had no Plan B other than to own up. 'OK, you got me, detective. I don't have any relatives of the victim getting on my case and no, I don't know what her real name was, either. It looks like all the information she gave me when she hired me was false.'

'Then you don't have a client,' Miller said. 'Why are you calling me about this? Why haven't you moved on to the next case?' It was a fair question and I wished I had a really good answer. Saying that it didn't feel right probably wasn't the way to go, but it was the closest to honest I could have gotten.

I exhaled, probably in Miller's ear. 'I took her money,' I said. 'Whatever her name was, she had a valid bank account at Chase and the check cleared. So I'm looking into it because that's what I've been paid to do.'

'She knew she was going to be murdered and hired you to solve it?' Again, Detective Miller was employing sarcasm (which they issue to you at the New York City Police Academy when you become an officer) to point out that I was behaving like an emotional woman and not the tough New York cop he believed himself to be. I bet he would cry like a baby at a cute puppy video on YouTube.

'No, she hired me to find her birth father, but seeing how I have no idea who *she* was it seems unlikely I'm going to track him down.' If I wasn't going to get any new information out of Miller he would have to serve as the vent through which I would relieve my frustration with this case and the fact that my stupid brother had stormed out of the office and refused to tell me where he was.

'That's not my problem,' Miller said. He was right, but that didn't help.

'Come on, detective,' I countered. 'You've been there before. A case has taken a bite out of you and you need to see it through to the end. That's where I am. And anything that helps me get there would be sincerely appreciated. I can't be any clearer than that.'

Cops like nothing better than sounding world-weary and Miller was clearly a practiced user. 'You do realize that I have no obligation whatsoever to tell you anything, and that whatever is in the report, which is public record, is all you're entitled to know. Right?'

I don't know why but I felt encouraged by his patronizing me. 'Right.'

'OK. I'm not going to give you a quiz on investigation to prove you know what you're doing.'

'Big of you,' I said. Probably shouldn't have, but a girl has to stand up for herself, and I stand taller than almost all other girls.

Miller ignored my lack of gratitude. 'Here's what I can tell you without damaging the investigation, which is something I'm never going to do no matter how bad you feel about yourself.'

'Detective . . .'

'Just listen. The ME's report came back.'

Big news. 'I'm going to go out on a limb and say she was hit on the head with a great big brass candlestick and that caused enough trauma to her skull and her brain that she died, not to mention the loss of blood. What else is new?'

You could hear the smug smile in Miller's voice. Or at least I could. 'What else is new is that the blow to the head didn't kill Ms Whoever She Was. It knocked her out and caused some bleeding but she probably would have survived.'

That was weird. 'So what did kill her?' I asked.

'The amount of strychnine that had been injected into her body, probably in her neck,' Miller said. 'Likely took fifteen to twenty minutes for her to die because she couldn't breathe.'

FIFTEEN

I walked home.
That's what I do when I need to think. Trying to navigate the subway system takes too much energy and too much brain power, while walking (particularly when you are fairly immune to the people shoving their way through Manhattan streets) leaves me bandwidth to work out problems.

Strychnine? Where could you find strychnine? If memory served it was often used as a pesticide, so maybe you could buy it at a Home Depot or use it if you worked for a pest-control company or . . . if you were a building super and you had frequent calls from your tenants about bugs eating your plants on the terrace or something. What was the name of the super at Evelyn Bannister's building? Gus? I'd have to go talk to him.

Tomorrow. I'd talk to Gus tomorrow. I was walking in the wrong direction right now and wanted to talk to Ken. I was sufficiently charged but even then I could get fatigued like anybody else. I do sleep at night, even after a plug-in.

My phone buzzed in my pocket and the ID showed MANK. I wasn't going to RICH yet in my contacts. He'd have to show me a lot more than one plate of primavera for that.

Still, I had asked him to do some more research and he was calling so I picked up the call. You kiss a guy a few times and he calls you the next day? For some girls, that's a keeper all by itself. I was convincing myself to be a little bit more hard to get. If I was going to get got at all.

'What's up, Mank?' I said. I wanted him to know we were on a professional call here and that was what I was going to call him.

But he was even more professional than I was it seemed. 'I've been shipped a package that was addressed to you,' he said. 'I'd appreciate it if you'd come to take it off my hands.'

OK, that was weird. 'What's in the package?' I asked.

'The package is your brother,' he said. 'The cops in Englewood, New Jersey just drove him over and dropped him on my feet.'

My stomach clenched. Was Ken dead? Mank didn't sound that alarmed. 'What were the Englewood police doing with my brother?' I asked.

'Denying me my right to assembly!' I could hear Ken somewhere near Mank's desk. So he was clearly alive, and I rolled my eyes because he was being Ken.

'They were deciding whether to arrest him for trespass and disturbing the peace,' Mank said. 'Apparently he was crashing a funeral.'

'Don't tell me,' I said.

'Yup. Dr Mansoor.'

I hung up the call and changed direction to get to the precinct and go sign out my idiot brother. But I took my time. Let Ken think I *hadn't* been worried about him and feeling, just for a moment, terrified at the prospect of him dying. I'd walk all the way there (which was admittedly only about ten minutes out of my way but I was making a statement). Let Mank put up with my brother's antics for a while and see how he liked it.

I called the office and got Igavda, as I should. I asked her if there had been any messages or visitors during the day. She said an older woman had come by, didn't want to say what her case was about and didn't leave a name. I wondered if Evelyn Bannister's birth mother had somehow heard about her death. I told Igavda to call me if the woman came back and not to let her leave. I was pretty sure Igavda understood what I told her. It's not always easy to know with Igavda.

Other people don't seem to have this problem, but I really can't walk the streets of Manhattan and do research on my phone at the same time. I'm so old-fashioned. But I could make a list of things I wanted to find out and they contained:

- Find out who Evelyn Bannister actually was;
- Find out if her mother's name actually was Melinda Cantone, and if so, where the hell she was now;
- Talk to Gus about the possibility of exterminators being on the premises of Evelyn's building recently;
- Find out if Dr Mansoor had actually bio-engineered Ken and me;

- Find out if Dr Mansoor had recently discovered something about my parents that would endanger Ken and me
  (he had said it was urgent);
- Figure out what the time difference was to London so I
  could call Sotheby's and see what I could find out about
  the $1.2 million ukulele;
- See if Augustus Bennett had left any traces, and if he
  was a ukulele freak.

And that was just the highlights. Realizing exactly how
much I didn't know right now was a sobering experience. If I
was a person who could walk and chew phones at the same
time I might have diverted myself with whatever the latest
game app obsessing half of America might be, but I'm not, so
I just walked to the precinct and went inside to retrieve my
'package.'

Mankiewicz was sitting at his desk, but where I had expected
to find him absolutely exasperated with Ken, I found my date
from the night before in the midst of hysterical laughter, in which
my idiot brother was joining him.

'She really thought the song went, "Down came Lorraine
and washed the spider out?"' Mank clearly thought this was
hilarious, and Ken was helping.

The 'best' part? They were talking about me, and it was a
story from when I was all of four years old.

Families are such a joy. I'm told.

I approached the desk and looked not at Mank but at Ken.
'Do I have to tell him the story about your prostate cancer?' I
asked him.

Ken's face fell so dramatically he almost had to pick it up off
the floor. 'Don't do that,' he said quietly.

Mank looked concerned and I could tell despite not looking
him in the eye. How dare he take Ken's side when he wanted to
date me! 'Did you have prostate cancer?' he asked Ken.

'No,' my brother mumbled.

Mank looked at me. 'I don't get it,' he said. 'What's funny
about that?'

'Nothing,' Ken said.

'Let's just say that young Ken, without so much as a glance

at WebMD, once believed himself to be suffering from prostate cancer,' I said. 'But he had misdiagnosed himself.'

'What did he have?' Mank said, still looking concerned.

Ken looked at me with pleading eyes. I had to remind myself that he'd vanished without telling me where he'd gone, and had then gone precisely where I'd told him not to go. He had earned this.

'His first boner,' I said.

It took a moment to register with Mank, during which time Ken lowered his head and put his hand to his forehead. Then Mank began to laugh and with each shudder of his shoulders endeared himself back into a man I'd date more and more.

'I was eleven,' Ken said weakly.

That started off another round of hootin' and hollerin' until we were finally laughed out and even Ken had joined in a little, strictly out of the contagious nature of laughter.

'Fine,' he said. 'I was an idiot.'

'Watch your tenses,' I told my brother. 'There's still the matter of being arrested at a funeral I specifically told you not to attend.'

Ken stuck out his lower lip. 'I was right to go.' He glanced at Mank for fear of saying more than he should.

I ignored him, which is my default move, and looked at Mank. 'Is he being charged with anything?'

Mank shook his head. 'The Englewood police just wanted him to go away, and were happy to provide him with a ride to guarantee he'd do so. But *I'd* like to know exactly why you thought this was a good idea, Ken.'

'You can find out stuff from people when they're emotional,' was the best my brother could do.

Luckily I'd already consulted Mank on the Dr Mansoor problem, so he could fill in the blanks on what it was Ken had been trying to find out at the funeral. I guessed they'd had enough of a chance to chat about the subject before I'd arrived and I didn't want to give away too much no matter how good a kisser Mankiewicz was. 'Can I take him off your hands, then?' I asked him.

'Yes, but keep him away from Englewood, New Jersey and call me later.' There was a specific look in Mank's eyes that I chose not to acknowledge for the time being.

'OK,' I said, meaning yes to the first part and I'd decide about the second. I gestured to Ken that he should stand up, which takes a good few seconds with my brother. He gathered himself to full height and already managed to dominate the room. I pointed toward the door. 'Thanks for babysitting,' I told Mank.

'I charge by the hour, normally.'

I chose not to answer and ushered my supposedly contrite brother out of the precinct house.

For reasons I can't entirely explain I didn't want to talk to him while we were still out in the street. It wasn't that I thought the odd passerby was an agent for whatever dark force was monitoring us and probably chasing our parents, but on the other hand how did I know they weren't?

Ken tried a couple of times to explain himself as we walked but I refused to discuss it, instead talking about what we'd do for dinner that night and anything else I could think of so innocuous no dangerous spy would be the least bit suspicious.

So I was completely pent up and fully loaded once we closed the door to our apartment. 'What the hell were you doing going to Dr Mansoor's funeral?' I screeched at him. 'Didn't I tell you that was exactly what you shouldn't do?'

'Since when do I have to take orders from you?' he countered. 'I thought we were supposed to be equal partners in this business. In fact, if you count the money that went into starting up, *you* should be taking orders from *me*.'

We like to ease into our arguments in my family.

And I'll admit, Ken's tirade caught me a little off-balance. 'You've never shown any interest in doing investigating on your own before,' I said. 'Besides, this wasn't for the agency. It was about Mom and Dad.'

Ken plopped himself down on the rickety sofa, which I feared for a moment would cause damage to the ceiling of our downstairs neighbors. Not to mention the sofa. 'Yes it was. Now do you want to hear what I found out, or not?'

If I was going to be the grownup – and I always was – I'd have to be the first to break the mood and speak in a calm, interested voice. 'OK,' I said. I sat down on one of the 'dining' chairs next to the door table and faced him. 'What happened at the funeral?'

Believing he'd won that round (which, for the record, he hadn't), Ken allowed himself a tiny smile. 'Well, I didn't see our parents, if you were wondering.' He's so bad at coy.

'And how would you know if you did?' I asked. 'We haven't seen a photo of them more recent than thirty years ago.'

His smile flattened out. '*Anyway*, there were some people there who had heard the names Olivia Grey and Brandon Wilder. Specifically, there was a woman there named Eve Kendall who looked about the right age to have known Mom and Dad – and Dr Mansoor – at Rutgers. She said she hadn't worked with Mom but she knew people who had.'

'Amazing, Holmes. So what?'

'Dr Kendall was close friends with Dr Mansoor and I think she might know why he was calling you.'

I felt my mouth curl up on the right side. 'Based on what? Your best assembled-man's intuition? Ken, just because someone was at the same university as Mom, and I guess Dr Mansoor, doesn't mean they've been carrying the answer to our origins around with them for decades.'

Ken folded his arms 'Dr Kendall heard from Dr Mansoor the same day he called you, the day he died.' He held up his head a little, better for the purpose of looking down his nose at me.

'How exactly did you broach this subject at the man's funeral?' I was dodging the fact that he might actually have some new information, and that I might have to admit that he was right to go crash the memorial.

'You're at a funeral of a guy who died very suddenly a few days ago. Asking when the last time was she heard from him made plenty of sense,' Ken said. He was having a high intelligence day and I was a good few steps behind him.

I don't know how this had become a competitive event, but now I felt like I had to reestablish my credentials as the brains of the investigation outfit. I put my left hand on the corresponding hip; that would teach him. 'So what amazing nugget of information about our parents did you get out of your new buddy?' I asked.

Suddenly the ceiling of our apartment was fascinating to my brother; he couldn't take his eyes off of it. 'Well, I didn't find out *that* much. As soon as I told her my name she asked how I knew Dr Mansoor and I said I really didn't, and that's when she started to talk loudly and the next thing I knew the police were there.'

'The cops came because you weren't invited? Can't anybody go to a funeral if they want? Sounds like this woman is fairly nuts.' I picked up our pile of takeout menus because Aunt Margie wasn't coming to cook tonight and I'd decided that I wasn't either. Ken might have tried but we didn't have fire insurance. That's not fair; he can cook when he wants to.

That spot on the ceiling was clearly a source of unending entertainment. Ken wasn't even blinking. 'It's possible that I suggested someone might have killed Dr Mansoor,' he said.

All of a sudden the choice between takeout barbecue and pizza didn't seem quite as urgent to me. 'You said what?'

'I was trying to stir the pot a little bit. I wanted to see who'd react.' Now Ken closed his eyes. Maybe whatever was on the ceiling had been too disturbing, but he sure as hell didn't want to look me in the eye.

'But you know nobody killed Dr Mansoor. He died in a car crash on West 48th Street.'

'Yeah, and our parents died in a car crash on the New Jersey Turnpike, remember?' Ken opened his eyes and looked at me with a speck of fury in his eyes.

'Nobody killed them, either,' I reminded him.

'Are we a hundred percent sure of that? We don't know where they are and we don't know what they're doing, if anything. It's possible they are dead and someone was sending Aunt Margie CARE packages for us to keep the illusion alive. Funny how those ran out the past few years, isn't it?'

I stared at my brother for an extended moment. 'You're one of those nuts who thinks Stanley Kubrick faked the moon landing, aren't you?'

Ken waved his right hand to declare the subject irrelevant. 'Never been proven either way,' he said. 'The fact is, Dr Kendall knows more than she's saying and we don't know for sure that Dr Mansoor just lost control of his car. Something might have happened. We don't know anybody in that precinct.'

'We will soon. Bendix told them who I am and let's face it, they already had my phone number. I'm surprised I haven't heard from the cop in charge of the investigation yet.' Pizza. It's the easiest thing in the world to order for dinner and it's cheap. My two favorite things, cheap and easy. Wait. That didn't come out exactly right. The only problem is that Ken likes pepperoni and I like meatballs. We could get half and half.

'Car crash. How much are they going to investigate?' Ken said. 'We should look into it. I'll talk to Dr Kendall about it when she comes for dinner.'

Hold on. 'When who does what?'

Ken smirked. 'I invited the good doctor here for dinner tomorrow night.'

'Was that before or after she insisted at the top of her lungs that you be removed from the premises?' I asked.

'Amazingly, after. I asked her before but just when the cops were *suggesting* that I leave with them, Dr Kendall looked at me and said, "See you at dinner tomorrow." Then she texted to get our address and I gave it to her. You can see for yourself.'

I found myself shaking my head involuntarily. 'You never cease to amaze me,' I told Ken.

'Thank you.'

'I didn't mean it like that. Mom and Dad left us because they were afraid for our safety and, we can imagine, their own. They thought people were watching them and trying to get at their research. *We're* their research. And you walk up to a random woman at a funeral that you think might have been made necessary by a murder and give her our home address and your cell number?'

Ken pondered that a moment. 'Well, when you put it that way . . .'

We ordered pizza. And I made it all meatballs.

SIXTEEN

I spent much of that night (after Ken went out to meet his ex-roommates for a drink in order to evade my accusatory stares) finding out all I could about Augustus Bennett, which wasn't much more than I already knew. His business interests had never been made public so there was no record of where his money might be going and no resource that could list his holdings, particularly of stringed instruments, like perhaps Harpo Marx's favorite harp not to play in *Duck Soup*.

But I did have something of a lucky break when Robert Van Houten himself decided to call me back. You never know.

'This is Ms Stein?' The voice was far too deep to be Ms Stein, and I knew that was probably me, so I assumed the man on the other end had dialed me on purpose.

'I don't recognize your number,' I said. Never say 'yes' when someone you don't know calls. They can record that and use it. 'Who is this, please?' It might be a potential client. I had to at least pretend to be polite.

'This is Robert Van Houten.'

Of course it was. Billionaires call me up every day.

'Excuse me?' I was taken by surprise. Yes, I'm embarrassed I couldn't do better.

'My name is Robert Van Houten. I have a note here that you called me about a ukulele.'

Right! The ukulele! 'Yes I did, Mr Van Houten. I was a little surprised that you called me back.'

A chuckle. 'I get that a lot. Just between us, it's one of the reasons I call people back.'

'I guess so.' It was a placeholder. 'Mr Van Houten—'

'Rob.' *Wow* this guy was working hard to be approachable.

'Rob,' I agreed.

'And your name is Frances?'

'Fran,' I corrected. If I was calling him *Rob*, after all.

'Nice to meet you, Fran.'

'Glad to meet you too. Mr . . . Rob, I'm told you have an affinity for rare stringed instruments, and I'm looking for one that appears to be fairly unusual. I thought you might be able to give me some idea as to where I should look.' It's best not to tell someone right off the top that you're thinking about them as a possible deadbeat adopted dad (the 'deadbeat' part was just because he had all that money, although Evelyn Bannister or whoever she was had done just fine for herself as far as I could tell) and maybe murderer. Tends to make them clam up a tad.

'A ukulele. Not usually my area, I'm afraid.' My new buddy was being coy; you could hear it in his voice. 'But if you give me a few more details I might be able to point you in a direction. I know a few people.' No chuckle there; he wasn't trying to be self-deprecating.

I explained to him about Evelyn Bannister's uke in the same detail I've told you, minus the fact that it was possibly auctioned off in London recently, that a case which might have fit it was found in her apartment, and that next to that case had been Evelyn's dead body. You don't have to tell a client *everything.* And he wasn't even a client.

'So your client is seeking out this ukulele not because he or she wants it, but because it might lead to an adopted parent?' There was no hint of anxiety in Van Houten's voice. He was not worried that the uke might lead to him, or was extremely good at covering that up. He merely wanted to understand the circumstances under which the question was being raised.

'Essentially,' I said. Finding Evelyn's father, whoever he might be, was no longer a priority for her, whoever *she* might have been. This was more in the area of a murder investigation but I didn't see any reason to mention that. 'My client believes the instrument might be in their father's possession, or used to be, and thinks it would be possible to trace him back if we had an idea of where and when that might have been.' You have to dance around conversational English a lot when you're trying to keep your client's identity, gender and non-living status secret from the person you're talking to about her missing rare ukulele. In case you ever run into a similar situation.

'Well, I'm familiar with the general status of that kind of instrument,' Van Houten said. 'It's rare but not *that* rare, although

I have read about something very close to what you describe being auctioned off in London recently for more than a million dollars. Might that be the one you're seeking?' Wow, and he could use the internet, too. This guy was going to be quite the catch for someone one of these days. Or maybe already was, for all I knew. He wasn't *that* transparent.

'To be brutally honest, Rob, I don't actually know. I read about that sale and thought it was a heck of a coincidence, but so far I don't have any evidence that it's the one I'm looking to find.' There was no advantage in lying about this. On the other hand, who was I kidding? That had to be Evelyn's uke.

'Well, from what I can tell the buyer was anonymous and it's pretty much impossible to squeeze any information out of Sotheby's when they don't want to tell you.' Van Houten seemed to find the pursuit of the uke charming. 'I'll tell you what I'll do. I can't give you private phone numbers or email addresses of the people I know who might have some interest in such an instrument. One of them might be the person you're looking for and might not want to be found, and the others would be mad at me if I leaked their private contact information. But I can call around to a few of them and see what I can find out. How does that sound?'

I was going to have Robert Van Houten, the Pacific Northwest's answer to Bruce Wayne, act as an operative for my agency? 'That sounds pretty good to me, Rob. I appreciate your offering to do it.'

'Not at all. It should be fun. Shake a few of these rich geezers up to suggest they might have a child they don't know about.' The chuckle was back. 'It's been nice talking to you, Fran. I can find you at this number?'

'Day or night.'

'Perfect. Give me a couple of days.'

Hell, take a week if you want, Rob. 'I really do appreciate it,' I said.

'Happy to do it.' And then he hung up. We'd concluded our business and that was it. But I felt like I'd made progress even if Van Houten couldn't find out anything, or wouldn't tell me what he did find out. I'd made a new, valuable friend.

I've always had trouble making friends for a lot of reasons.

One was that I have always been, to put it mildly, noticeable in a crowd. I tower over a lot of people, and in school that meant I seemed intimidating and *different* (which, let's face it, I am). Those aren't popular qualities.

Once I was in college I'd already built emotional walls around myself. Nobody was ever going to understand what it was like to be me, not even Ken. Being enormous and noticeable are very popular qualities for boys. Every year the school would want Ken to go out for the football team and every year Aunt Margie would forbid it, fearing that a broken bone would lead to X-rays, which would possibly lead to questions when that USB port in Ken's left side was discovered. Nobody wanted that.

OK, somebody did. Probably the FBI or a related agency. But we were dedicated to their not finding out about us, so that was kind of an issue.

Anyway, Ken didn't play football, but girls liked him – a lot – and the boys liked him because girls liked him. Ken doesn't have the same problems I do with getting to know people so it's difficult for me to talk to him about it.

I have, over the years, managed to cultivate a few friendships. With Mank, for example, although that was threatening to turn into something way scarier. But there was when I was studying for my master's at Fordham I met Shelly Kroft and we'd hit it off, being the only two women in the program at the time. (There have been more since then.) I call Shelly when I need to remind myself that not everyone I meet thinks I'm a freak of nature, even if I'm a freak not so much of nature. Shelly is six feet tall and loves it.

Right now I felt the urge to call and I didn't resist it.

'Fran!' Shelly always sounds happy to hear from me and I always think that's surprising. Yeah, I know I should be in therapy but there are things I really can't tell *anybody*. 'How's the finding-pcople's-parents business?' Shelly stayed with the law enforcement end and is now a U.S. Marshal working in Portland, Oregon.

'It's more the looking-for-people's-parents-and-hoping-you'll-find-them business,' I pointed out. 'What's new in kicking down doors?'

'It's hell on my stiletto heels. Seriously, how are you?'

'I'm good.'

There was a pause. 'Are you?'

'I'm in a moment,' I said. 'I had a case go sideways on me and I'm blaming myself and Ken's being Ken.'

Shelly chuckled. 'I can't help you with your brother, Fran. He's a force of nature. But the case. How bad?'

'My client got killed.'

I could hear her digest that information. 'OK, that's pretty bad. What happened?'

I recounted pretty much everything about the Evelyn Bannister case except the name Evelyn Bannister, since it might not have been real anyway and I have this obsession with protecting my clients' privacy even when they're dead. While I was doing all that recounting I started straightening up the living room because it seemed we were going to be having company for dinner the next night. Just to spite Ken I decided to invite Aunt Margie along too.

'So your client is dead, it's not your fault, you're not being paid, and you're still investigating this because, why?' Shelly has a very practical sense of life and besides, she's on a full-time government salary and is probably one of the last fifteen people in the country who still has a pension plan.

'I took her money to find her dad,' I said. 'I haven't done what I'm contracted to do. So I'm doing it.'

'Who are you gonna tell when you've done it?' she asked.

'Ken,' I said. The living room was straightened up and didn't look that much better.

Shelly takes me at face value and is one of the few women I know who can look me in the face, even if at the moment she was almost three thousand miles away. She took a long time to respond. 'And you think that the name she gave you was fake, she probably *wasn't* looking for her birth father, she might not even have been adopted, and on top of all that she's dead. Am I sizing this up about right?'

'You've hit it on the head,' I admitted.

'OK, then. What can the U.S. Marshals Service do for you?' That's a friend.

'Honest, Shell, I wasn't calling to ask you for a favor. I just needed a friendly ear.' Immediately I felt guilty, thinking Shelly would assume I saw her just as a source of aid and information and not as a friend.

'I know that,' she said. 'If I thought you were just using me I wouldn't have picked up the phone when I saw it was you. So what can I do to help you?'

'You can see if there have been any reported thefts in the country of a Gibson Poinsettia ukulele,' I said. 'I know there haven't been any in New York but I don't have access to records outside the city and officially, I don't have access inside the city, either.'

'I'll say this for you, Fran. It's never boring when you call.' I could hear Shelly scribbling down the information. 'I'll take a look and get back to you. Because now I'm on ukulele patrol.'

'Somebody has to be,' I said.

SEVENTEEN

'Thai. For sure this time,' Rich Mankiewicz said.

'I can't tonight,' I told him. 'I'm having company for dinner.' Of course that was true but I didn't see any reason to explain to Mank exactly why a clinical biologist named Eve Kendall was visiting my apartment tonight for a dinner of roast chicken and risotto, which probably didn't go together. Since when was I a master chef?

Mank didn't react, which was good. We weren't a couple and in my mind we weren't officially dating. Jealousy at this point (because he didn't know it was a middle-aged female biologist showing up at my apartment tonight) would have been overstepping by a long stride. 'How's Sunday night, then?' he asked. 'My next night off.'

'I'll check my calendar.' I wasn't sure about this whole thing and now, standing in the squad room at Mank's with Bendix in earshot I really didn't want to discuss it.

'Your calendar's in your phone,' Mank noted.

I didn't answer him. Enough of this witty banter; I had a purpose in this room. Now. What was it?

Oh, yeah. 'What do you know about Detective Bernard Miller of Midtown North?' I asked Mank. I'd tried calling Miller on the number he'd given me and gotten his voicemail seven times. I was starting to think Miller didn't want to talk to me again and figured I should find out if it was my breath or something.

Mank shook his head. 'Never heard of the guy,' he said. Then without prompting he looked over at Bendix. 'Hey, Meal.' They call Bendix 'Meal' because his first name is Emil, and because he looks like he's always just finished one. 'You know a guy at the 19th named Miller?'

Bendix, for him, looked thoughtful. 'Maybe. Who wants to know?' Like I wasn't standing right there where – let's face it – he could definitely see me.

Mankiewicz indicated in my direction and then spread his

hands in front of him toward Bendix, essentially telling me with one gesture that if I wasn't going to answer him about dinner I could deal with the man myself. It was cruel but fair, so I walked over to Bendix.

'I do,' I said. 'He's investigating a crime that's connected to a case of mine and he won't answer my calls. I'm trying to figure out why.'

'Geez, Gargantua, did the mean policeman hurt your feelings?' Bendix probably can't figure out why women don't like him. Everyone else on the planet can. 'You can't just go up there and ask him yourself?'

I took a step closer so I could loom over Bendix a little bit more. If Shelly Kroft thought height could be an advantage I was in no position to argue. The problem was that leaning in too far would put Bendix's chin within a few inches of my cleavage and that was the absolute last thing I needed.

'I would, but the guy's like you and that means he's afraid of strong women,' I said. 'I could ask him all I wanted but he wouldn't tell me anything. But if you'd prefer for me to think that you don't know anything about it I can do that and walk away. It's been a laugh and a half, Bendix.' With that zinger delivered I turned to head back to Mank, who looked like he couldn't open his mouth for fear of the gales of laughter that would undoubtedly result.

But Bendix surprised me. 'I'm not afraid of strong women,' he said. That part *didn't* surprise me, because that's what all men who are afraid of strong (or to be honest, any) women say. Then he added, 'But Miller is. He's not, you know, *woke*.' Now it would be necessary for *me* to suppress the urge to laugh. 'Get your buddy Mankiewicz to call him and you'll find out more.'

Mank held up his hands like he was surrendering to a bank robber in Dodge City and turned back toward his desk. He sat down and pretended to be madly absorbed in his computer screen. He leaned in so hard I couldn't see his face, probably because the hilarity he'd been holding back could no longer be denied.

I looked around, trying to determine how I had come to a point in my life where I had to rely upon Emil Bendix for assistance in something that was important to me. Lord, this place was depressing! The NYPD seemed to feel it was best if the people who worked for them never had so much as a sliver of sunlight or hope. Maybe that was a motivator.

Deflecting? Me? Perish the thought.

I walked over to Bendix and did not loom. 'Would you help me please, Sergeant?' I said as sweetly as possible, which wasn't very sweetly at all.

'Me? A man who hates strong women?' Bendix was enjoying this and I had to overlook it. Or I could go home, remember that I had no living client and move on to the next thing, which as I recalled had to do with finding the birth mother of a man in his sixties because of course she'd be living and desperate to know how his life had turned out. 'I don't think you'd want *me* to step in for you.'

'I didn't say "hate," Bendix.' It was better not to reiterate what I *had* said, which wasn't much better. 'I just hoped you would be able to make a call to your friend at the 19th and ask about a case. You don't have to mention my name at all.' In fact, it would be better if he didn't, but I wasn't about to say that.

Bendix took a long look at me, but not in the leering way he usually did. That was probably due to the fact that I have a long reach and could easily have decked him, Evelyn or no Evelyn, if he'd sized me up with a glint in his eye. 'I can do that, Gargantua. You just had to ask nicely.'

In this case, 'nicely' included not clocking him upside the head, so I didn't do that. 'Thank you,' I managed through clenched teeth. I really didn't want to see Mank right now, and he didn't want me to see him if he ever wanted to kiss me again.

Since I wasn't about to get down on my knees and genuflect, Bendix took what he'd gotten and walked over to the phone on his desk. These newfangled mobile phones were OK for some people, but not Emil Bendix.

He dialed away for a while. It was like he was calling Belgium and not an affiliated precinct maybe four miles away. Eventually the button pushing ended and Bendix waited a few moments. 'Detective Miller,' he said to whoever had answered the phone.

'Barney?' I guessed it was Miller himself who had picked up, and that meant Bendix had already made a tiny fool of himself, something I could expect only to escalate as the conversation went on, if previous experience was any indicator. 'Oh. Sorry.

Bernie. Yeah, it's Emil Bendix from the 13th. Bendix. B-E-N
. . . that's right.'

Mankiewicz was holding a piece of paper up in front of his
face, pretending to read it. It was shaking.

'Yeah, I'm calling to ask about a case you're working,' Bendix
continued, unbowed by the tidal waves of disrespect coming at
him from around the room. He checked the slip of paper I'd
given him with the one significant detail on it. 'Evelyn Barrister,'
he said. Then he listened for a second. 'Yes. Bannister. Just
checking on it because we have some interest in it here in the
precinct.'

All of a sudden Bendix looked stumped. 'Why?' he said.
'We're cops.'

The paper in front of Mankiewicz's face shook harder. I scrib-
bled something down on another piece of scrap paper from Bendix's
desk and handed it to him while a light chuckle from nearby
cubicles filled the air. Bendix looked down at the paper.

'We have a similar case and we're trying to figure whether
it's a copycat or the same perp,' he said, reading in a tone that
a fourth-grader might have used in a school play about why
racism is bad. Which, for the record, it really, really is. 'No, it
hasn't hit the system yet. We're not really sure. Wanted to check
on yours first.'

Like I said, I just jotted it down. I didn't promise it would be
brilliant.

It took a long moment for Bendix to do anything except stand
there with his mouth open for no particular reason. But eventually he said, 'Yeah. Strychnine. We haven't gotten the screen
back from the ME yet but it could be. Did you hear anything
about a guy with a limp in his left leg?' You have to trust me; I
did *not* feed Bendix the guy with the limp in his left leg. Bendix
has been on the job for decades and still thinks all criminals are
in some way deformed and scary to look at. Still, it was a good
way – whether he intended it to be or not – to get more information out of Miller.

'No guy with one leg?' Bendix pretended to sound surprised.
And now his imaginary suspect had a complete leg missing.
'What does your suspect look like?' He nodded, like Miller could
see him, and reached on to his desk blindly, holding the phone

up to his face with his chin. I handed him the wad of scrap paper and a pen. How the man got dressed in the morning all by himself was something of a mystery. He immediately started scribbling madly without acknowledging me in any way. 'How do you think they got the poison into her?' More scribbling. 'Uh-huh. And was anybody else in the apartment as far as you know? Yeah. No, just one last thing. There's like a valuable guitar or a violin or something that was missing? A *what*? You're kidding. So where did that end up? Any idea? OK.' Bendix had filled about four pages of scrap paper, proving that he could write and talk at the same time. I would not have bet on that before he picked up the phone. 'What's that? Our guy? No, it doesn't sound like a match. Our guy got shot.'

Mankiewicz's head dropped down almost at a ninety-degree angle from his shoulders and he was shaking it.

'Yeah well, thanks for the help. Feel free. Take care, Barney. Bernie. Right.' Bendix hung up the phone.

For three desks in every direction the detectives stood up and applauded.

I turned and looked at them, mostly at Mank. 'Yeah, go ahead,' I said. 'But Bendix was the only one who offered to help me.' The cops sat down and started looking at their screens again.

Bendix, surprisingly, did not seem to appreciate my grand gesture. He glowered at me and flattened his mouth out. 'They were applauding me,' he said. 'After what I did for you, I'd think you'd at least let me enjoy the moment.'

'They were—' I stopped myself. Let him have his delusion if it got me the information I needed. 'Sorry, Bendix. What did Detective Miller say?'

'I'm not sure I'm going to tell you now.'

Really? He was going to be a six-year-old? I looked back around the room. 'Another round of applause for Meal Bendix!' I shouted. All the cops, including Mank (who smiled at me, understanding), got up and clapped again.

This seemed to placate Our Hero and after everyone got back to whatever it was the city of New York was paying them to do he sat down behind his desk and shuffled the pieces of paper in his hands.

'Your friend Miller says they don't have a whole lot on the

murder you're asking about,' he said. 'The woman in question was probably injected with strychnine after being hit on the head and landing on the rug.'

'I knew that already,' I told him.

Bendix looked up, annoyed. 'You want to hear this or not? Because I have real cases I can be working on.'

'You're right. Sorry.' That was the third time I'd apologized to Bendix today, beating the record I'd had up until this day by three times. 'Please. Tell me what you found out.'

Bendix nodded, accepting his overdue respect. 'They've canvassed the victim's floor and the ones above and below it but nobody heard or saw anything. They haven't been able to find any survivors, and the ID in the woman's purse didn't check out, although it was a really good fake. You figure she just wanted to get into some bars and she wasn't twenty-one?'

'Evelyn Bannister – or whoever she was – was easily in her thirties, Bendix. She was carrying fake ID because she didn't want anyone to know who she really was.' Had I overstepped? Would Bendix now clam up and pout?

'I knew that, Gargantua. I was being sarcastic.' Of course he was. The man has to save face on a daily basis and keeps saving that one. It boggles the mind. 'Anyway, they're working on who she was. No prints in the system match hers, so she never got arrested or applied for a government job and she was never in the military. What were you doing for her?'

'Looking for her ukulele,' I said.

Bendix curled his mouth up like a kitten taking a nap. 'You know, I don't *have* to help you out on this.'

'I'm serious. Evelyn Bannister came to my office and asked me to find a ukulele because she thought it could be a link to her birth father, whom she had never met. I think she really wanted to find it because for some reason I can't figure out yet it's really valuable and she wanted the money. I think she found it, or something that looked like it, and somebody killed her for it.'

'That's the nuttiest story I've ever heard,' Bendix said. 'And I used to work in the Village.'

I shrugged. 'So it has to be true, right? Why would I make up something like that? Anyway, if Miller can't figure out who she was and nobody saw anything, what are they working on?

Did I hear you say they thought they had a suspect?' Better to refocus his attention on his call to Miller before he decided the story about the uke was too stupid to believe and clammed up.

'They don't have a suspect in custody,' he said, forgetting to be offended (and apparently forgetting that he heard about the Gibson Poinsettia from Miller; Bendix has the attention span of a flea). 'But they're looking for a guy who was seen outside her apartment right before you two got there. Short, gray hair.'

'What about the theft of the ukulele?' I asked. The case had been on the floor open and empty. Clearly something had been taken out of it.

'No prints on the case but they did find a couple on the dresser behind it and they're thinking those could be from the guy outside the apartment. Should find out soon if they get a match.'

Of course, there was someone else who had touched that dresser, someone whose prints would be in the system because he'd been fingerprinted when he applied for a private investigator license.

My brother.

EIGHTEEN

'I didn't know your parents well,' said Dr Eve Kendall.

We were seated around the door table, which I'd disguised with a tablecloth I'd found in a closet that was probably meant to be a flat bed sheet but I wasn't in a position to be picky. I'd 'roasted' a chicken, in the sense that I'd bought a roast chicken at Trader Joe's and dressed it up nicely in the center of the table, and had 'cooked' risotto in much the same way. Trader Joe was doing himself up proudly tonight.

Aunt Margie, who is as much a cook as she's actually our aunt, certainly didn't notice the difference and besides, her attention was riveted on Dr Kendall, whom she had told us she had never met before. Kendall turned out to be an attractive woman in her early sixties, serious without being pompous and intelligent (as the Ph.D. might indicate) but not stuffy. The bottle of red wine (yes, red wine with chicken and leave me alone because it had a picture of a bird on the label) had helped to loosen up the mood nicely. For my family. Kendall had been drinking water exclusively, to the point that I wondered if she was a recovering alcoholic. I was drinking water because I didn't want to find out if I was an alcoholic.

I'd had the requisite argument with Ken when I'd gotten home from the precinct house and told him that Det. Miller had probably found his fingerprints at a crime scene. Ken had said that since the cops obviously knew we were there (we had called in the emergency) that didn't mean a thing and could I please just concentrate on our guest for the evening, who at that point hadn't arrived yet?

There are days when everything just flows beautifully and there's no sense of stress at all. This had not been one of those days.

'But you did know Dr Mansoor,' Aunt Margie said. 'Do you know why he was in New York and why he might have contacted Frannie?' Aunt Margie has never really understood that I'll let her and Ken call me 'Frannie' but no one else can do that. Or she simply doesn't care, which is another completely plausible explanation.

'I knew Aziz.' Kendall's face got a little dreamy, the way a face will when remembering a dear friend, but not a lover. Her respiration did not increase and she appeared relaxed. 'He was a very fine man and had decided to live here in New York after he left the employ of a small town in Minnesota, where he was working in the medical examiner's office. Aziz was a medical doctor but he liked being a pathologist because he didn't have great social skills and didn't like to see live patients.'

'Why not?' I asked. 'You clearly liked him a lot so he couldn't have been too antisocial. He had friends, like Ken saw at his funeral.'

Both Ken and Kendall (which would have been a great name for a vaudeville act) looked a little uncomfortable at the mention of Dr Mansoor's funeral. But Kendall managed to shake it off quicker because I'd asked her a question. 'Aziz liked people too much, maybe. He never wanted to tell them bad news,' she said. 'If the prognosis wasn't favorable he preferred to have someone else deliver it.'

That immediately sparked a thought. 'If he would rather not deliver bad news, then when he called me he must have had good news, right?' I asked Kendall.

'I'm just guessing but that sounds right. I mean, all doctors have to tell patients and families something they don't want to hear every once in a while, and Aziz wasn't pathological about it, if you don't mind the pun.' It took me a moment to remember that Dr Mansoor was a pathologist. 'He'd do it if he had to, but he did his best to avoid that part of the job when he could. My guess is either that he had news he thought you'd want to hear, or it was so sensitive and private that he couldn't trust the information with anyone else.'

Trader Joe had supplied a coconut cream pie along with the rest of dinner so I started to clear the table but to my shock Ken stood up and said he would handle that. I let him; I'm not crazy.

Aunt Margie looked a little skeptical of Kendall the whole evening and I couldn't get her aside to ask why so I filed that away in my head for later. Right now, masking that edge of suspicion, she asked Kendall what she remembered about our parents.

The doctor took a sip of water and thought. 'I never really knew them well, you know,' she said. 'It was such a long time ago and they didn't stay in New Brunswick very long after you and your brother were born, Fran.'

Whoa! 'You remember when we were born?' There was a word I didn't use very often in relation to Ken or myself.

Kendall tilted her head to the right in a *sort of* gesture. 'I remember hearing about it. I knew Olivia and Brandon wanted to have children and then I heard they had the two of you. I hadn't been in touch in a little while, and after that they left for New York and we didn't see them much at all.' She paused and I saw part of why Aunt Margie might be on alert: The look of sadness Kendall adopted was not convincing. 'I was so sorry to hear about the accident.'

'Thank you.' I put an air of *I don't want to talk about that* into my tone. Because I didn't. I wanted to sound interested but not like I was grilling our guest. 'What were they working on when you met them?' I asked. That doesn't sound like grilling, right?

'Oh, that was very secret. I never really knew. I think it had something to do with speeding up recovery times, but that was your mom. Your dad didn't work at Rutgers like she did.' Not like I didn't already know that, but it was best to let Kendall think she was enlightening me. Loosen her up. It'd be even better if she'd drink some of the wine and not just the water on the table.

'He was a medical doctor.' Ken walked back into the room and sat down hard (as always) on the dining chair. We had to get extra sturdy ones just for him. I've learned to sit more demurely. Big doesn't have to be clumsy. Ken wasn't clumsy so much as he didn't care about furniture. 'Was he working out of a private practice?' Again, my brother was asking a question to which we already knew the answer. I don't know if he was testing Kendall or just thought he'd get information in that direction. But I still wanted to know more about Dr Mansoor and why he'd called. And I had reached the conclusion shortly after we started talking that Kendall couldn't answer that last – and most crucial – part.

'No, I don't think so.' Kendall looked thoughtful and that one appeared to be a sincere look. 'He was in practice with some other doctors and he had privileges at Robert Wood Johnson in New Brunswick when I knew them. But I heard most of this from Aziz.'

Perfect. There was a way back into the topic I most wanted to explore. 'When did you last hear from Dr Mansoor?' I asked.

Kendall let out a long breath. Her friend was gone and I was making her remember it. I could consider it retribution for bringing up the death of our parents, but then I remembered they weren't dead as far as we knew.

'Aziz called me the day before his death,' she answered after a moment. 'We spoke for a couple of minutes about getting together for dinner sometime this week. In fact I think it was supposed to have been tonight.' She brushed away what appeared to be a real tear.

'Did he mention me or anything about my parents?' I asked. I might as well get to the point.

Kendall shook her head and sniffed just a little. 'No. I'm sorry. Before I met Ken at Aziz's funeral I hadn't spoken to anyone about your parents for years. I apologize if that sounds callous. People just drift apart over the years.'

'Not at all. I understand. I just thought I'd ask. Dr Mansoor left me a message the day of his accident and he said he thought our parents were trying to contact him.' I had to use the cover story. 'Did he believe in communication with the dead?'

Kendall looked puzzled and mildly surprised. 'No,' she said emphatically. 'Aziz was not a spiritualist. I can't imagine what that meant.'

I looked disappointed because I was, just not in the way I was trying to sell to Kendall. 'I thought if he'd discovered something interesting he might have told you.'

'I'm afraid not. But you're wrong about one thing. I don't think for a moment that what happened to Aziz was an accident.' Kendall's face took on a determined expression.

How should I ask this? No matter; Ken jumped right in. 'You think he committed suicide?' he asked.

'No. I believe Aziz was murdered.'

Well, *that* quieted the room for a while. Five seconds? Ten seconds? An hour and a half? Hard to know.

Ken caught his breath first. His eyebrows met in the middle (which isn't a good look even for him) and he said, 'Why do you think that, Eve?' Ken had decided because he met Kendall first – at a funeral where she asked for him to be removed – they were now friends.

'I knew Aziz. There's no way he fell asleep behind the wheel. That man was caffeinated beyond comprehension. I guarantee you they found a container of energy drink in that car.' Kendall looked past Ken like she was seeing the wreckage of Dr Mansoor's Infinity and couldn't take her eyes away. 'And he didn't just lose control of the car unless someone did something to it or there was something wrong with the steering. Aziz was meticulous in everything he did. More than that, he was a defensive driver. I've ridden with him and he was without question the most careful man behind the wheel I have ever seen.'

'Still, things happen that you can't plan for,' I suggested. Kendall was sounding a little like a person who didn't want to believe what had happened and was creating an alternate reality that would make it weirdly easier to accept. In other words, the typical concoctor of a conspiracy theory.

She nodded, coming back to our dining 'table.' 'That's true. But here's something you should know, Fran. Aziz wrote everything down. *Everything.* If he knew something about your parents that he thought he should tell you, I can pretty much tell you without question that it was in his car.'

'Probably burned up,' Ken, ever tactful, said.

'Maybe,' Kendall agreed. 'But maybe not. I said Aziz was meticulous and had a small streak of paranoia. He carried a fireproof box with him in every vehicle he ever owned. If he had notes on something important, they'd be in that box.'

Even Aunt Margie looked impressed by that. Her eyes were wider than usual and her right hand was not exactly pointing in Kendall's direction, but was resting in a way, with the index finger extended and pulsing up and down, that indicated she was trying to figure something out. I'd seen it a thousand times. Aunt Margie had decided she'd met Eve Kendall before and was sifting through her memories (which she did *not* keep on paper in a fireproof box) to recall exactly where.

Aunt Margie was doing her thinking, but I had another thought, and that was: *I need to see the inventory from that car.*

NINETEEN

'I think I've got something,' Ken said.

Under normal circumstances I would have made a hilarious crack instructing him not to get too close to me so I wouldn't catch it, but I had asked my brother, who has better hacking skills than I do, to try and get a handle on who Evelyn Bannister might really have been. Now he was saying there could be a lead, so devastating him with professional-level humor seemed unwise. For now.

'You know who she is?' I said. I leaned over his shoulder. I was standing behind Ken in his bedroom (which was disgusting but his) as he sat on his bed and flailed away at his laptop computer.

'No, I don't know who she *was*,' he answered. 'But I might have a line on how to find out how to find out.' No, that's not a typo; it's how my brother communicates.

'Speak to me in Human,' I said. We exchanged a look that took our relationship to humans into question. But we both knew we weren't some other species.

Ken turned back toward the computer and I couldn't see his eyes but I was willing to bet he was rolling them at what a complete and utter failure his sister is with technology, despite being made partially of technology. We live in ironic times.

'OK,' he said. 'I found some of Evelyn's past addresses, so she'd been using the name for at least two years. She moved around a lot. Look here.' As most tech-savvy people do, Ken thinks that he needs to point at things on the screen to get the rest of us Luddites to understand. I dutifully moved my face in the direction he indicated. 'This is a list of properties on which the name Evelyn Bannister was used when signing a lease. It goes back two years and then nothing. So you have to figure she'd been changing names for a while and had really good fake IDs.'

'There are four apartments listed there,' I pointed out because

I'm pretty sure Ken can't count (that's a joke, Ken). 'How did she keep getting out of the leases in each one when she left?'

Ken held up his index finger like a philosophy professor whose student just correctly identified a theory of Kierkegaard's. 'She didn't. That's the thing. She just kept paying rent at each one until the lease ran out.'

This offended my sensibilities as a New York apartment-dweller in ways that I don't think I can adequately describe. But I tried to rehabilitate my opinion of Evelyn: 'So she sublet every time?' I asked.

Ken shook his head. 'Nope. The places stayed empty and she never even contacted the landlord until it came time to not renew the rental agreement.'

'I'm starting to hate Evelyn Bannister,' I said.

'I totally get that, but it was your idea to keep investigating her murder. Now, there had to be a reason she kept moving from place to place every few months. I mean, we're pretty sure the government or somebody is hot on our trail and yet we've lived here all our lives and nobody's found us.'

Nobody until you let your pal Dr Kendall visit, I thought, but what was the point in saying that now? Besides, I didn't really think Kendall was part of the rumored conspiracy tracking down Ken and me roughly since we first started taking in air. But I didn't know for sure, did I?

Once Kendall had left after dinner (without having had any coconut cream pie because nobody seemed to be in the mood) Aunt Margie had confirmed for me what I'd suspected from the look on her face. 'I've seen that woman before,' she said. 'A long time ago. Something with your parents. But I can't place her exactly.'

'You seem worried about it,' I said. I was washing the dishes by hand. This was not because we have such precious china but because we don't own a dishwasher. It's an old building.

'I'm not *worried*.' Aunt Margie wouldn't admit to being worried if the house was on fire. 'But I get the feeling wherever I saw your Dr Kendall before, it wasn't good.'

'She's not *my* Dr Kendall. She's *Ken's* Dr Kendall.'

'Whoever's. Be careful when she's around. And when she's not around. Just be careful, Frannie. If I remember anything else I'll tell you. Now hand me that glass.'

'I just washed that glass.'

'That's what you think.'

So the mysterious (sort of) Dr Kendall was now on my list of things to be concerned about, which had been growing by leaps and bounds every day since 'Evelyn Bannister' asked me to find her a uke. Which reminded me that I wanted to go visit Gus the super in Evelyn's building. Maybe bring him a bottle of something to show what a nice person I was. How do you know what a superintendent drinks? What if he was a recovering alcoholic and I nudged him over the edge? Nothing's simple.

I did need to find out about Dr Mansoor's car, though. Very next thing on my to-do list. After Ken showed me what marvelous information he'd uncovered, which seemed to be getting less marvelous every minute.

'So Evelyn moved a bunch of times in the past two years and used a number of identities,' I said. I was mostly thinking out loud but Ken was welcome to join in if he didn't have something especially bro-ey to say. 'It's possible she thought someone was after her, but maybe we're overlooking other possibilities. Why else would a woman want to be someone new a few times a year?'

'Maybe to keep attracting younger guys.' Bro-ey. Like that.

'Maybe she was in a cutthroat business where it's better to be anonymous,' I suggested. Again, I was talking to myself because I was clearly the more mature audience. In fact, now I was hoping Ken wouldn't respond at all. Attracting younger guys. You should see how I'm rolling my eyes right now. 'Like maybe . . .'

'Smuggling rare and possibly stolen stringed instruments for collectors who might be wealthy and not all that concerned about the supply chain?' Ken said. Once in a while he manages to say something intelligent. You have to wait, but it's often worth it. 'It's possible. In fact . . .' He was back in tech genius mode and started clacking away at his keyboard. I thought the laptop might start to emit smoke and then got hung up on the fact that the port that charged the computer was similar to the one that charged me and I got distracted. Or did I say that already?

'What?' I said. 'In fact, what?'

Ken's voice took on the dreamy quality it has when he's

talking to you but thinking about something else. 'We never really did check into that ukulele sale in London,' he said.

'Sure I did,' I said. I get defensive in a hurry, or did you not notice that already? 'But the buyer was anonymous and trust me, I've tried but you can't get Sotheby's to give that information up even if you threaten to blow up their building.' Which, I feel obligated to point out, I have never done.

'Yeah, you checked about the buyer and of course you couldn't get a name,' Ken said, still clacking with some serious vigor. 'But you didn't check to see about the agent who handled the bid.'

I looked over his shoulder again. 'Was it Evelyn Bannister?' I asked. I saw a website that appeared to have records of every auction sale in the world since someone invented auctions. It was, dare I say it, a lot of sales. But Ken was scrolling through them at warp speed and I couldn't make out any names, even from just a few feet away.

'Maybe, but she wasn't using that name. That's why it didn't set off any alarms for us when we checked on it before. Hang on.' He scrolled some more until he got to a page that looked to my eye exactly like every other page he'd looked at before. But clearly to Ken this was the White Whale he'd been searching for. 'Here. A sale of one Gibson Poinsettia ukulele, circa 1926. Original finish, unscratched. Painted poinsettia on front. With "The Gibson" on the headstock instead of "Gibson" to document its age and rarity. This sounds like our uke, all right.'

OK. I gave up the ruse; that was Evelyn's ukulele and it had sold for a literally ridiculous amount of money. I'd just have to live with it. 'Who brokered the sale?' I asked because he kept moving his head and I wasn't about to climb on the bed behind him.

'It went for $1.2 million and that still doesn't make any sense,' Ken said. 'Even a site that called it "The Holy Grail of Ukuleles" priced it at eleven thousand.'

'Who brokered the sale?' I repeated. Yes, the extremely inflated price was important, but the identity of the person making the deal was a little more urgent.

'Whoever bought it did so through a broker and on the phone,' he went on. As if I hadn't spoken. 'Didn't even bother to come look at the thing for themselves. Why?'

'I'm sure the obvious answer is they were not in London and couldn't show up in person for the auction. It happens all the time.' I stood up taller because my neck was starting to ache and besides Ken wasn't showing me anything in the least bit interesting anymore. 'Why does it matter?'

My neck was achy. Maybe I needed a charge soon. It's one of the signs.

'It matters because the item being sold here is a rare instrument and there are only so many people on the planet who can authenticate something like that,' my brother answered. 'Somebody spent a million two on a thing that should have topped out at eleven grand. It would be interesting to know exactly who they consulted to prove it was worth the money, and whether that person was getting a cut of the take.'

He was making good points. But when a Van Gogh is sold for umpteen millions of dollars, it's a rare object that's authenticated by an expert. I asked Ken why this was different.

'Everybody agrees a Van Gogh is worth ridiculous amounts of money,' he said. 'In this case, everybody agrees a ukulele isn't worth anywhere near this much. So you have to cast some suspicion on one or both of two people: The agent who brokered the deal, and the expert who said the lot in question – the ukulele – merited overpaying by a factor of more than a hundred times.'

'I was told there would be no math,' I said.

'You were lied to. This is all about the math. What inflates the price of an old Hawaiian mini-guitar to the point that a member of the one percent needs to buy it? What makes *this* ukulele that valuable when literally no other instrument like that on the planet is worth anywhere near as much?'

I sat down on a chair Ken keeps at a desk next to his bed that he never uses. That wouldn't normally bother me, but his desk is better than the one in my bedroom. 'The whole thing hinges on those two people,' I said. 'Do you have a name for the agent or the ukulele expert?'

Ken was so deep into his screen that he didn't answer for close to a full minute. Luckily, I had Words With Friends on my phone and beat Shelly Kroft in a game using the word *suq*, which to my knowledge isn't a word but the game will accept it. Finally Ken took a semi-deep breath and turned away from his laptop, which I wouldn't have thought was possible only seconds before.

'I have a line on both the agent and the ukulele expert,' he said. 'It's actually pretty public so it didn't take a lot to get those names.'

'Is either one of the names Evelyn Bannister?' I asked.

'No, but is that surprising? She had more names than the directory of the American Dental Association.'

That was an odd choice but I let it go. 'Was either one a woman?' I said. 'I'd bet my last dollar Evelyn was a woman.'

Ken pointed a finger at me like the barrel of a pistol. 'Yes,' he said. 'The broker who arranged the purchase was a woman named Patrice Lancaster. It'll take some digging to find out whether she might also have occasionally been Evelyn Bannister.'

'I take it our uke maven was not female,' I said.

'You are correct again and thanks for playing our game.' My brother thinks he's amusing. 'Authenticating the, you know, authenticity of the Gibson Poinsettia was a Mr Langley Comstock, Ph.D., of McLean, Virginia. He appears to be legit from what I can tell.'

'With a name like that? Practically screaming he's from the CIA?' Seriously, *Langley* of *McLean, Virginia*?

'I know. The hairs on the back of my neck stood up, but he seems to have never even met anybody in the CIA. Just a weird name, I guess.'

'Can we be sure? How can we feel safe?'

Ken swung his legs off the bed and they pretty much already touched the floor. 'Two very good questions. But if you don't mind I promised Igavda that I would come by and help her with her citizenship test. She's taking it next week.' He stood up.

'Whoa!' I barked at him and Ken stopped to look at me. 'You're leaving in the middle of this?'

'I did what I do. Now you do what you do. Find out whether the woman who died on the Upper East Side sometimes called herself Patrice Lancaster. You know how to find me.' He turned again to leave.

'Ken,' I said. I stood up to look him in the eye.

He did a *why me* shoulder shrug and looked at me. 'What?' The question was practically an accusation, although I wasn't sure of what.

I walked over and blocked his path to the door. Then I put a hand on his forearm. 'You know that I got mad at you yesterday just because I worry about you, right? I mean, you are truly the only person in the world who understands what it's like to be me and when I think I might lose you I get really upset. You're my brother and I love you.'

Ken's eyes softened and he put both his hands on my upper arms 'I know,' he said. 'Now if you don't mind I have to go help a very hot immigrant become a citizen.' He lifted me up off the floor, moved me out of his way and placed me back down without so much as a grunt. 'I'll see you later.' Then he was gone.

That is to say, he left. We don't have the power of vanishing or anything. We're just big and strong and we plug into the wall every now and again. Other than that, just like you. With a few improvements.

I fumed a little bit because I felt like I'd just opened up emotionally to Ken and he had treated it like a joke. But that's Ken and there isn't much you can do about it. Or at least there isn't much *I* can do. I imagined there were things Igavda could do but it was better not to think about that.

After a short while I gave up on the fuming because it wasn't doing me any good and would continue not to do me any good. Besides, I had major decisions to make.

But first there was a text from Shelly Kroft, as reliable as a sunrise. *Gibson Poinsettia stolen from private home in Portland, ME. Has not been recovered.*

At the moment I had two major concerns (beside my usual cases, which were getting my attention but which I'm not detailing here because my clients are entitled to anonymity): I could look into Evelyn Bannister's (or Patrice Lancaster's) ukulele, her phony missing birth father and, just as an aside, her murder *or* I could concentrate on Dr Mansoor, his *possible* murder – although I was fairly sure Dr Kendall was way off base on that one – and more to the point, his connection to my parents.

Paying (or having already paid) customers first. It was Evelyn's murder that came up first. Because at least I had an idea of where to go about that, and I needed to get out of the apartment. You do enough research online in your pajamas and eventually you really feel the need to be outdoors, even in Manhattan, where the sky is often obscured by all the other people looking for the sky in even taller buildings.

I'd go talk to Gus the super, I decided. I'd bring bagels from a place I had spotted close to Evelyn's apartment building. Because even carb addicts don't get offended when you bring them bagels.

It was a hot-ish day with some cloud cover and I was way past looking up for the sky because what am I, a tourist? But it did feel good to be out among humans and even the subway gave me a little sense of familiarity that I needed today.

Eve Kendall's visit had shaken me more than I wanted to admit. There were people out there, and I had no idea how many, who had known my parents under the names Brad and Livvie or others I didn't know. And if Kendall was to be believed, there was someone out there who had killed Dr Mansoor right at the time he was trying to contact me with some answers.

I know. I just said I didn't believe Dr Mansoor was murdered. And I didn't. But that's how my mind works sometimes: Consider the worst-case scenario and how you'd handle it, and then you can work your way down to what's more probable.

Having pondered this for some time I almost missed my stop but the Q train has a way of reminding you when you're getting where you're going. It stops. That woke me up enough to get out and retrace the steps I'd taken with Ken on the day we found Evelyn's body in her bedroom.

I was approaching the building and noting the car parked right near the front door in an illegal spot when a call came in from Mank. I had sufficiently forgiven him for whatever it was I'd decided he did that deserved forgiving that I picked up.

He didn't even say hello. 'Somebody's following you,' he said.

That seemed like an odd game to play and I was just about to say, 'What?' but I never got the chance.

Instead I felt someone put a hand over my mouth and pushed me hard to the left. Normally that wouldn't have even set me off-stride but I wasn't expecting it and I fell toward the street. I dropped my phone, but hands I suddenly couldn't see caught me and after a quick moment of wondering why I was blind I felt the black cloth bag over my face, I was sitting down and heard a car door slam. And I felt a little pinprick in my right hip.

I don't remember a whole lot after that for some time.

TWENTY

I t would be such a cliché to say I woke up and asked, 'Where am I?' And I didn't say that, I promise.

Of course, it wasn't that I didn't want to know where I was; it was more in the area of there was no one in the room with me and asking myself wasn't going to get me anywhere.

What appeared obvious and equally ominous was that I was in an operating room. The equipment I saw stacked around me in the surprisingly small area was consistent with what I'd seen on television shows about doctors, but theirs were always a lot roomier and more upscale. The TV people had the finest in medical equipment and I could just as easily have been in one of the better auto body shops in Queens. I didn't have anything else to use for a comparison. I'd never been to a doctor before but I had seen more than one car repaired.

Most worrisome was that I was on a gurney and strapped down so efficiently that even I couldn't break the bonds. On the plus side I was relieved to see there was no IV line running into my hand.

There was also a security camera positioned directly down at me from the ceiling. Whoever was watching me wasn't particularly worried that I'd find out. I couldn't blame them. I was, after all, strapped to a gurney. It was unlikely I'd be doing anything particularly natural or unguarded right now.

After testing my bonds a number of times and realizing they were more up to the task than I was, I decided on the direct approach. 'Hey!' I yelled. 'I'm awake! Let's get this show on the road! I have a date tonight!' I had no date because I was playing hard to get with Mankiewicz (and what was that about how someone was following me?), but they didn't know that. I hoped.

Nobody appeared immediately, which frankly got me a little insulted. Here someone went to all the trouble to abduct and confine me and now they weren't interested enough to come in and explain themselves? What was I, chopped liver? (Shelly Kroft taught me that one.)

Don't get me wrong: I was also absolutely terrified. I wasn't accustomed to feeling helpless. A person like me – and there are only two – is generally able to deal with pretty much any situation that requires physical strength. The fact that this gurney had restraints with steel cuffs and solder instead of bolts indicated that it had been built specifically with me in mind. That was not a comforting thought.

But one thing I have discovered over the years is that showing fear is almost always the wrong strategy. I'm not often afraid but when I am, my immediate instinct is to go straight to snark. And it has rarely failed me.

'Yo, fellas!' I got a little louder this time. 'I'm gonna need to pee soon and you definitely don't want to be here for that!'

You'd think the thought would have brought in my captors, or someone carrying a bucket, but no.

I had to focus. Look around the room. See what my possibilities, however limited, were. The place was tightly packed with electronics and what I could only assume was diagnostic equipment. It looked like where they'd sent everything when all the Radio Shacks closed. There was a flat-screen monitor affixed to the wall up above the door. It was turned off at the moment. There was also a very suspicious-looking mirror to my right that probably showed whoever was in the next room what I was doing. I was doing remarkably little but you never know what some people find entertaining.

It was a relief that there were no surgical instruments in sight but that didn't mean they wouldn't appear at any moment. If someone was into vivisection here they weren't tipping their hand. That wasn't stopping me from worrying.

Don't ask me what was behind me because that simply wasn't an option from my perspective. There was no mirror on *my* side of the room.

'Seriously, I drank a whole large bottle of water with lunch!' I yelled. 'You really want me off this table fast!'

Nothing. These people had no common courtesy and no sense of hygiene. Clearly they were fiends.

And that, finally, just pissed me off (so to speak). 'Get your asses in here *now*!' I screamed. 'The last thing you want is me for an enemy! And I have friends who are bigger and stronger than I am!' OK, not so much a friend as a brother but that wouldn't have sounded as ominous: *Just wait until my big brother finds out.* Not quite the same panache.

It did leave me to wonder if Ken had any idea I was missing yet. I had no clue how long I'd been in transit or how many minutes/hours/days I'd been on this table. That's the thing about anesthesia: It's not like a nap. You have no idea that anything at all happened to you except you were in one place and now you're somewhere else.

The rage I was feeling was real and it inspired me to try pulling on the restraints one more time. They didn't come loose, but my right arm, the dominant one, definitely felt a very slight give. If I were here for another three days I might be able to pull that one free.

Just as that thought occurred to me the door swung open slowly and in walked . . . a person. It was hard to tell what kind of person this was, as he/she/they was dressed in very loose surgical scrubs, a surgical mask and cap, and a plastic shield over the face that reflected light. It was like being stopped by a state trooper wearing mirror sunglasses all over his face.

'It's about damn time,' I said before the anonymous figure could speak. 'Now let me up so I can use the bathroom.' I'd been telling that lie for so long I was starting to believe it myself.

The person didn't speak, but turned on a monitor to my left which showed my heart rate and oxygen level courtesy of a clip mechanism my captor attached to my left index finger. They (the heart rate and oxygen level) were fine for me. A little slow (heart) and rich (oxygen) for a regular person, but nothing a doctor would be likely to find alarming.

'Hey! RoboDoc!' If you annoy people enough they tend to react. At least that has been my experience. 'You gonna tell me who you are and why I'm here? Because when my friends from the police department get here I want to be able to give them accurate answers.'

Mank knew I was being followed, he'd said. Did he have eyes on me? Was he on his way? There was no evidence I knew of that anybody had even noticed I was missing yet. Maybe I *wasn't* missing. Maybe I was dreaming right now. I mean, it seemed real enough, however weird, and I didn't tend to dream but there's a first time for everything.

The automaton in the surgical garb didn't talk, but there was a voice that came over what was clearly a very efficient audio system in the room. No static. Very clean sound, but the voice was being distorted electronically. And the person speaking was oddly not standing next to the gurney. 'The police aren't coming.' Male voice. Not familiar. 'No one is coming.'

'Yeah?' I was reduced now to arguing with the ceiling because that's from where the voice was emanating. 'You underestimate me, and that's your mistake. Now why don't you come in here, tell me who you are and why you kidnapped me, and then we can have a reasonable discussion before I tear your head off.'

'We can have any discussion you like right now,' the disembodied voice said. Calm as could be. Cool as a cucumber, assuming all cucumbers are cool. My mind was wandering. I was feeling the need for a charge more since the shock of waking up. It was probably a bad plan to ask the anonymous being in all the HazMat gear next to me, now attaching a blood-pressure cuff to my left bicep, to plug me in for an hour or so. 'For example, you can tell me exactly where the people who constructed you might be found.'

It's not that I didn't suspect all this sci-fi melodrama was connected to my own bizarre origin story. It's not that I thought this man, hiding behind walls and electronic devices, didn't know there was something odd about me more than the obvious, that I was tall and strong. But hearing The Voice say that, so matter-of-factly, sent an actual chill up my spine. Turns out that's really a thing. I think, to my eternal embarrassment, that I gasped audibly.

I tried to cover for it. 'It's hard to breathe with all this stuff tying me down,' I said, like that made any sense. 'What are you talking about?'

Having finished taking my vitals, the person in the head-to-toes PPC removed the cuff and hung it back up on the monitor. He/she/they turned toward the badly disguised one-way mirror (and it should be noted that all mirrors are one-way mirrors; this one simply had a window on one side) and held up a hand making the 'OK' sign. Whoever it was did not speak and the voice of my tormentor didn't address any comment to them. But there must have been some kind of communication device included in the hood because the person inside it nodded. Clearly it is best to spend the extra money on your evil equipment because you get the optional features.

There was no way I could get myself out of these restraints. Pulling with all my might had just tired me and not weakened the wrist or shin cuffs (not ankle, which was odd I thought) at all. But if the medical assistant made the move I wanted them to I might at least have a chance to see the evil genius – we were in that territory, let's be real – in person. That would be something, anyway.

But I needed that human (an assumption, but at least a likely one) to move to my right and that hadn't happened yet.

It was a very narrow room made narrower by the tons of equipment. You had to wonder what the landlord must have thought when all that stuff was being moved in. I despaired for the fact that my captor might lose his security deposit. But the tight quarters might very well play to my advantage.

'You know perfectly well what I mean,' The Voice said. 'The people who constructed you, or grew you. Where are they? Tell me and we'll remove your restraints and send you on your way.' This guy clearly grew up watching James Bond movies and rooting for Ernst Stavro Blofeld.

'I don't know who you're talking about,' I said. 'If you mean my parents, they were killed in a car crash when I was little.' I was watching my new friend the service technician, who was adjusting levels on various devices. But on the left side. I needed them on the right side.

'Don't insult my intelligence,' The Voice said with a weary tone.

'Don't insult mine,' I said back with what I hoped was a sneer. 'You didn't put a bag over my head and bring me to the crazy man's Mayo Clinic to ask me questions about my parents. You have some medical reason for me to be here. So let's put our cards on the table. What do you *really* want? Because I'll tell you right now, what *I* really want is to get up off this gurney and spend five minutes in a room with you.'

I was not pleased when the medical technician reached into what appeared to be a sterile chamber of some kind (it actually looked like a microwave oven but I was willing to bet it wasn't) and pulled out some vials and a syringe. I'd never had a blood test before and didn't know if anything unusual would show up. Not to mention I figured I needed all the blood I had in stock.

But I *was* pleased when the tech did something I wouldn't have expected: As they crossed in front of the gurney, they felt down with their foot and I could feel the front two wheels unlock. The mask was pointed directly at me, so I figured the tech was looking at my face while doing that, so it must have been deliberate. Maybe I was about to be moved, but I didn't have to go along with their plans. The tech's move gave me exactly the advantage I'd been hoping for, even if I couldn't figure why the wheels had been freed up.

'What I really want,' The Voice said, 'is to get the whereabouts of the people you call your parents.'

'If you believe in heaven, I think that's the area code you're looking for,' I told him. 'So now that we're done, how about telling your pet robot here to let me up?'

That was when the medical technician first spoke and asked exactly the question I wanted to hear. 'Are you right handed or left handed?' A woman's voice. Go figure. In stupid action movies the evil minions are usually men. Except the ones the hero is going to sleep with.

I looked at her and tried to put on an expression of worry. 'Left handed. Why?' I was lying, but I knew why she asked and was hoping she'd react accordingly.

'OK,' she said. 'Then I'll do this on your right arm.'

Oh, yes. Please do.

She held the syringe, with a newly unwrapped sterile needle attached, straight up to avoid unintentional contact. Then, nodding, she walked around the gurney and picked up a cotton swab and some alcohol from a cabinet on her way. Perfect.

She got to the right side of the gurney. Before she could even consider tying off my arm and jabbing that thing into a vein, I reached out as far as I could with my left foot.

Like I said, the room was very narrow and there was bulky

equipment everywhere. I kicked as hard as I could against a heavy unmovable object, some computer equipment I couldn't identify, on my left. The force (I was pretty strong even if I needed a charge) moved the gurney – with its front wheels unlocked – directly into the tech and pinned her against the wall without noticeably injuring her. Even better, I could still reach the computer console with my left foot (this place must have been a closet before they'd moved in half of NASA) and maintain the pressure on the woman in all the PPC. She gasped, as it caught her directly in the abdomen. She dropped the syringe.

'What are you *doing*?' The Voice demanded.

I looked the tech directly in the mask. 'You have a choice,' I said. 'You can unlock my right hand or I can push a lot harder and cause internal bleeding and you can die.'

That was not much of a choice, I knew, and without speaking the tech reached over and unstrapped my right hand. She reached for my right foot but her arms just weren't long enough.

Not a problem at this point because I had already undone the restraint on my left hand and was working on the right foot.

'Brenda!' The Voice scolded. 'What did you *do*?'

By then I'd freed myself completely and was getting ready to jump off the gurney when the tech suddenly put her hands on my right triceps. I looked in her direction. She reached into her pocket and pulled out my cell phone, which she handed to me.

'Run,' she whispered.

I figured that was a pretty good idea and was at the door and through it into a corridor before The Voice could protest any further or send any extra minions in my direction. I looked back at the tech before I bolted and she was just standing where I'd left her, pushing the gurney far away enough that it wouldn't be painful anymore.

It was as nondescript a corridor as I'd ever seen and I had no idea which way to run, so I just chose a direction and hauled ass. At the end of the hall was a doorway that led to stairs and I flew down three flights until I finally made it to the street. I'd never been so happy to be engulfed by my fellow New Yorkers.

This wasn't a neighborhood I knew well but it's hard to be in Manhattan and not find your way. I tried to look normal, like I wasn't fleeing a mad scientist out to collect my blood and track down my parents, because the average NYC resident can sense that on you.

Luckily there was a subway station at the end of the second block and I blended into the usual mélange of humanity submerging themselves into the bowels of an island in the hope that they can get to their next meeting faster. I figured calling Ken or Mank or Aunt Margie (who I always wanted to talk to when I was scared) could wait until I was as far away from this building as possible. And until I could figure out what I wanted to tell Mank. *Hi, I got abducted by a mad scientist who knows that I'm a freak not of nature and wants to experiment on me and find the parents I told you were dead.* That didn't seem like a great strategy no matter how good a kisser the man was.

I tapped my phone on the scanner and blended as well as someone who looks like me can blend into the crowd. There wasn't an open seat on the train, which was kind of comforting.

At least *some* things were normal.

TWENTY-ONE

A unt Margie's apartment is laid out a lot like the one Ken and I share. This is not surprising, given that it's one floor below and two doors down from us. She has decorated in a slightly different style than our Early Goodwill motif, with real rugs and tables bearing tablecloths as well as actual art on the walls. In our apartment we have the occasional concert poster, unframed and stuck up with masking tape, or a plant I'm in the process of killing with inattention.

I went straight to Aunt Margie's from captivity. She's the closest thing I have to a mom present in my life and I love her dearly. She was also an excellent crime reporter in her time and knows the things I don't about law and its enforcement. So today, given that I (1.) needed a hug and (2.) had just been kidnapped, she was the perfect person to seek out.

I got the hug. That was first, and it was a good one that lasted a long time. Aunt Margie loves Ken and me like we were her own children, and even though we tease her about it sometimes, we know that we'd literally not be alive today without her.

Once we sat down she got out a box of Oreos and some milk because she's Aunt Margie and knows what's necessary, and two coffee cups because that is unquestionably the best way to dunk Oreos. I told her my whole bizarre story (the one she didn't already know) and asked her advice.

'I can't call the cops,' I said. 'They'll ask me questions I can't answer. And that's especially true now, because this must mean that the suspicions Mom and Dad had about people trying to find us were right. We have to be even more careful now. Maybe we should move.'

Aunt Margie sat back in her chair a little, seemingly stunned. 'Move?' she said. 'Out of the apartment?'

'Out of New York,' I said. 'If they know we're here. It could be dangerous.'

She waved a hand to knock the idea down and squash it.

'Dangerous. For you everything is dangerous, Frannie. But nobody's come here to the apartment. Your home address isn't listed anywhere. You have business cards circulating, apparently all over the place because a doctor you never met had some in his car, and yet nobody's come to your office looking for you.'

I told her that Igavda had mentioned a middle-aged woman who'd come in and left without leaving a name.

'That was probably a prospective client and you know it, Frannie. Let me tell you something about danger.'

'You know danger?' From my memory, she sat in a studio and read news copy. But it just that moment occurred to me that Aunt Margie had probably given up the more perilous aspects of being a crime reporter when it had become obvious she'd have to be taking care of two very unusual children full-time.

'I've seen a bit of it,' she said with a smile. 'And I can tell you this: Danger is something you can run away from or you can run at. If you run at it and you look determined enough, danger tends to turn tail and run. Danger, my dear, is a bully and a coward.'

Aunt Margie took a dunk of Oreo and ate it. She has a dramatic sense.

'So you're saying I should welcome danger?' This was not what I'd been taught growing up and I'd been taught by this very same woman.

'No. You don't seek it out. But if it comes for you, that's when you charge it. And today, it came for you. I think you found out something about yourself today. You might have been scared . . .'

'*Might* have been?'

'Let me finish. But you dealt with it directly and you found a way out of the problem.' A little milk dribbled down her chin. It's an occupational hazard with wet Oreos. She had a napkin handy. Being prepared was what Aunt Margie was all about.

I thought about that. 'Mostly I was rescued by the lab technician,' I said. 'All I did was kick the wall.'

Aunt Margie extended her index finger and shook it. 'Now that's interesting,' she said. 'You didn't recognize this woman, you said?'

'I said I couldn't *see* this woman, at least not her face,' I answered. 'She was wearing so much protective gear I was starting to wonder if they'd exposed me to plutonium while I was unconscious.'

Aunt Margie leaned forward. 'Did you recognize her voice? Think hard.'

I did as she suggested and scoured my brain for any familiar tones. 'No. At first I was suspicious that maybe it was Dr Kendall because you said you thought you recognized her from somewhere, but I don't think I'd ever seen or heard the tech before. Maybe she was just a kind soul who didn't like the way I was being treated.'

'Then she used a really lousy temp agency when she was looking for a job,' Aunt Margie scoffed. 'No, she was there working at something she at least didn't have a problem with and then you showed up.' Aunt Margie, unlike many others, doesn't get quiet when she's thinking. She talks everything out and makes every possible suggestion. 'Would it do any good to stake out the building and wait for her to leave?'

I shook my head. 'I have no idea what she looks like,' I reminded her.

'I thought maybe by build or the way she carries herself or something.' She was covering for the fact that she hadn't thought of that. Then she looked me in the eye. 'What about letting yourself get captured again? Ken and I could be trailing you and follow.'

The thought of that absolutely turned my stomach. 'Not a chance,' I said. But the mention of being followed reminded me of Mank, who had left four text messages and two voicemails on my phone that I hadn't yet answered. 'What's my story going to be?'

'Your story?' Aunt Margie was confused.

'I've got to tell Ken and Mankiewicz something. I mean, I have to tell Mank because he called me and said someone was following me. And I *think* I have to tell Ken, because they might try again.' That thought wasn't doing my digestive system any good either. 'I've got to call Ken.'

Aunt Margie nodded. 'Right now,' she said.

Ashamed of myself for waiting this long I punched in my brother's number and he answered on the fourth ring because why not make me wait. 'Listen,' I said before he could tell me about how far he'd gotten with Igavda (which I was willing to bet was nowhere at all). 'Someone kidnapped me off the street today and strapped me to a gurney.'

There was a long pause. A very long pause. 'Wow,' Ken said finally. 'They got you too?'

I made him come home. This wasn't a conversation for the telephone; it was one I wanted to have when there was a two-by-four nearby to smack Ken upside the head with if I didn't get the answers I wanted. We have a very loving sibling relationship.

While we were waiting for him to make it home from our office I caved in and called Mankiewicz without a full story in place. I figured I'd wing it. OK, so I had no idea at all what I'd do but I knew I had to do something so Mank wouldn't be putting out an APB on me.

'Where've you been?' he asked. 'I've been calling all day.'

'Yeah, I was out of range for a while,' I said. That didn't actually mean anything in the English language but it was weirdly accurate in its own way. 'You said someone was following me.'

'And you hung up on me,' he answered back.

'It wasn't intentional.'

'Nevertheless,' Mank said.

'What did you mean by that? Who's following me?' This was no time for him to try to be cute. I mean, I'd just gotten up from a gurney and I hadn't asked to be there. Of course Mank didn't know that, but I didn't see the relevance in that fact at the moment.

'You walked by the precinct this morning and I happened to be looking out the window,' he said, now in cop voice. 'There was a guy definitely tailing you. He stopped when you stopped, started when you started. I'm surprised you didn't notice him.'

I was kind of surprised by that myself. 'What did he look like?' I asked.

'Medium height, but I was looking down from the second floor so it's hard to gauge. Wearing a hat so I didn't get to see his hair. Had on a dark coat, like a trench coat, which is weird in this weather. I only got a glance at his face. Caucasian. No facial hair. That's the best I can do. Fran, what are you up to that somebody would want to put a tail on you?'

That was an excellent question, but the only honest answer would have required a very long conversation and probably some smelling salts for Mank. I'd also need to trust him a great deal more. He was a nice guy, but my kind of secret is just for family. And Mank wasn't family.

'I honestly don't know,' I told him. Which was at least defensibly true. I didn't know why some guy was following me on the street. If it had been The Voice he'd been behind me the whole way to his evil lair, including the trip on the Q train. 'I guess it could have something to do with Evelyn Bannister's murder, but it's not like I'm carrying classified information around with me.' Well, it mostly wasn't like that. Depended on how you looked at it.

'You didn't see him at all?' Mank asked. 'I told you that and all of a sudden you vanished.'

OK, how much was I going to lie? Telling him the truth would open up a whole police investigation into my abduction and the best-case outcome to that would be the cops finding The Voice and arresting him, at which point he'd drop the bomb of my odd existence and the *National Enquirer* would be at my door in minutes. Not to mention whoever The Voice was affiliated with, because I figured he wasn't acting alone. Mom and Dad had warned Aunt Margie about possible government affiliations or other groups looking for them and us. I didn't think it was just one guy with an odd technology fetish.

'I didn't *vanish*,' I said. 'I lost my cell phone signal and I was working on a case so I wasn't answering the phone, no matter how cryptic a message you were leaving. I called you as soon as I got back.' *And had a long talk with Aunt Margie and ate seven Oreos and called Ken, who'd told me they were after him too, and by the way he hadn't mentioned that before.*

'You need to be on your guard,' Mank said. 'Do you want me to get a cruiser to pass by your building a little more often?'

It was a kind offer, but a mostly ineffectual one. 'What are they going to see?' I asked. 'It's an apartment building.'

'I'd feel better.'

He was such a sweet guy but I felt that my ability to pin a sympathetic lab tech to a wall using just one foot was evidence (that Mank didn't have) that I could rescue myself when neces-

sary. 'I promise I'll be watching and I'll call you if I see the guy
in the dark trench coat, OK?' I said.

'OK.' He didn't sound happy. Men like to protect women,
whether we ask them to or not. It's kind of a weird compulsion.
But then, most women aren't quite as strong as I am. But I'd
have to plug in soon if I wanted to stay that way.

I promised him we could keep our dinner date for the next
night and got off the phone. Ken would be home any minute and
that was going to be a conversation that would take some time,
and restraint on my part to keep from bashing my brother with
the nearest heavy object.

I looked over at Aunt Margie. 'You know you're the best ever,
right?' I said. She was the absolute tonic for my day, which had
been a doozy and wasn't close to over yet.

She walked over and put one arm around me. 'I'm in the top
ten,' she said.

And that's when Robert Van Houten decided to call me.

'You lied to me, Fran,' he said by way of a greeting. I miss
the days when you didn't know who was calling you and people
said hello. I'm an old-fashioned girl. Meaning I was fashioned
by people who were a lot older now. 'You said you were looking
for a client's father and in fact you were looking for your client's
murderer.'

Wow. He was good.

'You can pretty much find out anything, can't you, Rob?' I
said. 'Yes. I was hired to find my client's birth father but she
was murdered, I think because of the instrument I asked you
about. And since I can't do what she asked me to do, or at least
I can't give her the information she requested, and I've already
cashed her advance check, I feel an obligation to bring her killer
to justice in her name. Should I have mentioned that when we
spoke the last time?'

People with power or money are rarely spoken to with anything
but deference. Some of them are glad about that, but others are
happier when they're treated like normal humans and called on
their attempts to act imperious. I was about to find out which
kind Robert Van Houten might be.

He laughed a little. 'You really are a person of character, Fran.
I admire you continuing on even though your client can't pay

you. So suppose I hire you to investigate the death of the woman you knew as Evelyn Bannister.'

'I'm already doing that,' I told him. 'I appreciate the offer, but my client paid me and I'm doing at least some of what she asked me to do. But you can help, which is why I assume you were calling to begin with.'

Van Houten chuckled again. 'You're right about that, but I'm not sure how much help I can be just yet. I've made a few phone calls and emailed a bit about the Gibson Poinsettia.'

'I'll bet you found out it's a somewhat rare but not terribly expensive vintage ukulele and nobody knows why someone would pay $1.2 million for it, assuming it's that uke. How am I doing so far?'

His voice no longer had the edge of amusement. 'I'm afraid that was the information I could gather. At the beginning. But then I got in touch with a friend who – strictly by chance – was actually present at the auction in London.'

OK, that knocked some of the snark out of me. But just some. 'Your friend saw the sale happen?' I asked. 'I was told the trans-action was conducted on the phone.'

'That's so twentieth century,' Van Houten said. 'It's all done via text message and email now. But yes, my friend was there when it happened. He said the room was audibly stunned by the bidding, which kept going skyward until one of the two anonymous bidders dropped out. And as you know, that was at the price you've already quoted. A million two.'

'You're not going to tell me who your friend is, are you?' I asked.

'No. Suffice it to say I trust his word.'

That didn't tell me much more than I already knew, which led me to believe Van Houten was building toward something. He came across as the kind of man who would want to maximize the dramatic effect so he would be even more universally admired. 'Was he there to bid on the ukulele?' I said.

'No,' Van Houten answered. 'He was looking into another instrument, a violin, which I believe he ended up buying for considerably more than the Gibson.' OK, so the guy had rich friends. He was all kinds of wealthy and those people tend to hang out together. Nobody else can afford the restaurants they go to. 'But he paid special attention to the lot we're discussing because the bidding was so unpredictably high.'

'The agent for the buyer was a person named Patrice Lancaster,' I told Van Houten. 'Does that name sound familiar? Did your friend mention it?'

He took a moment to think about it. 'I don't recognize the name, and of course I didn't ask my friend about it because we hadn't spoken about her yet. But there was, as there always is, a certified expert on hand to attest to the authenticity of the instrument.'

'Langley Comstock,' I said.

Van Houten sounded disappointed. 'Yes. And apparently no one in the UK thought to check on someone with such an outlandish alias.'

'Was it an alias?' I asked. Ken had thought otherwise.

I looked over at Aunt Margie, who was doing her very best to avoid looking like she was trying to hear my conversation. I had no issue with her hearing it but didn't think Van Houten would want me to put the phone on speaker. I gestured for her to sit next to me on the sofa but she gave her head a little shake and put up her hands to indicate she didn't want to. Even with her hands Aunt Margie was a lousy liar.

'I wondered about that,' he answered. 'The fact is, Langley Comstock is registered in the UK, and in five states in America including New York and California, as an expert in vintage stringed instruments. Has been for fourteen years and has authenticated as many as six hundred purchases. There have been no complaints lodged against him and he is in good standing in every jurisdiction where his certification is recognized.'

That seemed . . . unlikely. 'But is that his real name?'

Van Houten took a moment. 'I mean, I didn't think so, but I don't have any evidence that he's ever been called anything else. You know, this isn't my full-time job.' I think he thought he was being folksy and self-deprecating there but it didn't really land.

'I appreciate everything you've done, Rob,' I said.

'Wait, don't hang up,' he said quickly, as if that had been what I was planning to do. 'I left the best for last.'

Now I gestured vehemently for Aunt Margie to get closer so she could hear the call, and seeing the way I looked she didn't hesitate. I held out the phone a bit to make it easier for her to eavesdrop.

'I'm all ears,' I said, not mentioning that at the moment there were four listening to him.

'It's about the buyer of the ukulele,' Van Houten began.

'I thought you said Sotheby's wouldn't give out that kind of information under any circumstances,' I, well, interrupted.

'And they didn't.' The air of amusement had crept back into my billionaire buddy's voice. He was going to drop a bomb and he enjoyed being the bombardier. 'But my friend who was there got to talking to another bidder who dropped out very early. And that person – no, I'm not going to say who – knew something about the uke and something about the people likely to be obsessed enough to overspend broadly on such an item.'

'Do we trust this person's information?' I asked.

'I think we do. I have asked them about things in the past and the answers I've gotten have always checked out to the letter. Always.'

Aunt Margie leaned in a little; her left ear is stronger than her right. All those years of radio through headphones.

'So what questions got answered this time?' I asked Van Houten.

'First, I was told a little something about the ukulele itself. Part – and only a very small part – of the reason its price escalated so much was that it was briefly owned by George Harrison, who toward the end of his life became very fond of ukes.'

Interesting, but hardly an earthquake. 'And that's only a small part of what made it so valuable,' I said. 'What other factors went into that?'

'My source didn't know about that,' Van Houten answered. 'There were some rumors that Bob Dylan had it for a while, but once a Beatle was involved I'm not sure Dylan was going to add hundreds of thousands of dollars to the price. What's more interesting is that my source believed there was only one person in the community of collectors who would be that hell bent on obtaining such an instrument, someone who actually beat out a bidder like Augustus Bennett.'

Bennett! 'He was the other high bidder?' I asked.

'The man himself. Well, not himself, of course. He bid through a reputable agent, Eduardo Cabrini of Rome. But Bennett didn't get the uke.'

OK, it was time to drop the straight line so Van Houten could have his moment. 'Who did?' I said.

'The name probably won't mean much to you,' Van Houten said, sounding a little sheepish. 'But what's interesting about it is that I spent the better part of a day researching it and found absolutely nothing. No mentions anywhere ever. And that simply doesn't happen.'

No, I was sure it didn't. It's easy enough to Google a name and you very rarely come up with no hits at all. A man with Van Houten's resources would be able to do a hell of a lot more than that.

'What's the name?' I reached for a pad Aunt Margie keeps on a side table for grocery lists and a pen I had in the pocket of my jeans.

There was the sound of rustling pages. Van Houten must have kept notes on paper, too. 'It's Brandon Wilder,' he said.

I almost dropped my phone. Aunt Margie looked like she'd literally seen a ghost. 'Brad,' she said aloud.

Brandon Wilder.

My father.

TWENTY-TWO

'That doesn't make any sense,' Ken said.

Aunt Margie and I had moved upstairs to my apartment after I'd gotten off the phone with Robert Van Houten, who was pleased that I was dumbfounded by his information but stumped as to why an obscure name would have such an effect on me. I'd said it was because I wasn't sure what to do with that information, which was the understatement of the millennium.

Until, of course, my brother arrived home and wanted to talk about the call with Van Houten rather than my recent abduction and his admission that he'd had a similar experience. We had, to put it mildly, different agendas.

'Of course it doesn't make any sense,' I said. 'But that's not the point. It's not the headline right now. At this moment, I'm still shaking from having been kidnapped and threatened by some maniac with a strange knowledge of us and I'm wondering why you haven't told me before that someone's been after you too. Did they take you prisoner like me? Want to experiment on you?'

Ken spread out his hands, palms down and kept flexing his elbows like he was trying to push something to the floor. 'I can't do that now,' he said. 'I need to know what your pal the gazillionaire meant when he said Dad was the guy who bought Evelyn Bannister's ukulele. *Then*, I promise you, we can talk about the other thing.'

The other thing. My brother was so shaken by the evil scientist and his operation that he needed to process before he could even talk about it. Fine. We could do it his way but then we'd do it my way and there would be no postponing that.

'OK,' I said. I looked over at Aunt Margie, who was behind Ken and therefore not in his line of sight. She nodded; I was doing the right thing. Aunt Margie tends to referee when Ken and I are having, you know, sibling discussions. 'Let's start with that. You're right that Dad's name showing up in connection with the uke doesn't make sense.'

'Somebody killed Evelyn Bannister, maybe in connection to that ukulele,' Ken said, pacing our living-room floor, which was dusty and unwashed at the moment. Who had time for cleaning? I'd been busy being abducted, but hey, we weren't talking about that yet. And was I upset? Nah. 'It was just after the auction and there was an empty ukulele case next to Evelyn's body. There isn't any way on this planet that our father could have been even remotely involved in that.'

'And yet it would be the world's biggest coincidence if his name just showed up in the middle of this investigation about Evelyn Bannister that had nothing to do with him, right?' I asked. It was a wordy question but I think they were all necessary to the point.

'Yes.' Ken countered with one syllable. I wasn't letting him get away with that so I sat and watched him pace. Aunt Margie didn't offer anything but she did pick up a piece of knitting from her canvas bag and started in on a row. Aunt Margie had lately taken up knitting and it was never a calming thought to think of what she might be trying to create.

After looking at my blank face (intentional) for about ten seconds my brother broke under the pressure. 'You're right. Coincidences like that can't be trusted.'

'There's a third possibility,' I said without having detailed the first two. 'Dad's name could be a signal to us.'

Ken, who had been searching the screen on his phone for something I couldn't possibly identify, looked up. 'A signal?'

But Aunt Margie got it right away. 'You mean someone associated with that auction was trying to get your attention and then Evelyn Bannister was murdered?' She shook a little, like a literal chill was going up her spine.

I nodded. 'Let's say Evelyn Bannister was a red herring, or at least was intended to be. Someone with knowledge of our existence, Ken, wanted us to know they were aware of us. They sent Evelyn to hire us so we'd be aware of her and of the ukulele. The auction happened just about then and just to be sure they used Dad's name as the winning bidder.'

'Wouldn't Sotheby's be suspicious of someone using a false

name?' Aunt Margie asked. Then before we could answer I saw the gears in her head spinning. 'Someone with that kind of money could get really great false documentation.'

Ken stuck out his lips a little in an expression of disbelief. 'There are so many holes in that theory it could double as a piece of Swiss cheese,' he said. 'First of all, there is no one who has any knowledge of us.'

'Dr Mansoor would disagree, if he were here,' I pointed out.

'He knew Mom and Dad. He didn't necessarily know anything about us or how we came to be. He just tried to get in touch, maybe just to reminisce the way Eve Kendall did.' Ken didn't want to believe the idea about Dad's name being a signal. He had a couple of decent points, but so did I.

'We don't know *what* he knew or didn't know,' Aunt Margie piped up. 'We never got to find out.'

'I need to see the items taken out of his car,' I said, largely to myself. 'If Kendall is right, he'd have written stuff down that could actually help us and maybe give us an idea where our parents are right now.'

Ken put his phone in his pocket; whatever he'd been looking for either hadn't been about our conversation (which was unlikely) or hadn't panned out (likely). 'Put that aside,' he said. 'Let's say Dr Mansoor did know something. OK. He didn't do anything about it, or if he did, we don't know what. Forget Dr Mansoor. Why send a signal through the auction of a weird ukulele? There are so many easier ways to get our attention. Why bother with all that? Set up Evelyn Bannister, whoever she was, to be a client so we'd know about the sale, so we'd find out the name of the winning bidder? What were the odds? If you didn't know a crazy billionaire who likes to buy things for no reason we never would have known our father's name was even mentioned. Plus, it's possible that there's more than one Brandon Wilder in the world. It's not that unusual a name. It's not even Dad's real name, as far as we know.'

OK, so he had more than a couple of decent points. 'It's too big a coincidence,' I said again. 'And two people died around the sale of that uke, both of whom were attached in one way or another to us. That's unsettling, and we'd be idiots if we didn't get a lot more careful while all this is going on.'

Aunt Margie nodded. Ken just looked resigned to an idea he didn't care for. Being extra-vigilant puts a damper on his love life. Or so he thinks.

'OK, given that you were taken on the street I think you're right about that. We do have to be more careful. Especially you, Frannie.' He smiled a little bit at that last part.

I folded my arms for the express purpose of looking at him disapprovingly. 'Really. And when I told you about that, you said, "They got you *too*?" Now's when you tell me exactly what *that* meant.'

Ken nodded his head like a guy who just accepted the challenge in a bar fight. 'OK. All right. You want to talk about that. Right.' Aunt Margie and I waited and he didn't say anything else.

'And?' Aunt Margie prompted.

'Yeah. Yeah. So about a week ago a guy tried to hustle me into a van,' Ken said. Then he looked away.

'How does that information add up to you being embarrassed?' I asked. 'And what do you mean, he tried to hustle you into a van? This unnamed man tried to talk you into getting into his van? Did he offer you candy or tell you there was a puppy inside?'

Ken stopped looking away long enough to give me the stink eye. 'Cute, Frannie.'

'Well?'

'I'm saying I was out about a block from the office and there was a black van parked on the street in an illegal space. I was walking by, not really even noticing it. Then this guy moved out of his way to hip check me in the direction of the van. But I guess he didn't know how strong I am because he just sort of bounced off.'

'Was he wearing a dark trench coat?' I asked.

Ken stared at me. 'You think I remember what he was *wearing*?'

Aunt Margie, always a careful listener, wrinkled her brow. 'So you bumped into a man in the street and you think it was an attempt at abduction?' she asked.

'No, there's more to it than that.' Now my brother seemed to think we were in some way attacking his manhood. He might be artificial, but he's a man for sure. And I don't necessarily mean that in a nice way. 'When he saw he couldn't shove me into the van he tried to block me in the street and said he needed some help moving something out of the back.'

'What did you do?' I asked.

'I kept walking. I'm a New Yorker.' Ken also thinks being from New York means that he always has to be rude; he takes that as a badge of honor. It's not true, of course, but Ken still has a decent amount of maturing to do. I decided not to challenge him on his manners just now.

'And then what?'

'What do you mean, "and then what?"'

He can be a little slow on the uptake, but Ken's not dense. 'What did you do after that?' I asked.

'I went to get a sub sandwich.'

Then it hit me. Because otherwise I would have hit Ken. 'That's exactly what happened to me, except they put a bag over my head instead of trying to hip me into the car.'

'What did they look like?' Ken asked.

'I didn't see the person who shoved me into the car,' I told him. 'They *put a bag over my head.*'

'And no one on the street yelled or anything?' Ken sounded appalled.

'They were New Yorkers.'

'What about the man your friend the cop saw?' Aunt Margie asked.

Ken looked confused so I told him about the man in the dark trench coat.

'Frannie,' my brother said, 'this is serious. Somebody knows about us and they want something from us. If the guy was following you and Mankiewicz could see him . . . where was this?'

'Right in front of the precinct,' I said. 'Where's a cop when you need one?'

'That's in our neighborhood,' Aunt Margie said with a catch in her voice. 'If they were following you that soon after you walked out the door they might know where you live.' She started knitting faster. Whatever it was she was making might be finished in another hour. The only thing I could tell you for sure was that it was green.

We sat there silently for close to a full minute. Then I stood up and felt a little lightheaded. 'I've got to charge,' I said.

Nobody stopped me with an encouraging thought so I went into my bedroom and plugged myself into the wall.

TWENTY-THREE

I was not familiar with the 18th Precinct. I had never been there before and didn't even have the cache of saying that Mankiewicz or (heaven forbid) Bendix had sent me. I was a private investigator walking in with questions, and the one thing you can say about that situation is that cops really don't like it unless the PI is an ex-cop, in which case they slap him on the back and still don't tell him anything.

The cop in question on this day, after I'd recharged myself, had dinner and slept nine hours without talking about our predicament to Aunt Margie or Ken, was Sgt. Hank Klinger. It was a serious effort not to make *M*A*S*H* jokes, but I managed it. I loved that show when I was a teenager. People stuck in a bad situation being wiseasses. What was there not to like?

Klinger – the one in front of me – was a guy in his late thirties or early forties whose respiration and heart rate had increased when he'd gotten his first look at me. It's something I notice but try not to resent. They don't *try* to make their respiration and heart rates jump. He did, to his credit, keep his gaze on my face and that was an improvement over the norm.

'It was a car crash,' he said once I'd explained my reason for being there. 'It's not mysterious. He drove too fast and lost control, rammed into a tree. It happens.'

OK, so Klinger wasn't the most sensitive of people. That too is not terribly unusual in police officers; they see a lot of stuff that citizens do to each other and it's rarely pleasant. You need to grow a hard shell to survive.

'I understand that,' I said, although I harbored at least some suspicions about the crash that had killed Dr Mansoor. 'But I'm curious about what might have been found in the car. Do you have an inventory?'

'Yes, I do,' Klinger replied. Then he sat down behind his desk, which was a welcome conglomeration of papers, staplers (three), paper clips, a phone and various and sundry other items I couldn't

see because all that stuff was obscuring them. 'But I can't for
the life of me think of a reason why I should share it with you.'
He didn't smile when he said it. He wasn't being smug or
cute. He wasn't trying to impress me. Even his respiration had
returned to normal. He gestured to a guest chair in front of his
desk but I remained standing.

'You should share it with me because it can be very helpful
to me in a case I'm working,' I said. It wasn't exactly what you'd
call true in the legal sense but it was in the emotional sense. I
had decided as soon as Ken and I opened the agency that trying
to find out about our parents would be treated like any case. I'd
deal strictly with facts and not let any emotional baggage influ-
ence my decisions. 'You should share it with me because I might
be able to help you score some points with it and clear your
paperwork. And mostly you should share it with me because it's
a matter of public record and I am a member of the public you
serve.'

You'd think a speech that eloquent and forceful would have
dented Klinger's armor, but he didn't even look impressed. He
refrained from putting his feet up on his desk, which I appreciated in retrospect, but the arms folded across his chest were not
a sign he wanted to collaborate.

'The incident report is a matter of public record,' he said
without so much as a blink. 'The inventory of items recovered
from the car – and believe me there weren't many given the
damage that vehicle had sustained – is not. Now suppose you
tell me why you're so hot to get your hands on that list and then
maybe I'll decide that I'll be a nice guy and help you out.'

I sat down.

'Look,' I said. 'The man who was killed in that crash was a
friend of my parents. They died in a similar incident when I was
only three. He left a voicemail for me that day saying he had
information about them and I never got a chance to talk to him.
I'm hoping there might be something retrieved from that car that
might give me a hint about what he meant. Is that too much to
ask?' I let there be a slight tremor in my voice but avoided letting
a tear fall from my eye strictly because I didn't think Klinger
was the kind of guy on whom that would work especially well.
I can do it when I want to.

Klinger smiled. With some people that would mean they were enjoying your pain but it didn't seem that way with him. The crooked grin still had an element of victory in it, though. 'See?' he said. 'You can do so much better when you just tell the truth. That was the truth, wasn't it?'

'Every word.' Except most of them.

'Let me find the file.' I thought Klinger was going to start typing away on his keyboard, but apparently he was one of the odd breed of humans still hanging on fiercely to the concept of paper documents because he started picking up manila folders from his desk, glancing at them and then tossing them aside. He had a filing system like Ken's. Mine was a little more organized. Igavda had learned from Ken. My office was a place of chaos if I didn't go in often enough. 'Ah! Here we go!'

He pulled out a completely nondescript file and instead of handing it to me (as I would have wanted but didn't expect) he leafed through it, actually licking the pad of his index finger to do so. I fingered the vial of hand sanitizer in the pocket of my jeans but left it there.

Klinger reached into the file and pulled out a single sheet of paper, clearly a printout of the form that the cops on the scene of the accident had filled out. It was unlikely a plain-clothes detective had been dispatched given that Dr Mansoor had clearly died in a car accident. There is a collision investigation squad that looks into every fatal crash, but when it's a one-vehicle incident like Dr Mansoor's, the investigation is into how it happened and not necessarily if someone else was involved.

'This is the list of items found in the car, at least the ones we could identify,' Klinger said. 'See if there's anything that can help you.'

What could have helped me would have been seeing the rest of the documents in that file but that didn't seem likely so when Klinger extended the single sheet of paper toward me I took it and smiled at him like he was doing everything he could for me. You can lie in smiles, too.

The form was standard and had been filled out by an Officer Patel whose first name was in such a scrawl that I couldn't possibly make it out. That wouldn't much matter unless I had to talk to the officer and there was more than one Patel working at the precinct.

At first glance it didn't look like there was anything of interest listed on the sheet and I was prepared to pout, hand it back to Klinger, and shuffle off into the night (it was mid-morning) with a storm cloud over my head. There was a bottle of spring water found in the back seat, split open and empty. There was a comb, a cloth handkerchief (Dr Mansoor was old school), two canvas shopping bags from Gristedes, the iPhone discovered lodged under the rear seat that had probably saved it, and a dog training pad. Apparently the doctor had a dog who did not treat car upholstery well. The dog had not been in the car at the time of the crash.

Just before I was going to give up, though, I saw a separate list in another section of the form, this of items discovered in the car's trunk. Of course there was a spare tire (donut) and jack, a tire iron, and a pair of jumper cables. There was Mansoor's medical kit in case of emergencies. There was a sweater, gray wool.

And there was a metal lock box, just as Dr Kendall had predicted, containing a second cell phone. A Samsung.

It would probably have been a mistake to look too excited when I asked Klinger about that, but I was encouraged. A second phone could mean that was the work one, the phone issued by a company, agency, or hospital (Mansoor had been working at New York Presbyterian Hospital part-time) and not the one on which he would have been saving personal contacts. He had called me from the iPhone. So maybe there was little chance Dr Mansoor had kept his notes, if there were any, on his second phone. But maybe he had. I didn't have access to either device at the moment and needed to concoct a decent argument that Klinger should let me have both to look at.

'Not terribly interesting, is it?' I said, trying to sound dejected. Best to give him the impression I was going to give up; he could go on with his day and feel like a hero for showing me the one measly form.

'They usually aren't,' he answered, reaching for the form. I'd pretty much memorized it so I handed it back without protest. 'I'm sorry I couldn't help you.'

I stood and picked up my purse, the large one I carried for business. I couldn't store a laptop in it, but my phone does almost everything I need when I'm not in the office or at home. 'Well, thanks for the look.'

Klinger nodded and made a show of reaching for another file on his desk, indicating he was getting on with his important work and not the whims of some silly, if unusually tall, woman.

Then I went full Columbo on him and turned just as I was about to walk out. 'Just one thing,' I said. 'Do you know if he had any notes on either of his cell phones?'

'Notes?'

I assumed he wanted an explanation and not a definition of the word. 'Notes. Like things about what he was working on, appointments he had, that sort of thing.'

Klinger's eyes narrowed. 'You think he was getting ready to meet with your dead parents? Because it's possible he's having lunch with them as we speak.'

I put a hand on my hip to show some irritation. Because I was, you know, irritated. Talking about my dead parents – who quite probably were not dead – like that? Rude. 'He called *me*,' I said with an edge. 'Maybe there's some indication of what he wanted to talk to me about.'

'I'm not going to show you the dead doctor's phones,' Klinger said. 'There could be personal stuff on there and that's unethical.'

'Have you looked at them?' I turned back toward him. It wasn't meant to be a threatening move but sometimes I intimidate people by being me. Klinger backed up in his chair an inch or so. It wasn't much of a move but I could see it, which was probably not what he had in mind.

'Of course I did,' he answered. 'It's my job.'

'Did you take notes?' I took a step forward to see what would happen, but this time Klinger was ready for it and nothing happened. You can't win them all.

'Yeah, but I'm not showing you those, either.'

I put both hands on my hips. It made me look like I was pretending to be Superman, which was only partially the effect I was hoping to have. 'So I'm guessing you can tell me if my name was mentioned.'

Klinger exhaled dramatically. I considered nominating him for a Tony Award but remembered a Broadway theater needed at least five hundred seats to qualify and the precinct couldn't have held more than seventy-five. 'Stein, I never so much as heard your name before the dispatcher called and let me know you wanted to come in and ask me questions about a dead doctor's telephones.'

The hip thing wasn't working so I folded my arms to look more authoritative. 'Dr Mansoor had an FBI file,' I said.

Klinger blinked. Twice. 'Why?' he asked.

'Let me see the notes on Dr Mansoor's phones and I'll tell you.'

He pursed his lips, which didn't do very much for his face. 'You're bluffing.'

Fully charged, I was feeling strong and my mind was operating at its fullest potential, which is either a good or bad thing depending on your estimation. I go back and forth on that one. 'I'm not bluffing. I don't know the whole story and I haven't seen the file but I know it exists and I know why. If you'd like me to tell you that, you can show me the phones or the notes you took on them.'

Klinger gave that some thought; you could tell by his eyebrows, which met in the middle, dropped, and then returned to their respective corners to prepare for the next round. He dropped his hands on his desk like they were just too heavy to hold up anymore. 'I'm not letting you touch the phones,' he said.

'The notes, then.'

He nodded with a frown. I made a mental note to send his ego a sympathy card when I got home. Klinger rifled through the file on Dr Mansoor's crash again and came up with a copy he'd made of handwritten notes. I was impressed because I didn't think anyone wrote in cursive anymore. It was even legible.

After reading the notes over and determining, I guessed, that they didn't contain anything leading to the overthrow of the government, he handed me the pages. It was a considerably more substantial document than the accounting of items from the car had been and it took me a couple of minutes to scan through it.

Most of what he'd written wasn't relevant to my situation. There were lists of appointments that he wasn't going to keep and some reports about cases he'd consulted on with the patients' names replaced by numbers. Dr Mansoor had been very scrupulous about keeping his records private. His grocery list, however, had been very searchable and included such items as red leaf lettuce, bananas, and whipped cream. It was eclectic, or he was planning on making one weird salad.

In the middle of the second page, however, were notes regarding people he identified only as 'B & O.' At first I thought he was referring to the railroad in Monopoly, but as I read I realized Dr Mansoor had been talking about Brad and Olivia.

My parents.

Aunt Margie referred to my mother only as 'Livvie,' so it didn't immediately occur to me she was the 'O' being discussed here. And it became fairly clear in a short period of time that Dr Mansoor had been just a little obsessed with Mom.

O develops KXD3, one note read. *Most amazing discovery since Radium. Should have Nobel. O says it doesn't matter.*

Says? That's the present tense. Was Dr Mansoor in touch with my mother at the time he'd died?

B is in Paris, another note said. *Coming Sunday. Find space. Only 48 hours.*

Dr Mansoor's message on my voicemail had suggested I had forty-eight hours to contact him about my parents, and he'd died less than three hours later. Had he found them a place to stay for those two days? Was he being tracked? Were they?

Before Klinger could object I took out my phone and snapped a picture of the page. 'Hey!' he yelped. 'Who told you it was OK to take pictures?'

'Who told me it wasn't?' I took one of the next page just in case.

Klinger reached out to grab my phone and I snatched it out of his reach. I put the phone in the hip pocket of my jeans, daring him to reach for it now. Showing some good sense, he didn't.

'No more pictures!' he said. 'That's a rule.'

'OK, OK. Fair enough,' I said. Then I noticed references to 'O' and 'B' on the fourth page and memorized them because I didn't think I could get my phone out fast enough. They read: *B to NY LHR-LGA O to NY AF1355 CDG-LHR-ORD-EWR.* They were dated just under two weeks earlier, and I figured if I had alphabet soup later I might be able to figure those notes out.

There were no other 'O' or 'B' references in the document. Which was probably good news for Klinger although he didn't know it. I'd be out of his (thinning, I noticed) hair shortly.

'Quid pro quo,' he said. 'Why is there an FBI file on Mansoor?'

Fair enough. 'Because apparently some of his work involved eugenics,' I told him.

Klinger wrote that down without so much as a raised eyebrow, then looked at me. 'What's eugenics?' he asked.

How to boil this down? 'The idea of genetically engineering people to be whatever the scientist or the people the scientist is working for believes is superior,' I said. 'The Nazis were big into it.'

Klinger wrote *NAZIS* on the page next to his previous note. I held my breath in the hope that he would not ask me who they were.

'OK, that's bad,' Klinger said

I agreed and thanked him but did not hold out a hand to shake. Klinger looked at me curiously and his respiration did not increase. 'I have a totally unrelated question,' I said just on an impulse.

Immediately he looked suspicious. 'What?'

'What could a person hide in a ukulele that would be worth more than a million dollars?'

Klinger squinted at me as if I were very far away, or standing in the direct path of the sun. He spoke in a faraway voice. 'Not drugs,' he said. 'Maybe precious stones or some kind of information stored on a chip. Anything else would be too big or heavy.'

It was, possibly, the first useful piece of information I'd gotten all day.

TWENTY-FOUR

Since I was already uptown I figured it was best to go check in on Gus the super from Evelyn Bannister's apartment building. I still needed to ask him about the use of strychnine as a pesticide under his watch. I guessed that Det. Miller had already interviewed him but oddly Miller wasn't sending me regular updates on his pursuit of Evelyn's killer.

It would be a crosstown walk to get to Evelyn's building. It was a nice (if hot) day so that wasn't an issue, but I did find myself looking behind me more often than I normally do, which is to say I was looking back quite a bit and I usually don't at all. There was, for the record, no sign of a man in a dark trench coat.

Just to be safe I dug my phone out of my hip pocket and FaceTimed Mank. If anyone came up behind me while I had the video running he'd see it happen. And if it was the guy in the dark trench coat there was the slimmest possible chance that Mank would recognize him.

OK, I was grasping at straws. But calling Ken right now wasn't going to do me any good and Shelly was probably busy US Marshalling, so it made the most sense to check in. Calling Igavda for office information was about as useful as an umbrella stand in the Sahara.

Mank had a puzzled look on his face when he picked up. I could see the walls of his cubicle behind him; he was in the precinct. 'What's this all about?' he asked.

'I just wanted to check in on this restaurant we're supposedly going to tonight,' I lied.

'What do you mean, "supposedly?" And how come you're video-calling me when you're walking out on the street?'

The second one was actually a good question and I couldn't be too outlandish in my explanation. Aunt Margie always told me it was easier to remember the truth. 'I wanted to be visible in case the guy in the trench coat is following me again,' I said.

Mank nodded. That made sense to him. 'Let me see,' he said.
I angled the phone to view behind my right shoulder. 'How's that?'

'Nobody there,' Mank said. 'I mean, there are people, but none of them looks like they just left the set of a Humphrey Bogart movie.'

'Good,' I said. 'I'm heading to Evelyn Bannister's building to talk to her super.' Probably more information than Mank needed or cared to have, but I figured if I was thrown into a car and ended up being vivisected it would probably be best if he knew at least what neighborhood I was heading for.

Paranoid? Me? Does it count as paranoia if you've actually been abducted in the past twenty-four hours?

'You think the super killed her?' Mank asked.

'No. What possible reason would he have to kill Evelyn? I'm going to ask him if there was rat poison on the premises because that's a common use of strychnine.'

'Maybe he asked her out on a date and she said she was "supposedly" going,' Mank said. 'People have been killed for less. Or so the homicide guys tell me.'

A woman walking in front of me was trying to negotiate a stroller around an open basement door and finding it difficult with people walking in the other direction. I couldn't get around her either, so I reached my free hand out and lifted the stroller over the open door without dangling it over the opening. I placed it down on the pavement again just as the woman began to scream at me.

'What are you *doing*?' she yelled. 'You could have dropped my baby!'

I decided not to tell her she was welcome and passed her, noting that the stroller held a small Yorkshire terrier who didn't seem the least bit perturbed over his apparent flirtation with death.

Leaving the woman and her dog behind I looked back at my phone. Mank seemed amused. 'Placing people's children in jeopardy?' he asked.

'It was her dog.'

'Worse yet. So what about this "supposedly?"'

I didn't have a coherent answer to that question, now that he'd asked it three times, so I changed the subject. 'Mank, do you think whoever killed Evelyn was doing it just for the ukulele? I mean, once they knocked her out with the candlestick they could have taken the uke and run. Why bother to inject her with poison?'

'Why not just keep bashing her over the head if you wanted to kill her?' he countered.

'Maybe he's squeamish.'

'How do you know it's a he?' Mank asked. Touché.

'They,' I said. I'm accepting of all gender pronouns.

'From what I've read, why not take the ukulele case?' he said. 'Whoever it was just left it sitting there for the cops to find.'

I hadn't thought of that. 'Yeah. Why the hell not?'

'It's a good question. I wish I'd thought of it.'

I tilted the phone to show Mank behind me again and he assured me my shadow was nowhere to be seen. I worried that I'd done something to offend the man in the dark trench coat, or that he was so easily discouraged that he'd give up after one day.

'Maybe the ukulele is just a red herring,' Mank said. 'Maybe the idea always was to kill Evelyn Bannister, or whoever she was.'

'You're paying an awful lot of attention to a case that's not even in your precinct,' I noted.

'I need dinner conversation for my date tonight, which I'm definitely picking you up for at seven thirty.'

I was only a block away from the building at that point so I figured it was safe to hang up on Mank, just to keep him wondering what I'd meant by *supposedly*. Because the truth was that I didn't know why I'd said that either.

Evelyn's building was a tall one, but not especially so by Manhattan standards. It couldn't be seen from space. There were choices of thirty-two buttons in the elevator but knowing how most such apartment buildings work, I pushed the one for the basement. If the super lived on the premises, which the landlord corporation's website insisted was the case in all their properties, and that's almost always where you can find them. Just one way in which the person who actually keeps the building running is treated with the utmost in respect. The meager paycheck was no doubt another one.

A third probably would have been the apartment itself but I

never got that far. The basement looked like another floor, albeit a considerably less luxurious one than those assigned to the tenants. There must have been another area of it, probably behind a locked door, where storage and building materials were kept.

There were a number of doors, fewer than on a residential floor because the spaces must each have been larger, but only one marked *S-1*. In case the super had for some reason forgotten his job after a day of fixing broken toilets and replacing batteries in smoke detectors for people who could easily have done so on their own.

I wondered if Gus ever thought about this stuff when he came back to his underground apartment at night, or if he was just so tired all he wanted was to flop on the couch and watch *Real Superintendents of Beverly Hills*. Or something.

Considering that he might be out when I got there I had decided against bringing him bagels, which would have gotten moldy and inedible in the basement I had been expecting to find. I'd brought nothing because it was weird, finally, to bring a gift to a man because he was going to answer your questions when it wasn't really costing him anything but a few minutes. And now, of course, I felt like a cheapskate.

If Gus gave me any useful information, I decided, I'd send him some designer popcorn. Everybody likes popcorn.

There was a doorbell on S-1 so I rang it, assuming that Gus would be upstairs in someone's apartment, superintending. So I was mildly surprised when the door opened.

I was more surprised when the man standing in the doorway, a large man wearing a blue polo shirt and work pants, was considerably not Gus. His roommate? His son? A visiting relative?

'Hi,' I said, looking the man in the eye. 'My name is Fran Stein.'

It was not at all hard to understand that the man didn't widen his eyes in recognition of my name. But I waited a moment and got no response at all.

'I'm looking for Gus,' I said. 'Is he in?'

The man's mouth widened, closed, as if he were tasting something bad. 'Who's Gus?' he asked.

'The super?' Suddenly it seemed to be more like a question.

The mouth got wider yet. I worried he might hurt himself. 'I'm the super,' he said. 'My name is Harry.'

Sure he was. Sure he was. Harry. Harry the super who looked nothing like Gus the super, who was there in the apartment being questioned by the cops when I'd called them to look into Evelyn Bannister's murder. That Gus.

Maybe the trauma had been too much for Gus. 'Did you just start working here?' I asked.

'Lady, I've been the super here for seventeen years.'

Well. So much for the designer popcorn.

TWENTY-FIVE

A Taste of Athens was definitely not, by anyone's definition, a Thai restaurant. Rich Mankiewicz had sheepishly announced that the place we were supposed to have dinner had suffered a kitchen fire and would not open again for at least a month. I didn't especially care about that but I was not above teasing Mank mercilessly about it as if he had set the place ablaze himself.

I cut into my pastitsio with my fork and tasted it carefully. 'They make a really unusual mango chicken here,' I said.

Mank, who knew what he was in for when he asked me out, nodded. 'You're hilarious,' he said.

'Please. My modesty.' It was actually really good pastitsio. I tried not to eat like a hungry rhinoceros because I was just ravenous. 'Mank . . .'

'You really can't just call me Rich?' he said.

I would have put down my fork to make a point, but pastitsio. 'Here's how I see that,' I said after the interval when there was food in my mouth. 'Anybody can be a Rich. You're unique because you're you, so I call you Mank because I don't call anybody else Mank.'

'Bendix calls me Mank,' he said.

OK, that was worth thinking about. 'He calls me Gargantua.'

'The man has an impish sense of humor.' My date, whose name I was still pondering but it was going to stay Mank, was having spanakopita, which looked good. He seemed to be enjoying it.

'I'm gonna call you Mank.'

'Of course you are.'

A guy two tables away with a truly revolting combover was staring at me like I was a freak. I mean, he wasn't entirely wrong, but he didn't know that. I immediately checked to see if he had a dark trench coat draped over the back of his chair, but it was a leather bomber jacket the guy probably believed made him look cool. In any event, he was getting on my nerves.

'Hey,' Mank said. 'I'm over here.'

I diverted my attention back to him. 'Sorry. There's a man over there ogling me like I was a side of beef and he hadn't eaten in a month.'

Mank started and quickly stopped himself, not wanting to be obvious in his glance at my admirer. 'The bald guy?' he asked.

'Almost entirely.'

'He should stop that,' Mank said.

'Yeah, but he won't. I get that sometimes.' I shouldn't have mentioned it. Mank could obsess, especially when he thought someone was disrespecting me. He knows I can take care of myself, but he calls whenever a mysterious man in a dark trench coat is following me down the street. And he didn't even know that I'd been abducted right after that.

Could combover guy be The Voice? That would be so disappointing. He looked less like an evil genius and more like a regional representative of National Nut Products who'd had a couple too many ouzos.

'You shouldn't have to put up with it.' Mank was working himself up. I was really regretting broaching the subject at all, but it had taken my mind off all the things I had failed at over the past few days: Finding Evelyn Bannister's biological father, stopping her from being murdered, finding out who she really was, figuring out the deal with the $1.2 million ukulele, not being kidnapped, taking Dr Mansoor's call, finding out why he'd been trying to contact me and what it had to do with my parents, and most recently being able to question Gus because apparently there was no Gus and probably never had been.

Ken had been unusually serious when I told him about the Gus development when I was getting ready to meet Mank. 'I don't understand,' he said, watching me try out a number of pairs of earrings. He had a befuddled look on his face, which I could totally understand right now. 'Why don't you just put on a pair of earrings and go?'

Perhaps I was overestimating my brother.

'They have to look right. But this Gus thing is what's got me going right now.' The fake emeralds didn't look any better than the fake sapphires. Hell, it was Mank. I'd known him for more than a year and I'd bet money he wouldn't be able to say which earrings I'd had on ten minutes after we parted for the night. Maybe even while I was sitting right in front of him.

'Yeah, that's a problem,' Ken agreed. 'But it puts our old pal Gus, whoever he is, right at the top of our suspect list. So it really simplifies matters. All we have to do is find out who Gus is and we have the killer. Then we can go back to working on *paying* jobs.'

'This *is* a paying job,' I corrected him. Simple gold hoops. I'd be the only one who cared anyway. Might as well wear the ones I liked best. 'Evelyn's check cleared and we kept the money. But that's the thing that's bothered me right from the start.'

Ken sat back in my desk chair and laced his fingers behind his head. 'That we got paid?'

'No, but you are in fact hilarious. It's just my amazing ability to control my impulses that's allowing me to refrain from dissolving into hysterics. No, Ken. The thing that's bothering me and has since we took Evelyn Bannister's check is that nobody in this case is who they say they are and we have no clue who we're talking about. We never had a name for Evelyn's father and it turns out he might not be her father at all. Then Evelyn wasn't really Evelyn, but someone who might or might not be Patrice Lancaster. And even Gus the super, who just came in to tell the cops he'd been meaning to fix the pipe under Evelyn's sink, wasn't even Gus the super. There never was a Gus the super. The real super is a guy named Harry who thinks I'm a lunatic. And yes, I checked with the company and the super is a man named Harry.'

Strikingly Ken didn't take the opportunity to be a wiseass. He nodded while I was talking, indicating he was actually thinking. Then he unlaced his fingers and leaned forward, elbows on his thighs.

'We have to start with Gus, whoever he was,' he said. 'He was close by when Evelyn was killed, which we know because he showed up immediately after you and I called the cops. He had access to strychnine in pesticides if he was in the maintenance area at all. He lied about being the super and got out before the cops could check his story. Evelyn, or whoever, was clearly trying to find an older man who she told us was her birth father.'

I stopped on the left earring and looked at him. 'An older man like Gus,' I said.

'Bingo. Maybe he was a rival dealer in weird instruments and she was afraid he'd get to the million-dollar uke before she did. Your friend the US Marshal says there was a theft of a Gibson Poinsettia reported in Portland, Maine. Maybe Patrice was in on it, was about to take it to London to auction it and was worried he was on her trail and would take it from her. Maybe Gus stole it and was Patrice's supplier. Any way you look at it, our buddy Gus was tied to that ukulele. And for some reason it was worth a whole bunch of money, enough to justify – to him – killing Evelyn for it, lying to the cops and ducking out ASAP.'

When Ken decides to actually apply his brain, he can be something.

'So what we have to do is figure out who Gus really is and that might lead us to his whereabouts.'

'Yeah,' my brother answered. 'But how do we do that?' In our business, he's analysis and I'm strategy. Except those times when it's the other way around.

'Well, we have to make a couple of assumptions and then test them,' I said. 'First, it's a pretty decent bet his name isn't really Gus.'

'That's a pretty decent bet with anybody,' Ken pointed out. 'How many people do you know named Gus?'

I ignored that because I'm a grownup. 'And we have to assume that he's tied somehow to the ukulele, which is the only thing we know Evelyn was definitely interested in.'

'I'll check into Patrice Lancaster and see if she might be Evelyn Bannister,' Ken said. He couldn't add to my plan so he was going to steer the conversation toward an area in which he could be useful. But I wasn't done yet.

'So if it's a man whose name isn't Gus and who's interested . . .' I'm sure my eyes went dreamy and my face became blank. I was putting two and two together and for the first time in this case it was coming up four.

'What?' Ken said. It was a logical response to my suddenly becoming a pod person before his eyes.

'There's a guy who likes to collect rare stringed instruments. He can get obsessed with them when he's in pursuit. And nobody's seen him in at least five years.' It had all just come together in my head.

'Who is this guy?' Ken asked, still staring at me funny because of the faraway look in my eyes.

'His name is Au*gus*tus Bennett,' I answered.

Ken looked impressed.

Sitting here now with Mank at A Taste of Athens I was feeling like a failure. Ken was trying to dig up stuff I hadn't already found about Augustus Bennett and I was thinking of myself as a useless part of the K&F Stein Investigations team. All I could do was ask other people (like cops and marshals) for help and then assign the difficult computer work to my brother. When I went out to investigate I generally found that the person I was asking about wasn't who I thought they were, or I got taken off the street and almost subjected to unexplained medical experiments.

The one thing I definitely wasn't going to do, I decided on the spot, was ask Mank to help me with the case. Or any case. Ever. If we were out on a date, we were out on a date. Terrifying though that was to me, I was going to commit to the concept.

'That guy is staring at you,' Mank said. 'You want me to do something about it?'

Men. 'No, I don't want you to do something about it,' I said, perhaps with a little more testiness in my voice than was warranted. Or perhaps not. 'I don't know if you've noticed, but I'm pretty big and strong and I have no trouble defending myself. If it gets to a point where he's actually bothering me I can definitely handle it on my own.'

Mank nodded with a sheepish smile on his face. 'It just seems so un-chivalrous,' he said.

'Chivalry is overrated.'

'OK. Now. What about this murder case? You went to see Klinger uptown?'

I took another bit of the very good pastitsio, at least half of which was going to come home with me. Even people who were constructed from a set of Lego need to watch their diets. 'I don't want to talk about the case,' I said.

Mank looked concerned. 'Going that bad?'

'Well, yes, but that's not the reason. If we're going to be doing . . . this . . . I don't want to think of you as a resource. You're Mank. You're the guy I do . . . this . . . with.'

He laughed. 'And with a level of enthusiasm that would normally inspire me to go home, write a journal entry and have a cry.'

I studied him, thinking of Mank crying over me at night. 'Would you really do that?' I asked.

'No!'

But we didn't get past that. The guy with the combover, who clearly did not observe the same social boundaries as normal humans, reeled his way toward our table. He'd clearly had more than one drink tonight and it had, to the disadvantage of everyone in the restaurant, emboldened him.

'You're real big,' he slurred. He had to walk right past Mank to get to me, and had not so much as glanced at him. But I saw when Mank's hand tightened into a fist and when the other hand patted the pocket in which he must have been carrying his gun. This was a situation that would have to be defused quickly in order to avoid a *really* unfortunate resolution.

'Yes I am,' I said. 'Thank you.' Treating it as the advantage that height can be throws them off sometimes.

But only sometimes. 'And in all the fun places, too,' the guy said.

'Just keep walking, buddy,' Mank said. 'I'm NYPD.' Neither of his hands relaxed.

'I was talking to the *lady*,' the drunk said. 'I didn't break no laws.' That was technically true, if ungrammatical.

'Back. Off,' Mank said with a little more force.

Without delivering another lecture on my ability to handle my own problems, I stood up and faced the combover guy. Sort of. He was four inches shorter than I am.

'Wow,' combover guy said, staring at me not in the eyes.

'Sir, my friend and I are having a quiet dinner. So please have a nice night and move on, OK?' I gestured in the direction of the door in what I thought was a subtle but unmistakable fashion.

'You're really something,' the guy said. He was clearly a graduate of the Sorbonne. Such eloquence.

Then he reached up with his left hand and was about to place it in the area where he'd been staring. And that's where the line gets crossed.

Before Mank could say or do anything I hit the combover guy with a left cross and he went down in a heap on the floor. He didn't move after that.

The maître d', whom I guessed also owned A Taste of Athens, rushed over immediately. 'What did this man say?' he said, kneeling down to check on combover guy, who was breathing but not feeling at all well.

'Not so much what he said as what he was doing,' I answered. 'Sorry for the trouble.'

Mank just sat there looking stunned. But he did take his hand off the gun, which I supposed was a move in the right direction.

'We will call the police,' the maître d' said.

Mank coughed and then stood up. 'I'm a police officer,' he said.

The maître d' looked him up and down. 'You are?'

'*Yeah.*'

The guy I hit was starting to return to what I can only refer to as his senses because there's no other word for it. 'Somebody musta hit me,' he said. Stone cold sober now.

'I did,' I told him.

The maître d' helped him to his feet and he stood, a trifle unsteadily, leaning on our table for support. Mank looked like he wanted a crack at the man himself. But he wasn't going to get that. 'Do you need an ambulance?' the maître d' asked my latest assailant.

'What? Ambulance? No! I got hit by a *girl!*' With that he turned and walked out through the front door, saying, 'The stuffed grape leaves weren't that good, either.'

'My apologies,' the maître d' said. To Mank and me. 'Sometimes I think we should cut off some people when they're drinking. Please. Ouzo is on the house.' And he walked away before acknowledging the contradiction or determining whether Mank and I were people who should be cut off when they're drinking.

I sat back down at the table and took what I swore to myself would be the last bite of pastitsio for the night. But Mank stood there, looking at the maître d', then at the floor where combover guy had fallen. Then at me.

He took a deep breath and sat down. 'This is going to take some getting used to,' he said.

TWENTY-SIX

'So let's sum up,' I said. Immediately Ken rolled his eyes. His voice came out in a whine. 'Do we have to?' I thought back to when Aunt Margie would make him do his geography homework in fourth grade.

'Yes. It's my way of making sure I'm not missing anything.' I sat down at my desk and got out a legal pad and a blue Uni-ball micro roller (that's a pen) so I could make a list.

'It's not *my* way,' Ken protested. 'Why do I have to be here?' He was already at his desk, with its view of the reception area and Igavda. Ken had designed the layout of our offices so that would be the case.

'Because you have ideas that I won't have and you contribute useful things to the conversation.' I wasn't just flattering Ken to get him to stay, although that would have been enough. I needed him there for exactly those reasons. 'So shut up.'

'Don't see how I can contribute useful things if I shut up,' he mumbled, knowing full well I could hear him.

I overlooked his remark because it wasn't going to lead to anything productive. Today I was all about productivity. 'So Evelyn Bannister—'

Ken cut me off. 'I believe we can now say for certain her real name was Caroline Seberg,' he said.

That was news to me. I stopped writing the heading *Things We Know* on the left side of the legal pad and looked at him. 'Huh?' I grunted.

'Last night when you were out on your *date* I did some looking into the woman who told us she was Evelyn Bannister,' he explained. 'She had used a lot of names in her lifetime, and there were plenty of fake Social Security numbers for her, but only one birth certificate for any of the identities. And that was—'

'Caroline Seberg.' At least I had followed him that far.

He pointed at his nose to indicate I was correct. 'She was born in Evanston, Illinois on August sixteenth thirty-eight years ago. Had two perfectly intact parents, Jack Seberg and Hazel Francisco Seberg, for the first twenty-six years of her life. Then her mother died of breast cancer and her father died six months later of mental illness which brought on suicide.'

'Hazel?' I said.

'Nice being sensitive, Sis.'

'When did she start being other people?' I asked.

Ken tilted his head back and forth a couple of times. 'That's not entirely clear. She made a couple of slightly questionable real-estate deals under the name Penny Wilkerson ten years ago. But she might have been arrested as Carol Grande a year before that.'

'Arrested for what?' This was getting interesting. I had written only *Wow!* in the margin of my pad.

'Soliciting, actually. She got online and said the wrong things to an undercover cop. The conviction was eventually expunged after she did some community service and left Evanston.'

'When did the real-estate scam turn into weird auctioneering?' I asked. When Ken had actual information that he'd managed to dig up himself he loved showing it off and I'd learned to let him strut a little bit because he usually unearthed some really useful data. Which appeared to be the case today.

Ken was not referring to notes, which drove me nuts. He can remember things for inhumanly long periods of time and doesn't need any references. I write down lists of things I need to do in the next ten minutes.

'About two years ago,' he said. 'The first reference to Patrice Lancaster was then, on February twenty-seventh in Chicago. That seemed to be the name she used for the auction agent scam.'

'Was it a scam?' I said. 'I mean, you can be a legitimate auction agent.'

'Yes, I can. And you could. But Patrice . . . or Caroline, as it turns out? She never really did anything the way it is supposed to be done. In her case, she would dig up stolen property in pawnshops to begin with and then auction them off as rare objects. It was very small time until last December nineteenth when she moved up into the big leagues.'

'A forged harpsichord signed by Mozart?' I suggested.

He half-grinned, not wanting to give me the satisfaction. 'You're actually not that far off. She found a guitar she said had been handmade by Les Paul, which turned out to be just another Les Paul guitar manufactured by Gibson. It was a good guitar but the overwhelming odds are that Les himself never once held it in his hands. It's possible he and the guitar were never even in the same state at the same time.' Igavda must have stretched at her desk because Ken's attention was suddenly diverted in her direction.

'Did she get found out?' I asked, bringing him back into the conversation.

'Huh? Yeah, but not until it was far too late. She had already convinced the buyer of the Gibson Poinsettia that she was the right agent to make a bid for him.' Ken kept glancing over but Igavda, who was used to not doing much at her desk, had stopped squirming in what was, for my brother, an interesting fashion.

'Why did Sotheby's let her in if she had been found out representing a bogus Les Paul?' I asked.

'Because she was representing the bidder, not the object. The ukulele was brought to the auction by a company here in New York that never once tried to represent it as anything but what it was, a somewhat interesting curio.' He leaned back in his chair to get one more look at a woman he saw pretty much every day.

'And the bidder Caroline/Carol/Penny/Evelyn/Patrice was representing was using our father's name?'

'Well, the records aren't public but according to your pal Daddy Warbucks, yeah.'

Then something occurred to me in a flash. 'Hey. If . . . Caroline knew she already had the ukulele or that she was going to represent a buyer at auction, how come she hired us to find it?'

Ken stopped looking for Igavda, which is his chief occupation when he's in the office. (To be fair, Igavda seems to enjoy the attention but it's highly inappropriate coming from her boss, and Ken has never harassed her or asked her on a date because I told him we'd have to fire one of them if that happened and I was leaning towards him.) He frowned; he hates not having the answer to the question. He wants to show off how smart he is.

'You said maybe the people behind this were sending us a signal by sending Caroline and using Dad's name, or one of his names,' Ken said. 'What do you think they were trying to tell us? Because I'm guessing coming to the agency and telling a story about an adoptive father she never had wasn't Caroline's idea.'

'Neither was getting conked on the head and poisoned,' I noted.

'Fair enough. But what about it? What was this mysterious person, or these mysterious people, trying to tell us?'

That was a really good question. I got up from my desk and went to the small refrigerator I'd installed in the corner where the water cooler used to be. We were paying for the water every month and I was the only one drinking it so I got rid of it. Turned out Ken wanted a place to keep energy drinks and Igavda preferred green tea. This is what comes from polling the staff.

I reached in and pulled out a bottle of water. I took a long swig to mask the fact that I didn't really have an answer ready. OK, so I like looking like the smartest kid in class too. We do share DNA, after all. I'm pretty sure.

23 and Me would probably shut down its site if I sent in a saliva sample. I'm just saying.

'Well, let's think about that,' I said once my vocal cords were sufficiently moistened. 'They wanted to send us a message. We have to assume they wanted it to be a *clear* message. So what do you take from that?'

'How come I have to be the one to guess?' Ken asked.

'Because I asked the question. If I asked it and then answered myself I'd have to run for office and neither one of us wants that.'

He nodded to one side acknowledging my point. 'What I get from the message mostly is, *we know about you.*'

It's not that I hadn't been thinking that myself. I took another sip of water and walked to my desk to get comfort from my computer screen. It was showing the day's headlines, so that didn't work out great. 'That's a distinct possibility,' I answered. 'But I'm not sure it makes sense. If whoever this is had found out about us, I mean *really* found out about us like The Voice seemed to have, what's the advantage in telling us that? Aren't they giving up the element of surprise in whatever strange purpose they might have with us?'

Ken reached into his desk and pulled out a Kit Kat bar, which he began to unwrap. Everyone has their own office comfort food. Mine's water. 'Maybe it's the bat signal,' he said. 'Maybe whoever this is wants our help and thought that was the way to contact us.'

'Instead of phones and email?' I said.

'They want to be untraceable,' Ken suggested. 'They want our help but they don't want anybody else to be able to find them.'

'Then we can't find them, either.' This game wasn't going anywhere.

'Suppose the people trying to get in touch with us *were* our parents,' Ken said. 'They're in some kind of trouble and they need our help.'

I really hated that scenario for any number of reasons. But I also didn't think it held water. 'Well, without longitude and latitude I don't see how Mom and Dad would expect us to be able to find them,' I told Ken. 'Wait a minute. We've gotten off on this whole tangent because you found out who Evelyn Bannister really is. I thought I asked you to find out about Augustus Bennett.'

Ken eats Kit Kats by just biting into them. Everyone else on planet Earth breaks each row off and eats it separately. My brother just unwraps the thing and chomps away at it. Truly, there are days when I despair for him.

He compounded matters by speaking while he was still chewing the Kit Kat, an offense that should be punishable by at least six years in a maximum-security prison. 'What makes you think I didn't?'

'I'm sorry, that was so disgusting I couldn't focus on what you said.'

Ken scowled and swallowed his candy. 'I said, "what makes you think I didn't," because I have actually found out a few things about Gus Bennett.'

'I'm told he prefers August,' I said.

'He most likely murdered a client of ours,' Ken pointed out. 'I don't think his preferences should be a great concern to us.' He turned his attention to his laptop, which he prefers to a desktop computer with two monitors like I have on my desk. To each his own, even if his own can be proven by science to be completely wrong. 'Anyway,' my brother continued, 'the one thing we know for sure is that his name really *is* Augustus Bennett.'

'Refreshing,' I said and drank some more water. You can't talk and drink water at the same time, another advantage over the Kit Kat. But he was making me really want some chocolate now.

'He is fifty-two years old, five foot nine, one hundred eighty pounds.' Ken stared at his screen.

'You broke into his medical records? That's a violation of HIPAA laws.'

'No, I broke into the records of his gym. It's an especially expensive one. They don't think anyone will be looking.' Ken grinned.

'Does his physical description go beyond height and weight?' I asked.

'Not really. It's amazing how few pictures there are of this guy online.' Ken stood up and got himself a napkin from a stack we have on the filing cabinet. You get a lot of takeout in New York. He wiped his mouth of chocolate, which made him more palatable to look at.

'How many pictures are there of *you* online?' I asked him. We have made it a policy to be camera shy.

'Decent point.' Ken walked over to the fridge and got himself an energy drink, which on top of the Kit Kat seemed especially disgusting. Someday that guy was going to have to grow up. 'But I'm guessing our reason to stay away from photographers is different than his.'

I walked over and looked at the screen on his laptop. 'There are no images of him at all?'

Ken appeared behind me, gave me an annoyed look and walked around to sit in his chair. 'I didn't say that. I said there weren't many. The problem is this guy vanished about five years ago and nobody knows where he might have been since then.' He punched a few keys. 'This is what he looked like ten years ago.'

The picture that came up wasn't very clear. It was of a man of average height, perhaps a bit overweight, with a head of brown curly hair kept very well groomed. He was getting out of an expensive-looking car, from the rear seat, and looked annoyed that someone dared to take his picture. You got the feeling – or at least I did – that he took a swing at the photographer right after the image was taken.

'Fun guy to have at parties,' I said aloud.

'I think you could take him,' Ken said.

'So aside from his distaste for cameras what did you find out?' I asked.

Ken took another long swig of whatever the caffeine-fueled concoction he stocked was and sighed with satisfaction. To each his own. I still had a bottle of water and I returned to it by sitting behind my own desk.

'Your pal was right: Bennett is a very rich man who lived in an area not generally populated by very rich men. But he's not a tightwad. He'll spend tons of money on things that *he* wants and doesn't really much care about anything else. He bought, yes, a harp that Harpo Marx used, but in *A Night at the Opera* and not *Duck Soup*. And he paid a lot for it, over four hundred thousand dollars. Then after six months he sold it to an anonymous bidder for about thirty-five thousand.'

No sense was being made here. 'Why would a guy with that kind of money do that? How'd he make his fortune, anyway?'

'The old-fashioned way,' Ken said, staring at his screen.

'He earned it?'

He shook his head. 'He inherited it. He worked at a hardware store in Syosset until he got the money, and actually even for a couple of years after. Inherited it from his uncle, who it appears included no one else – not even Gus's sister – in his will. A cool thirty-eight million. The uncle, one Antonio Benedetto, made a huge pile in real estate and investments, chiefly by being smart enough to lock on to a little company called Apple when it was just starting out.'

There were puzzle pieces and they made no actual picture even if you put them together. I shook my own head out of confusion. 'So a hardware store employee gets tens of millions dumped in his lap and stays in his hardware-store-employee house but buys crazy stringed instruments and doesn't like people much.'

'That's right. No spouse, no children, no friends to be aware of. He has a sister in . . .'

'Sherman Oaks, California. Sylvia. She didn't get any of the cash?'

'Not a dime,' Ken said. 'This led to some friction when she asked Gus for a loan to get out from under a bad mortgage and he told her to suck it up like everybody else. Gus is not an especially lovable character.'

That was an understatement. 'I just want to let you know that if I inherit thirty-eight million dollars I will gladly pay off at least part of your mortgage,' I told Ken.

'I'm touched.'

'I know, but you're my brother so I make allowances. Did you find anything that ties our buddy Gus to the Gibson Poinsettia?'

Ken chewed on his lower lip. That's Thinking Ken, particularly when he's not feeling especially happy about what he's thinking. 'Well, you have to keep in mind that for the past five years there hasn't been an Augustus Bennett. According to the Syosset Police Department, he was reported missing by a housekeeper who only came to his place once a month, so he could have been gone for weeks before they knew about it. That was five years ago.'

'No sightings since then?'

Ken shrugged. 'He's the Loch Ness Monster. People claim to have seen him but nobody has any proof. Supposedly he was involved in an auction last year of the cello Yo Yo Ma played for John F. Kennedy when he was all of seven years old. Yo Yo, not Kennedy. But they didn't count on Yo Yo showing up to debunk the idea that it was his cello, which he did. Bennett never got the chance to bid because the auction house withdrew the instrument from any possible sale before it was supposed to have happened.'

Something about that got me suspicious. 'Who was the agent on that cello?' I asked Ken.

He grinned. 'You got it. Our old friend Patrice Lancaster.'

'Caroline Seberg,' I said.

'Evelyn Bannister.'

I leaned back in my chair. 'Well, you've given us a lot to think about.'

Ken stood and headed for the door. 'And we didn't even have the chance to sum up,' he said. 'Darn.'

TWENTY-SEVEN

A nalyzing Dr Mansoor's notes, which I'm sure he didn't intend to be cryptic, didn't take very long. Even without Ken in the room a minute or so of the most basic research (Google) revealed that of course the three-letter clusters were airport codes. Got that from JFK (John F. Kennedy in New York) and EWR (Newark), both of which I had visited in the past. And there are some who believe I *didn't* pass up a promising career at the NSA (which is not an airport code).

B to NY LHR-JFK IB4219 O to NY AF1355 CDG-LHR-ORD-EWR

So B – Brad, my father – was going to New York (NY) via JFK from LHR, which turned out to be London Heathrow, on Iberia flight 4219. Apparently my parents were traveling separately because O – Olivia, my mother – was arriving in the city from CDG, or Charles de Gaulle Airport, in Paris, with a stop in ORD, which is for reasons I could not discern, O'Hare Airport in Chicago, on Air France (AF) flight 1355.

Whew.

The problem – OK, one of the problems – was that there were no dates indicated by Dr Mansoor in his notes. Mom and Dad could have flown into the city (and not called – how many times had that happened since they'd left?) this week, last week or seven years ago for all I knew. I also had no idea what the purpose of their visit might have been. Were they coming to check in on Ken and me and had gotten thrown off track somehow? Were they on a mission about a new development in their work? Were they being followed by . . . somebody?

Let's face it: I didn't know anything more than I had before other than their flight numbers and the fact that they appeared to have been in separate countries whenever this travel had taken place.

It was a devastating blow, to have finally had some lead to follow and have it get me nowhere. But that was the defeatist attitude and I wasn't going to be that girl anymore. I got out my phone and called Iberia because I'd taken Spanish in high school. You don't have to tell me it was an irrational reason; I had two choices and I took one.

After the usual exhausting trip through the complex maze of a large company's automated phone system (I usually just keep pushing 0 until I get a human but that didn't work in this case) I found myself on the phone with a man named Miguel who had an accent that wasn't thick enough to be a problem and was actually kind of musical.

'My name is Fran Stein,' I said because it is, 'and I'm trying to get some information on a passenger who flew with you from London to New York on Flight 4219,' I told him.

'Was this today's flight?' Miguel asked. Truly, he sounded a little like Antonio Banderas, which was charming.

'Well, that's the thing,' I answered. 'I don't actually know when they were flying with you. I just know the flight number and the route.'

Miguel took a moment, probably to look at the person in the next cubicle and give them a look of incredulity: *This one is a doozy!* Assuming there's a word for *doozy* in Spanish. Mrs Culbreath in tenth grade never got to that one.

'I'm sorry,' Miguel said after he'd commiserated with his office mate. 'Without a date I really can't track a passenger. And we don't generally give out information on passengers except on the date they fly with us. If family wants to know whether they've landed yet or something like that.' All of a sudden his accent wasn't that charming.

I decided to go for pathos and see if that would stir his Spanish blood. 'Listen,' I said. 'I'm trying to find some information on my father. I haven't seen him since I was three years old and I believe he was in New York City recently. It's very important that I find him because I . . . might need to get a kidney transplant and he would be the only donor I know of who's compatible. So can't you help me out, please?' I crossed my fingers right after *important* because I didn't want to bring me or Dad bad kidney luck.

'I really don't know what I can do for you, ma'am,' Miguel said, sounding bored. Not only was he not trying to help, now he was calling me *ma'am* and that meant he thought I was old. This is how my mind works. There's nothing you can do about it.

The best strategy was just to plow on like he hadn't answered me. 'His name is Brandon Wilder.' I hoped that was the name he was using on the flight. Dr Mansoor knew him under that name, but then, so did The Voice and that was a problem. 'He was flying from Heathrow to JFK, and it must have been in the past three weeks.' That last bit was a complete guess but I felt that if it was longer ago than three weeks, I had no chance to find my parents anyway. I would probably call Air France at that point just to check, though.

Miguel let out a long breath that sounded to my ear like impatience. 'OK,' he said a little too loudly. 'Let me check if anyone by that name traveled on that flight in the past three weeks. But I shouldn't be doing this.' I disagreed, but felt it best not to point that out.

It took a good while of tapping on a keyboard without any word from Miguel before he came back on the line. 'Was that Dr Brandon Wilder, on a flight ten days ago?' he asked.

My heart leapt. He'd found my father. Now I could prove to Ken who the real brains in our agency really was. I could work a phone. 'Yes,' I said.

'I'm sorry but Dr Wilder did not travel on that flight,' Miguel said. 'It seems he passed away before it took off.'

TWENTY-EIGHT

The weird thing was, my first impulse was to call Mank. That made a grand total of no sense, and so I called Ken. He, of course, didn't answer because he's Ken, so I sent him a text: *Call me. Now.*

'What's up?' he said when I picked up. 'Did you find Gus Bennett under the couch in the charge-up room?'

I just . . . couldn't. 'Kenny,' I said, and then I started to weep like a six-year-old who's been told she can't have a pool party at her best friend's building because (it turned out years later) someone might see the USB port in her left side.

Ken's voice immediately changed tone. He was clearly outside from the noise on his end of the call but I could hear him clearly enough to know he sounded genuinely concerned. 'What is it, Frannie? Tell me what's wrong.'

It took a long while before I was able to speak again, and to his credit my brother hung on his end of the phone and didn't make any wisecracks. He did try to offer comforting words occasionally, saying whatever it was would be all right and he could come right back to the office if I needed him. But eventually I got hold of myself again and took a deep, cleansing breath.

'Kenny,' I said. 'Dad's dead.'

He knew. He knew from my tone that I wasn't kidding and I wasn't leaping to a conclusion. What he didn't know was that I'd thought Miguel had been lying to me and had run seven different internet searches on the name Brandon Wilder until I found a death certificate from the city of Boulogne-sur-Mer, France, filed exactly eleven days earlier. The date of death was given and the rest was in French. Google Translate had provided, for lack of a better word, an incomplete version of the text.

'Are you sure?' Ken asked.

'I saw a death certificate.'

'I'll be right there, but I'm betting it's not true.' And he hung up because he knew I was about to argue with him. Ken, for all his frat-boy bluster, is imbued with an optimistic nature and refuses to believe bad news until he absolutely can't avoid it. Of course he would say it wasn't true. I knew better because I'm a realist.

Our father was dead. We'd never get a chance to hear his side of our story, his explanation of the need for our parents to be absent from our lives all these years. We'd never get the sense of humor evident from what we knew of him and what Aunt Margie had told us about him. My first emotion, to my embarrassment, was anger. How dare he die before I could look him in the eye and tell him I'd needed him and he hadn't been there!

Wait. Aunt Margie. I had to tell Aunt Margie. But she was pulling a fill-in shift at the radio station, actually reading news every twenty minutes, and it was never a good idea to call her, even with very important information, if it could wait. This could wait. Dad would be dead forever now.

Had someone killed him, the way they'd killed Caroline Seberg, to get our attention? What would be the point of that? Did The Voice know about it, or was he a separate player in this melodrama? Had this whole plot, ukulele and all, been a set-up to get Dad to come out of hiding so they could kill him? Why hadn't I taken French in high school, so I could call someone in Boulogne-sur-Mer and get a fuller explanation? What time was it in France, anyway?

Now my priority had to be finding our mother. If she was in danger we could help. If Dad had simply died, wouldn't she have flown back to France as soon as she'd heard? How did I know she wasn't there now, or moved on from France to better stay undercover?

Every moment of every day now I knew less than the moment before. It was becoming a really annoying trend.

Ken arrived only a few minutes later; he hadn't gotten far away while I was talking to Miguel. He said nothing when he came in, barely glanced at Igavda, who had no idea anything was wrong, and embraced me as soon as he reached me. We stood that way for a while. My brother is very big and strong and leaning on him is like leaning against a very solid oak tree.

'It's true, you know,' I said. 'You have to realize that.'

He let me go and we walked, without discussing it, into the

side room we use when one of us has to charge up during office hours. There's a sofa in there. We sat down on opposite ends and faced each other. I thought I might burst into tears again and started wondering why. I'd barely known our father. It was like mourning a stranger.

'Here's all I'm going to say,' Ken began, just as I thought it was undoubtedly not all he was going to say. 'First, Brandon Wilder is not the most singular name in the world. It might not have been him.'

'There's Dr Mansoor's notes showing him on the flight when Iberia says it had booked a dead Dr Brandon Wilder,' I countered.

'Let me finish. Also: Mom and Dad have spent decades on the run. They've used a lot of names. We have no indication – aside from Dr Mansoor – that they're even still using the ones they had when he knew them. Dad's name got thrown around at the ukulele auction and I think we both agree that sure as hell wasn't him spending a million-two on Don Ho's favorite miniature guitar.' Ken was leaning his elbows on his thighs and holding his chin in his hands. That's not his thinking pose; that's his really determined pose. He was going to deny our father's death for as long as he could.

'Are you done now?' I asked.

'Not quite.' In the right mood Ken could get himself into a frenzy of oratory that would make Aaron Sorkin proud. 'Our father is well known to have a somewhat, let's say impish sense of humor. This is the kind of joke he'd especially love because it would throw off the people looking for us and our parents. He'd probably plan it for a time when he was going to come to New York, or pretend to come to New York, because that would make it more urgent and more plausible. He's probably off some-where laughing right now at the people who think he's really dead. And if that includes you and me, Frannie, then we've just fallen for the oldest joke in the book: faking your own death.'

OK, maybe not Sorkin. But he wasn't bad.

Ken took a moment and exhaled. '*Now* I'm done,' he said.

'Kenny, I don't want our father to be dead any more than you do and you're well aware of that,' I told him. 'But what you just suggested was nothing more than speculation.'

'It fits the facts.' He flopped down on the chair, which groaned despite being reinforced for, shall we say, heavier users. Ken qualifies because he's just generally enormous.

'Anything can be twisted to fit the facts,' I answered. 'The only facts we know for sure are that Dad was booked on an Iberia flight from London that he never got on, and there is in existence a death certificate in his name—' Ken gave me a look. 'OK, *one of* his names for the exact date that Iberia suggested. Weigh that against the absolutely no factual data you have. It's sad; it's even devastating. I don't know how to process it. But our father is dead and we have to figure out how to find Mom before something happens to her, too.'

Ken's face closed. He folded his arms and looked like a four-year-old who was about to threaten me with holding his breath until he turned blue. He took several breaths, at normal speed, in and out. Then he looked at me with fire in his eyes.

'We need to find Mom,' he said.

It took us a while to plan. I gave Air France a call to verify that our mother had not in fact died the day before *she* was supposed to fly to New York and after the usual rounds of being told they didn't give out that information, they gave out that information. She had indeed flown in to Newark Liberty International Airport eleven days earlier. She had not – and this really took some passive aggression to find out – booked a return flight. At least not on Air France.

I'd already resolved not to ask Mank for professional help, but was this really a professional matter? I didn't know whether I cared, but the fact was I'd already suggested to him that Olivia Grey was a person of interest to me, and asked if the FBI had opened a file on her. Asking him about her again would require a very plausible cover story and I wasn't sure I had one.

Nope, it was time to put on my detective shoes (they're really sneakers because who can detect things in heels?) and start doing the job all those classes and all the adoption cases had trained me to do. Find a missing mother? Hah! I did it all the time.

Yeah, this was different. I just couldn't think about that right now.

Ken had tracked down Eve Kendall via text and discovered she was at, of all places, JFK Airport waiting for her flight home.

He headed out to take the train and meet her there. What she knew about my mother (and more to the point, people my mother would know and possibly contact if she were in New York) wasn't a terribly promising lead, but it was a lead.

I went to a familiar place, the New York City Health Department at 168th Street. The Health Department keeps a registry of adoption records.

Now, I know what you're thinking: Adoption records? As Aunt Margie had explained it when we were old enough to understand, Mom and Dad needed to have some record of responsibility for us so we could go to school and participate generally in the city's society. They had known someone who was good at forging really convincing records like birth certificates and the like. But because there would be no record of Ken or me being born in a hospital, you know, anywhere, and because even births that take place at home have to be reported and confirmed (to make sure that no one is stealing babies), the birth certificates would list Mom and Dad as witnesses, not parents.

Adoption records would be beyond their friend's capacity to duplicate. So they went through the process of adopting us officially. And so here I was at the Health Department looking for those records.

Surely you're wondering at this point: Hadn't I ever gone in and requested these documents before? Good question! Yes, I had. It had taken the better part of a year to get just the rudimentary adoption records, and copies of those at best. For anything more detailed, our adoptive parents would have to sign a waiver form. And they weren't going to show up to do that anytime soon.

The 'biological parents' listed on the birth certificates were just other aliases Mom and Dad had used in the past. Again, unlikely we could get waivers from them. They'd have to exist first.

But maybe I could get some additional names, people who had vouched for the character of Brandon Wilder and Olivia Grey when they were trying to become the legal guardians of us two unfortunate foundlings. Because there's nothing that makes you think more like you're living in a Dickens novel than trying to unearth adoption records for anyone.

I'd been here a number of times, to the point that Clarice behind the main counter knows me by sight. Clarice has heard all the *Silence of the Lambs* jokes and I wasn't in the mood, so I got right to the matter at hand.

'I'm looking for adoption records and long-form birth certificates for me and my brother,' I told her.

Clarice's eyebrows rose a little. She probably wouldn't react for the normal patron of the place but she has seen me looking for everybody else's adoption records before and might not have been working at the DoII when I was searching for our birth certificates. 'You?' she asked. 'I didn't know you were adopted.'

'It's not a disease, Clarice.' I was in a lousy mood. My father was dead.

She sniffed. 'Never thought it was. You got the request form?'

'Of course.' Now I wanted to apologize for being snippy and didn't know how to do it. I handed over the filled-in form from a pile we have in the office. I'd filled in the relevant information and paid the fee with my phone. Clarice glanced at the form, nodded, and went into the back office to search.

'Long form? You running for president?'

'Not today, Clarice, OK?' She got back to the task at hand.

Most of the records are on the servers in the department's computer systems, but Clarice likes paper. She can scan it and send it to your phone but she wants to see it herself before she does and she doesn't trust pixels. 'Give me a paper form and I know it's real,' she's said to me on more than one occasion. There is no arguing with her.

When she returned she was holding a file that she did not offer me. 'I checked them,' she said. 'I can call them up and email them to you.'

'I'd appreciate it. Can I see the real ones first?' Maybe get on her good side by professing a shared belief in an antiquated method of data storage.

Clarice hesitated for a moment. She's not supposed to let anyone see the originals for fear of damage. But then she slid the file through the Plexiglas partition for me to examine.

The adoption forms were familiar from the first time I'd searched for them, when the red tape was considerably more dense than it is now, perhaps due to better digitization of the records. But they held more information. When you simply ask for the birth certificates and adoption records, some information might be redacted if the birth parents are not willing to release their identities to the child. In this case, nobody had been worried about being found out by Ken and me, but my parents didn't want their names to appear on official forms when they were assuming certain government agencies might be suspicious of them.

On the long form, which Clarice had handed me now, Ken and I were still named (and it's not 'Kenneth' or 'Frances;' it's Ken and Fran) and our vital statistics (ten pounds, six ounces if you must know) recorded. Although I'm pretty sure the length and weight numbers were fabricated because we were, you know, sort of assembled (they don't have assembly certificates) and even so would be larger than an average baby.

I didn't have to ask Clarice where to look for what I was hoping to find, and sure enough it was there. The adoptions had been witnessed and notarized.

The notary public listed had a name I didn't recognize but I would take note of it when Clarice emailed me the form. He was Richard DeCentis and he had probably just stood there and watched while Mom and Dad signed the papers, which is all he was required to do.

But the witnesses, whose names I had not seen listed before, were of more interest. One, of course, was Aunt Margie, or as the form had her listed, Margaret Lucille O'Sullivan. (I hadn't known about the Lucille before and was certain to tease her about it at some point but not today.)

The other witness was Eve Kendall.

I looked over at Clarice. 'I'm really sorry I snapped at you,' I said. 'My father just died.'

'Oh, honey,' she answered. 'I'm so sorry.'

'I've got to go,' I said. 'But I didn't want you to think I was mad at you.'

She shook her head. 'You were the most polite customer I've had all day.'

TWENTY-NINE

*D*on't let Kendall get on that plane.
OK, so maybe it was melodramatic but I texted my brother because I wasn't sure if Dr Eve Kendall was standing near enough to him to hear my voice. What was important was that she didn't leave until we got some answers.

I was already in a cab headed to JFK, which would only take maybe an hour in this traffic. If a tornado hit the airport and all flights were delayed I had a 50/50 shot at getting there in time.

Thank goodness Ken was actually looking at his phone. *Why?* he sent back.

She's lying. She knew Mom and Dad. She witnessed our adoption papers.

Ken's a strong, confident guy but he doesn't deal extremely well with pressure. I could picture him breaking into sweat and hear him starting to stammer as he spoke to Kendall. *Get Aunt Margie* was what he texted back.

I guessed this qualified as an emergency. Aunt Margie wouldn't answer her phone if she was on the air or about to go on. I asked the driver to turn on her station and her voice didn't come through. So I called her cell.

'What's wrong?' She began with that. Aunt Margie knew if I called during a shift it wasn't just to chat.

'A lot of things, but I'll tell you when I see you. Right now I need to know about Eve Kendall. You were right. You have seen her before.'

'I knew it!' There was a pause. 'When?'

'She was the other witness on Ken's and my adoption papers.'

'Oh shit!' That was unusually graphic for Aunt Margie. 'I *knew* I'd seen her before!'

I had no time, except that all the cars in the tri-state area appeared to believe I could spend a long weekend in this taxi. 'So she was lying about not knowing my parents well?' I asked, just to clarify.

'Hell, yes! She was the one they were grooming to help with the project after you guys.' Of course. She was the . . . wait. What?

'*What* project after us? Were they planning on making more people?' So Ken and I weren't enough for these ungrateful jerks? What kind of parents were they, anyway?

The cab driver turned his head just a bit. I lowered the volume of my voice.

'No!' Aunt Margie said. 'They had you guys and they loved you. But they were continuing your mom's work on healing and thought they might have actually found the pathway to a cure for cancer.'

OK, so they were the best parents ever and apparently amazing scientists as well. Hang on. A cure for *what*? 'They could cure cancer?' I said. This time the cab driver noticeably flinched. I was doing this very badly.

I could practically hear Aunt Margie smile and shake her head at my impulsive conclusion. 'Not yet,' she said. 'They said it was a possible *pathway* to a cure and could take years, maybe decades.'

'It's been decades,' I whispered. 'And Kendall is lying about what she knew. Do you think she's been in touch with them all this time?'

'How would I know?' she answered. 'I haven't heard from your folks in years. But Kendall was definitely in on it right before they left. Listen. I've got a news spot in forty-five seconds. Tell me what's wrong.' You can't fool Aunt Margie and she's never going to be distracted by a shiny object.

'It's something, I admit, but this isn't the time and not on the phone. When you get home, OK?'

'I don't like it.'

'Neither do I. Go read the news.'

She didn't have time to argue and I knew it, so Aunt Margie had to concede the point and disconnect the call. There was no guarantee she wouldn't call back demanding more information in three minutes but I couldn't worry about that just now.

I texted Ken. *If Kendall gives you a hard time tell her we know about the cancer cure.*

Ken is not unflappable. You can flap him pretty easily if you know which buttons to push. But he's generally good at dealing with situations (even if he's not calm about it), so I didn't get a questioning text. Instead it was: *Don't come to the airport. I'm putting Kendall in a cab. Meet us at the apartment.*

Have you ever told a New York cab driver you want to turn around and go in the other direction? They don't take kindly to it. This one mumbled things under his breath that he thought I couldn't hear, and they would have made me uncomfortable if I hadn't known for a fact I could pick him up and toss him across three lanes of traffic if provoked. There are advantages to being me.

As most disgruntled cabbies do, he growled a little more and then made the necessary U-turn and we were on our way back to my apartment. Along the way I decided I needed to get back to Mank because we'd left it in kind of a weird place and now my head was filled with all sorts of oddness. Mank is nothing if not steady. Steadiness seemed like a really valuable commodity right now.

I called instead of texting. Before I could even say hello, he was talking a mile a minute. 'I heard back from Detective Miller on your ukulele murder,' he said.

What? Murder? Oh yeah, Evelyn/Patrice/Caroline. That seemed like it had been weeks ago. That, and I hadn't been nearly vigilant enough about not being followed on the street today. Instinctively I looked out through the back window of the cab. There were cars behind us because, traffic. None of them seemed to be driving in a particularly suspicious manner.

'Why did Miller call you?' I asked Mank. 'You're not working that case.'

'He wanted to know about you and Bendix must have told him we knew each other,' he said.

I didn't like the sound of that. 'Does Miller like me for the murder?'

'No. But he said you'd been back to the building looking for the super they questioned that day and so was he. He wanted to know how reliable you are.'

So he called my not-quite-boyfriend? I was insulted. 'Why didn't he call me?'

'Am I his mother? I have no idea. If it was me, I would have called you. But the real piece of news here is that he thinks he found the ukulele.'

Whoa! Miller had found the Gibson? 'Where?' I asked.

'I don't know about where, but they don't have it in their possession yet and he wants to talk to you about it, apparently.'

'I *gave* him my business card.' This Miller guy was really starting to piss me off and I wasn't even talking to him.

'Once again, I'm not the one who told him to call me instead of you,' Mank pointed out. 'But if I were you I'd give him a call. And Fran . . .'

There was something in his tone. 'Yeah?'

'We need to talk.' The four most deadly words in relationship history. And I hadn't even wanted to date the guy. So why did my stomach contract when he said them?

'Do we?'

A pause. 'Yes. Because there's something you're not telling me and I think I need to know what it is.'

There was so much I wasn't telling him I could write an encyclopedia on the subject. 'Not today, Mank, OK? I mean, yes we should talk and I'll tell you what you want to know, but not today. I am having the day of all days.' I mean, I wasn't going to *really* tell him, but he wouldn't know what to ask and I could ad lib.

Steadiness returned to his voice. 'OK, not today. But maybe tomorrow. I know a place.'

'Thai?'

'No, you can dress casually.'

Understandably, I think, I hung up.

I got out of the cab right in front of Mank's precinct, which was a problem if he wanted to talk but a quick walk to my apartment. It was an incredibly hot summer day. I know from experience that the platform for the Lexington Avenue line at Grand Central Terminal is without question the most humid spot on Earth. So even without air conditioning but with open windows, the cab was decidedly better.

It isn't a long walk from the cop shop to my front door. This is Manhattan. If there's a square foot of space and nobody's making money from it, something has gone horribly wrong. But it was enough of a trip that I noticed the two men, coming from either direction, who seemed to be waiting for me to reach them.

They weren't wearing dark trench coats. Maybe that guy wasn't my only problem. I put my hand in the pocket of my jeans. I carried a Mace spray on my key ring that I had never used.

My initial plan was to walk by the men while paying special attention to their hands. The last time someone had (successfully) tried to abduct me I'd been injected with a sedative and woke up in restraints. And I felt just a little nauseated at the memory. That wasn't going to happen again. I'd just walk by them and get inside.

But Plan A wasn't going to get a chance to be implemented. The two men met right in front of the entrance and looked at me. I thought of asking if I could help them but then I realized I really didn't want to help them. I felt their purpose was likely something I'd be better off not participating in.

'Ms Stein?' The man on my left was speaking so I looked at the man to my right. Magicians like to work with *misdirection*, making the audience look in one direction when the work is being done in the other. I figured that's what they were doing, and as it turned out I was right.

The man on the right was just pulling a syringe out of his jacket pocket. Concealing it was the only reason to be wearing a jacket on a day this hot.

I didn't care if this guy wanted to inoculate me against every disease on the planet (you never know on the streets of New York) but he wasn't going to do it now. I reached out and grabbed his right wrist, the one holding the syringe, which had just cleared his pocket.

'Ow,' the guy said in a very conversational tone.

I twisted his wrist a little. A little for me, not for him. I heard something crack and he shouted out as he dropped the syringe. It was plastic so it didn't shatter but I made sure to step on it as I pivoted, still holding the guy's arm. I pulled him off his feet and tossed him directly into the other man, who had just realized something was amiss with their plans. While I did that I swept the non-syringe guy's legs with my left and he sat back, hard, on the pavement.

His friend (or colleague; maybe they didn't like each other) didn't fare quite so well. I saw to it that he paid for his attempt by landing on his face on the pavement in front of my building. The people walking by stopped for a moment to look and one thought about taking video on her iPhone but realized the fun stuff was over and she'd just be watching a guy bleed on the sidewalk. She moved on as well.

Syringe Guy was stunned, to say the least. He wasn't talking or opening his eyes, but he was breathing. I figured he'd be out for a few minutes. It's not like in the movies where someone is knocked unconscious and stays that way for hours without a mark on them.

I let go of what I assumed was Syringe Guy's broken wrist and turned my attention to the one sitting and looking embarrassed at my feet. 'Now that I have your attention,' I said, 'who sent you?'

'I don't know what you're talking about.' Seriously. He tried that one.

I took a step toward him and he scooted back on his butt, which couldn't have been fun. 'Don't insult my intelligence,' I said. 'Because I could do to you what I did to him, except now I'd have time to prepare.'

His eyes widened a bit and he made a noise like a mouse trying to squeeze through a hole that's too small for him. He swallowed. 'What do you want?' he said.

'I told you. I want to know who sent you.' Honestly. 'But first, I have a question I've always wanted to ask. How do you get a job like the one you have? I mean, is there a jobs site that lists openings for henchmen?'

Deciding he should show some bravado, even while on his ass in front of an apartment building, the guy curled his lip. The mouse, he was trying to imply, had become a rat. 'I don't have to tell you nothin'.'

'Not only was that poor grammar, but you also overlooked the fact that I can beat you to an unrecognizable pulp whenever I want. So you're going to tell me. Now. Who sent you?'

He looked at the ground in front of his feet and probably considered spitting. He wisely chose not to exercise that option. But he didn't look at me when he said, 'I don't know.' That was *not* a wise choice on his part.

I reached down and grabbed him by the front of his shirt. Then with one hand I lifted him up off the sidewalk. But I figured he didn't need to be on his feet yet so I took hold of his shirt and hoisted him about a foot into the air and held him there.

'Who. Sent. You?'

His eyes were the size of Eggo waffles. His tongue was hanging out of his mouth. His breathing was, to use a word, forced. 'What the hell are you?' he gasped.

It was a question I'd spent a lot of time mulling over and I still didn't have a satisfactory answer. Not that I'd give him one anyway. 'I lift a lot of weights. Answer the question or I'll carry you upstairs in this apartment building and drop you off the roof. Because nobody will ever believe that a girl could do that so I have nothing to worry about. This is the last time I'll say it before you take a trip upstairs: Who sent you?'

'OK, OK! I'll tell you. Just put me down.' He was staring at the pavement longingly, which nobody ever does in Manhattan.

'I don't think so,' I said. 'You're not that heavy and I can do this all day. So tell me now and then I'll think about letting you down.'

He nodded furiously. To be honest, my arm was starting to get a little tired but I didn't show that. 'I don't know that much. All I know is it was a guy named Elroy set me up with it. He told me and . . . that guy . . . what to do.' He tilted his head in the general direction of his prone friend, who moaned lightly every now and again.

'What were you supposed to do with me after I was sedated?' I said that because making fun of the name *Elroy*, no matter how enjoyable, would gain me no advantage.

'Take you to an address on West 79th,' he answered. No doubt the same address where The Voice had taken up residence. He knew I wasn't going back there even with the police because I couldn't risk him telling the authorities about me.

'How are they going to feel when you show up empty-handed?' I asked.

'I'm trying not to think about it. Can I get down now, please?'

He'd said the magic word so I lowered him down to the pavement and loosened my grip on his shirtfront. He was going to need a new shirt. I didn't want to think about his pants.

'Maybe I can help you out,' I said.

He looked at me like I had two heads, which was an innovation my parents apparently had either rejected or hadn't considered at all. 'Waddaya mean, help me out?' he rasped. I must have been holding him a little more closely than I thought around his neck.

The less conscious of my assailants was starting to come to and tried to raise himself up by pushing with his palms like getting up from a pushup position. Except I had done damage to his wrist so he yelped and collapsed again to the sidewalk. The more talkative of the two gestured toward me as if to ask for assistance, so I grabbed the guy by his belt and raised him to a standing position.

'I think I can keep you out of trouble with your employers,' I answered.

He still looked wary, as was only natural. I had threatened to drop him off a five-story roof, something I had never intended to do but it sounded good. 'How?' he said.

'I want you to set up a meeting with Elroy.'

THIRTY

K en got home only a few minutes after I made it upstairs, having made certain my two new acquaintances, who obviously knew where I lived, had left. The one with the broken wrist was in no mood to stay and the other one, his instructions received, slunk back down the street as his friend complained about the pain in his arm. I'd like to say I felt bad about that, except that I didn't.

As advertised, Dr Eve Kendall had accompanied my brother to our apartment and it was obvious from the moment they walked in that she had not been enthusiastic about changing her travel plans to have this little confab. She wasn't complaining, exactly – that wasn't her style – but she seemed disgruntled and looked at her wristwatch a lot, no doubt calculating the departure time of the next flight to wherever it was she was going.

'I really don't see why we couldn't do all this on the phone,' she said to Ken. She slumped down in her kitchen chair and was barely looking at me. Maybe in her time of being confined by my brother Kendall had developed Stockholm syndrome and now believed she was in love with him. But I doubted it judging by the tone of her voice. 'I could tell you all the same things and be home at the same time.'

I sat down behind the kitchen table and tried to catch her eye. 'The thing is, doctor, we're under some serious time constraints and we need to know what you know about our parents. And since you weren't completely forthcoming with us the other night . . .'

Kendall's eyes flashed in my direction. 'Are you saying I lied to you?'

Ken spoke to her as a tolerant parent speaks to a grumpy eight-year-old. 'Well, Eve, you did say you barely knew our parents and then Fran saw your name listed on our adoption papers as a witness. That would tell us you weren't necessarily telling us all you knew. And since we've gotten some new information about them lately, and we knew that Dr Mansoor was trying to get in touch with us, you were the logical person to ask.'

Eve Kendall shook her head. 'I was on the form because there was no one else around at the time they were signing the papers and they asked me to witness,' she said. 'If you'd listened when I told you this before—'

Forgive me, but I'd had a day, and in fact a pretty serious week. What with the whole kidnapping, escaping, being threatened and followed, not to mention the news of Dad's death, I was in no mood and Eve Kendall was going to be the person (besides the two guys I'd met outside) who was going to bear the brunt of my mood. I slammed my hand on the kitchen table. Luckily it's an especially strong table because it just shook and didn't shatter.

'Enough!' I shouted. 'Nobody has been telling us the truth and this is our family we're talking about. I think we're entitled to know what you know, Dr Kendall. And frankly, I think the fact that you've withheld it from us for all these years should make you feel quite guilty. We could have had a sense of the people who brought us into the world and you deprived us of that. So tell us, right now, something that we can actually use.'

Kendall set herself and breathed, thinking things over. 'Well, your father was a brilliant surgeon,' she began.

My brother, sensing my mood, decided to play good cop. 'Eve, Fran is under a good deal of stress. Reminding us of things we already know isn't going to help. We understand they were working on a cure for cancer, even after the time when we were told they were killed in a road accident. And your name came up when that project was discussed. So why don't you start telling us something we don't know? Like why they faked their deaths?'

The good doctor's lips straightened out into a flat line. 'We're being totally honest?' she asked pointedly.

'Totally,' I said.

'Then you already know precisely why they vanished and tried to make it look like they had died. That was because you two were constructed from some grown and some harvested body parts and they were afraid the authorities were going to find out about you and perhaps try to take you and your parents into custody. So since we're being totally honest, why don't you tell me what's really going on here?'

Ken and I stared at each other for a few seconds and then we each had the same reaction: We shook our heads like we'd just awakened and turned our attention toward Kendall. 'All right, doctor,' I said when I could. 'So we're all on the same page. Dr Mansoor's extensive notes, which you told me would be in his car with him, were right where you'd said they'd be. And inside there was flight information to New York for both our parents, from different cities, on different days, less than two weeks ago. I'm guessing if they were in touch with him, they were in touch with you. So why were they coming to the city and why weren't they going to contact Ken and me?'

The open candor seemed to invigorate Kendall; her eyes brightened and she sat up straighter in her chair. 'Brad did get in touch about a month ago,' she said. 'They've actually texted or emailed a number of times over the years.'

I'll admit that stung. Instead of cutting themselves off from everyone they'd ever known, it seemed that when my parents disappeared, they'd kept in touch with everyone they'd ever known except their children and Aunt Margie. The sadness must have registered on my face because Kendall said, 'Oh, they wanted to call you, Fran. They wanted to call both of you. But they were more worried about your security than their own and I know it took every bit of strength they had not to get in touch. They were scared, even after all these years, that you were being watched.'

We weren't playing poker but it was obviously time for cards on the table. 'They were right,' I told Kendall. 'In the past week both Ken and I have had abduction attempts against us. I was restrained and had to be rescued by a lab technician or I don't know what would have happened to me. I've personally beaten up two separate people trying to sedate and kidnap me.'

Kendall looked aghast. 'People have been coming after you? After all these years?'

My brother nodded and his voice took on an air of seriousness it rarely exhibited. 'And there's worse news than that, I'm afraid. Our father's name came up in connection with a very strange instrument auction for over a million dollars in London, and then today Fran heard . . .' He actually choked a little on his emotions.

'I was told, and confirmed, that our father is dead,' I said. 'It happened right before he was supposed to fly to New York. I don't know any other details except that he was in France at the time.'

Eve Kendall sat back as if punched. 'Brad's . . . dead?'

I nodded. 'I saw the death certificate. I don't speak French, but it was official and dated.'

Kendall's eyes narrowed. 'Do you have an image of the certificate?' she asked. 'I *do* speak French rather fluently.' Of course she did.

I got my laptop and called up the picture of our father's death certificate. 'What does it say?' I asked. I turned the screen in Kendall's direction. She reached into her purse, which she had brought but said she'd left her luggage with her airline, and brought out a pair of glasses which she put on. She looked very carefully at the laptop screen.

'Brandon Eugene Wilder,' she read. She gave the date of death and it was exactly what I'd said it was. 'Cause of death: vehicular accident.'

The three of us looked at each other and the same word came out of our mouths at the same time: *'Again?'*

Kendall read the rest of the certificate but there was no significant information on it. She looked up. 'I don't know what to make of it.'

'It's entirely possible it's true this time,' Ken said. 'I mean, I don't want to think that, but what possible motivation would Dad have to fake his own death now? And not Mom's?'

I had been thinking exactly that. 'I think we have to continue to assume he really is dead,' I said. Turning my attention to Kendall, I said, 'Would you have expected to hear from them when they were here in New York?'

She nodded. 'And it's very odd that if Livvie were here in the city I wouldn't have heard from her. I might not have actually seen them, but I would have gotten a call or a text at least.'

'You'd think,' I said sourly.

Kendall's face was compassionate and sad. 'Please don't ever think they didn't want to,' she said. 'I think it's done them considerable damage not to talk to you for all these years. And now with all this happening to the two of you, it seems like they had good reason to be.'

Ken, ever the pragmatist (I'm being sarcastic; he's an emotional volcano and acts on rash impulses all the time), stood up and started pacing. It's what he does when he doesn't have a tech screen to hide behind. 'Tell us about this cancer project,' he said. 'Could it have something to do with everything that's going on?'

'I don't think so,' Kendall said. 'Nobody knows about it.'

'Nobody knows about us, except all of a sudden everybody does,' I pointed out.

Kendall shrugged. 'You make a good point. The cancer project came out of some previous work of your mother's that they ended up collaborating on. It was a method of healing.'

My brother kept pacing but he pointed at her as an indication he knew what she was referring to. 'Yes. People would heal at a greatly accelerated rate,' he said.

'Exactly. That led to them working on . . . you . . . and once you were there and they were taking care of you, they turned back to the project.'

'How does that lead to a cure for cancer?' Ken asked.

'Well, it's the logical extension, isn't it?' Kendall suggested, although I didn't see the logic myself. She could tell that and added, 'If you're working on a method of getting cells to heal themselves very quickly, isn't the next step to try to get them to heal *before* anything really goes wrong?'

I was processing that but Ken got the science portion of our parents' brains, or at least some of it, so he added two and two faster. 'So it's less a cure for cancer than a vaccine against it?' he asked.

Kendall tilted her head from side to side. 'Sort of. It finds cells that are vulnerable to mutation and heals them before the mutation can occur. I'm not sure it would be a shot as much as a series of treatments, but it's still in the testing stages as far as I know.'

Ken knows science but I understand people. 'And that would be worth quite a lot of money, wouldn't it?' I asked. 'Billions?'

'More like trillions, probably.'

A thought chilled my stomach. 'And a lot of companies would be left with no business if it worked,' I said.

'A very real concern,' Kendall acknowledged.

'There are people who don't want it to happen and our father is dead.'

'Yes,' Kendall said.

THIRTY-ONE

Five minutes after Kendall left, presumably for the next flight to Denver, Ken and I were conducting our version of a war room, meaning we were each doing something separate but in the same room. Aunt Margie, whom I'd kept in the dark about our father's death, wouldn't get off her shift for another three hours so this would be a strategy session for just myself and my brother. We'd have to try to keep from telling each other just how stupid Ken had been acting (I might have edited that last sentence).

But before we could start disagreeing we hugged because our father's passing was still a raw wound, and we couldn't do that when Kendall had been here. Neither of us cried except me and then we sat down to sift through the rapid developments on two fronts: The people trying to abduct one or both of us, and Caroline Seberg's murder. The two did seem somehow to be connected but not in a way we could prove. The link was the use of the name Brandon Wilder when bidding on the Gibson Poinsettia and we only knew that based on the word of a source neither of us had ever met quoting a source whose name we didn't even know.

It was a little puzzling, you could say.

'Who's this Elmo character?' Ken began.

I knew he'd gotten it wrong for effect but I corrected him anyway because it showed I knew more than him. 'El*roy*,' I said, 'and even the guys who came to sedate and deliver me didn't know. My best guess is Elroy isn't The Voice himself, but someone who works for him and was given this task to complete.'

Ken likes to cook. He's even good at it when he sets his mind to it. But mostly it's about him doing something while he's working or thinking too hard. He's a physical man and can't sit around pondering life's troubles for too long. So he got up now and started moving pots around while I sat at the kitchen table and did my thing, which is making lists.

It was going to be too depressing to make a THINGS WE
KNOW/DON'T KNOW list so I avoided that and separated the
UKULELE and THE VOICE elements of our activities to see if
I could find a link. That's what we do while we're trying to work
together.

No family is entirely functional.

The lights flickered for a moment but stayed on. 'ConEd is
going to have a rough day with all the air conditioners,' I said.
'Do you know where our backup generator might be hiding?'

'Closet.' Ken's level of communication drops when he's
concentrating on a task. It's hard to imagine, I know.

'Which closet?' I was starting to get a little weary and knew
Ken had charged up the day before; we try not to plug in the
same day if we can avoid it. If there was trouble with the electrical grid in the heat wave, I'd need to get the generator to
plug in.

'Yeah.' He was chopping onions. Others would cry; my brother
becomes monosyllabic.

'So the meeting with Elroy is set for two hours from now. I
figure I'll go alone.'

That got exactly the reaction it had been intended to get. Ken
stopped chopping and glared at me. '*What?*'

'So you *are* awake. Good. Now. Here's how I see the plan.
You'll stay out of sight. I'll handle the talking and if anything
goes sideways you'll be there to back me up. Sound good? OK,
then.' I had three items in the UKULELE column and none in
the other. Because what I knew about The Voice amounted to
what it's like to be strapped to a gurney and hear a disembodied
voice threaten your life. Not terribly useful information under
the current circumstances.

Ken wasn't in a mood to argue with me, largely because he
knew I'd just played him like a . . . cheap ukulele, perhaps.
'Where's the meeting going to take place?' he asked. He went
back to chopping onions and went into the fridge for some garlic.
I didn't know what he was making but it was going to require
after-dinner mints for sure.

'You'll love this – first the guy wanted to come pick me up
and drive me to the meeting with Elroy.' Honestly. I practically
reduced his friend to a fine powder, held him up in the air by

his shirt, and this lunatic thought he could get me with a cheap ploy like that.

'So he could stab you with a needle and take you back to the lab of Dr Mengele?' Ken shook his head. 'Where's the beef cubes I bought?'

'I left them on the window sill during a heat wave. Was that wrong?'

Ken pulled the package out of the fridge and got a pan heating on the stove with a little olive oil. 'So after you threatened to drop him off the building – that's my favorite part of the story, by the way – what did he say?'

'There was a bit of negotiation and we finally agreed on Washington Square Park near the arch,' I told him. 'It's outside, there'll be the usual crowds everywhere and we'll be able to talk without anyone being spirited away for some quick genetic testing. I'll remember not to spit into a cup for him.'

My brother nodded. 'Decent choice. I would have gone to the South Street Seaport for the same reasons plus there's a good ice cream place there.' Ken never doesn't have an agenda. It's actually an admirable quality.

'Maybe Elroy is lactose intolerant,' I said.

'Bigot.' He started the onions in the pan, stirring until they were transparent, then added the meat. The garlic didn't need as much cooking and could go in later along with some bell peppers Ken was dicing now. He was definitely getting in his chopping therapy.

And that was when Det. Miller decided to bypass Mank and call me when he wanted to ask me a question. How quaint.

'There's a package in a locker in Grand Central Terminal,' he said. The man had a lively conversational style. 'We think it's attached to the ukulele murder.'

'So go get it,' I said. 'What do you need me for?'

'It's addressed to you and your brother.'

'And you can't get a warrant?' I said. I didn't need the uke and the cops wanted it. Let them take it on.

'I can, but it'll take time and I can get you the key in twenty minutes. You get it and you call me.' Miller must have trusted me to some extent or he'd have insisted on going along to pick up the package.

'Fine. Send the key over. But I can't go for a couple of hours.'

'Still faster than a warrant,' he said. 'Call me as soon as you get it.' And he hung up. Nice guy.

It wasn't until that moment that I realized the only address he had for me was at my office. 'We're going to have to swing by the office after Elroy,' I told Ken, looking at my list again. 'Then we have to go to Grand Central.'

Ken wasn't listening. 'Yup,' he said.

My list now consisted of six UKULELE entries, including the fact that the auction had taken place *before* Caroline Seberg was murdered. THE VOICE was offering such helpful tidbits as 'Definitely Male.' That reduced the suspect list to half the people on Earth. You laugh, but before that it was everybody except me and probably Ken.

'There's no connection except Dad,' I said aloud.

The beef and onions cooking were creating an aroma that was unexpectedly distracting. I remembered I hadn't eaten since this morning, and that had been a good ten hours now. Well, not a *good* ten hours. You know.

'What do you mean?' Ken asked. He was collecting spices and herbs from the cabinet and now I was lost because while I appreciate spices and herbs, I have no idea which ones go with what or why they should be incorporated into a meal.

I did have the ability to go into the small pantry (really a tiny closet) and pull out some Italian bread I'd bought the day before. I set up a cutting board on the door table and started to slice it. 'I mean, the only common element that our investigation into Caroline Seberg's murder and the person who tried to probe me in unspeakable ways is Dad. Obviously The Voice wanted to know about Mom and Dad and thought I knew where to find them. Then Dad's name was used as the winning bidder for the Gibson.'

'So what does that tell us?' Ken asked. He's good at keeping me directed. Maybe he won't answer the question but he can get me to answer it in ways I wouldn't have thought of on my own.

'Not necessarily that The Voice had anything to do with the auction,' I said, speaking at least partially to myself. I'm not great at slicing bread. Let's just say that I have a problem with consistent thickness. You get what you get. It's bread. 'I'm not really sure The Voice knew the names Mom and Dad were using. We're not even sure they're still using those names, but Dr Mansoor was still calling them Brad and Olivia as we can see by his notes about their flights to New York.'

'That's what it *doesn't* tell us,' Ken pointed out. 'What *does* it tell us?'

I had sliced the whole bread. Would we eat the whole bread in one sitting? Maybe; Ken eats like a beluga whale and maybe Aunt Margie would be home to eat a little later. 'Is there anything else you need sliced?' I asked.

'Stop deflecting. What does it tell us that both of our problems seem to involve at least one of our parents?' Ken was carefully stirring the food in the pan, making sure nothing was going to burn. He was sprinkling various things over the pan.

I wasn't getting off the hook. 'That the same people are behind both of them? That doesn't seem possible.'

'Maybe, but a lot of things don't seem possible. Like us. Let's pretend for a minute that it *was* possible and worry about the explanation later. How would that work? What does it tell us?' I honestly didn't think Ken had a particular answer in mind. He wanted to see what he could get out of me.

I drew a line from one side of the list, where I'd written *Dad's name on uke sale* to the side where I'd written *The Voice looking for Mom & Dad*. Underneath the line I wrote *message?*

'Maybe it tells us The Voice was at the auction,' I said.

Ken nodded as if he'd completely been expecting that response, and if he wasn't already dishing out his creation over microwaved rice, I would have called him on it. But now I was hungry.

'There's one other possibility,' he said. 'I think you're right about that and you should get on the phone to your buddy with the billions. But I think there's something that goes with it.'

I sat down at the table after getting a water bottle for me and a beer for my still-really-a-frat-boy brother. 'What goes with it?' I asked.

Ken sat down across the table from me. 'Maybe we're approaching this meeting tonight the wrong way.'

I dug in and it was really good, if simple. I don't mind simple when it's really good. Once I'd cleared my mouth I asked, 'How do you figure?'

'Maybe Elroy isn't working for The Voice,' Ken said. 'Maybe The Voice is working for Elroy.'

THIRTY-TWO

I t was summer, so the sun wasn't quite down yet even at seven-fifty. I could hear Ken in my earphones saying, 'Do you see them yet?'

I'd called him on my cell and then pretended I was listening to music. Whenever anyone walked by I started softly singing 'Godawful Things' by Lake Street Dive and that enhanced the illusion. I thought. Very quietly I said to him, 'Not yet. You'll hear when they show up, so stop asking me questions.'

I was standing near the west side of the Washington Square Park arch, the one that you've seen in all the movies and that was, decades ago, the center of the drug trade in New York City. Now drugs are spread around a little better and the park has become a tourist attraction for some and a refuge for others. One man used to come here with a portable piano and let you lie underneath it while he played a song you requested. It's a living. Or maybe not.

Ken was stationed somewhere nearby but I didn't know exactly where. Ken thought that was best because he was in his special commando mode and no, that doesn't mean he was without undergarments. At least, not that he told me, which was wise. I suppose he felt that under the duress of torture it would be wise for me not to know his exact location. That's how much confidence he had in me, and I had reminded him that I'd broken one wrist and caused a possible concussion only this very afternoon.

I was watching a man carrying some balloons because that seemed like the sort of thing an evil henchman would do for cover, but he walked right through the arch and made a right turn. I reminded myself to stop thinking I was in a spy movie.

The air was thick with humidity and very hot. Usually that doesn't bother me much but tonight it was especially noticeable, probably because I needed a charge. Everything is heightened when my batteries are running low.

I checked my phone and sure enough at eight p.m. exactly my

afternoon assailant who had set up the meeting turned the corner
on West 4th Street on to University Place. He was with two other
men, neither of whom was the one who had held the syringe this
afternoon and therefore had taken the brunt of the punishment.
That'd teach him to walk around with sedatives to force on
women, the perv.

Neither of his companions was wearing a dark trench coat,
which made sense when the temperature was 97 Fahrenheit. It
was a bit disappointing, though. I thought I could lay all my
demons to rest at once, but there would still be at least one of
them out there when this dizzy scenario was played out.

As the three men approached me I took the buds out of my
ears and pushed them into my left hip pocket. My phone was
hanging on my belt so Ken would be able to hear the conversation, but turned toward me so the three guys would not be able
to see it was on a call and not a music app.

'Where's your buddy from this afternoon?' I asked the guy I
knew. 'Is his arm still smarting just a bit?'

He smiled but it was more like a grimace. 'He sends his
regards. Sorry he couldn't make it.'

'I'll bet. Who are your new friends?' I emphasized the *s* for
Ken's benefit.

The two newcomers to our melodrama were a thin, small man
with a very small mouth who always appeared to be saying,
'Oh,' and a taller one, muscular and cold-looking. Tonight cold
wasn't such a bad thing, but he wasn't making it look good. I
turned toward the smaller one. 'You must be Elroy,' I said.

'Actually, that's me,' said the taller man, whom I had mentally
named Brutus. 'You called me here tonight, Miss Stein. What
exactly is it you want from me? It's a hot night and I'd prefer
to be indoors somewhere.'

'Well, you sent my two pals from this afternoon to drug and
abduct me,' I answered. 'I'd really like to know why.'

While his smaller companion continued to look like he was
constantly breathing in but never breathing out, Elroy let out a
sigh. 'Really? That's it?'

But I had noticed something about their posture. 'No. That's
not it,' I said. 'Right now I want to see everybody's hands.'

They stared at me.

'Out of your pockets. Now. I'm not kidding.' Anybody carrying a waiting syringe wasn't going to sneak up on me this time.

Elroy, naturally, had not bothered to keep his hands in his pockets; they were out where I could see them. He was the brains of the outfit. Any dirty work would be carried out by his minions.

I saw them each look at him and he nodded, although somewhat reluctantly. I guessed that drugging me up and 'helping' me out of the park had been next on the agenda. The two other men brought out their hands and showed them to me as if I were inspecting to see if they'd cleaned their fingernails.

'OK,' I said. 'Let's keep them that way. So. Who told you to kidnap me and why?' I turned my attention back to Elroy but made sure my peripheral vision wasn't letting me down. Elroy's respiration remained steady.

'I think you misinterpreted our intentions,' he said.

'Do you?' I folded my arms so they'd be higher up on my body if I had to hit people, which was not off the agenda just yet. 'Tell me. After I'd been sedated and abducted once on the streets and then approached by your pal here and his pal, who I assume had to visit the emergency room today, with a syringe in their possession, what *should* I have assumed they wanted? How come your two friends didn't want to take their hands out of their pockets? It's certainly not because it's so chilly tonight. So what?'

I wondered how close Ken had come. I didn't see him in front of me and wasn't about to give away our strategy by looking around for him. But I got the feeling this would not end as a quiet conversation. While I certainly could have handled all three of these guys if I had to, I hoped I'd have some help if/when the time came. Instead I was watching a young woman on rollerblades circling around virtually everyone in the park to the amusement of some and the annoyance of others. Everybody hadn't had the same day.

'OK,' Elroy said. 'We were hired to do a job. We tried to do it and you stopped us. Good for you. So what exactly do you want from me right now?'

'The name of the person who hired you.' That seemed simple enough.

Elroy laughed lightly. 'You can't really expect me to tell you that,' he said. 'I have a reputation in some areas, and you don't get to keep it if you run around telling everybody who hires you for things that aren't . . . typical.'

I let out a slightly theatrical groan. 'And on the other hand, I could easily beat the crap out of all three of you and then turn you in to the cops. That would be slightly worse for that cherished reputation, wouldn't it?'

It was Elroy's turn to fold his arms across his chest. He smiled sourly. 'Why didn't you?' he asked.

'Why didn't I what?' The woman on the rollerblades was heading my way.

'Why didn't you call the police? By your own admission you were drugged and kidnapped. Now, I don't know anything about that incident, you understand, but I'll take you at your word.'

'You can't expect me to believe—'

He held up a hand to stop me. 'Given that it happened, why exactly didn't you report that incident to the police?'

I definitely wasn't going to give him an honest answer to that one: *Yeah, it's because my brother and I are manufactured human beings and we don't want the authorities to know about us.* That wasn't going to happen. 'What makes you think I didn't?' I asked. Ball back in Elroy's court. The guy with the 'o' mouth inched a little toward my left side. I took a step to show him I'd seen the movement and he stopped.

'I have certain connections in this city,' Elroy answered. 'If that happened and there was a police investigation, I'd hear about it.'

'What, do they put out an Elroy signal from the roof of City Hall whenever you're needed?' Now the guy on the right was moving toward me in tiny increments. 'Don't,' I told him aloud. He held up a palm and stopped moving. I took a step back to even out the distance between us.

'So why didn't you call the police?' he repeated.

'Who hired you to take me?' *I* repeated.

'Fine.' Elroy spread his hands in a mock gesture of capitulation. 'I was hired by a corporation. My contact, who has a contact who knows the original client, is a person I know only by the name Myra.'

'Ooh, a girl,' I cooed sarcastically. 'How equal-opportunity of you. How do I find this Myra? Because I'm tired of being followed all over New York and not knowing who's doing the following or why.'

The woman on the rollerblades was getting awfully close, and fast. As she zoomed toward me I instinctively looked at her right hand.

It was holding a syringe with an exposed needle.

This wasn't 1976 and it wasn't that kind of park anymore but I didn't have time to think about that because just as she got to me she held it out toward my right hip. My guess was she planned to hit me with the needle and then one of the men would push the plunger to give me the sedative because she was skating way too fast.

At the same time the two men on either side of Elroy moved toward me, probably to grab my arms while the assault was being made. I had no time.

I moved my hip out of the way at the same moment that I could grab the skating woman's shoulders. I couldn't get a hand on her wrist because I needed both of my hands to lift her. That meant I wasn't able to twist the syringe out of her hand. It was important to stay clear of it.

The best way to avoid being injected was to create distance between myself and the person holding the needle, and I felt the best way to do *that* was to throw her, hard, into the face of the man on my right. He got caught in the mouth with a rollerblade, which I would have found amusing if I'd had time. It fell off and he was stuck with it between his teeth. What was left of them.

The syringe did not fall from her hand, though. She was good.

While she and the guy with the mouthful of rollerblade (and whatever it had skated over) were disentangling themselves I pivoted to the left to confront the guy with the O for a mouth. But I didn't have to.

Ken was already dealing with him, holding the man's arms behind his back with one hand and smacking him upside the head with the other. The guy never stood a chance. He dropped to the concrete like a ton of . . . well, a ton of anything weighs two thousand pounds, so fill in your commodity.

I thought that would leave us with just Elroy to subdue but Ken yelled, 'Frannie!' and pointed as he ran toward me.

The woman had gotten up and was charging at me again, this time on one blade (she was *really* good), still wielding the syringe. Even as she skated I saw her push the air out of the syringe. She wasn't kidding.

Because I'm faster than the average . . . well, any human, to be honest, I had just enough time to pick up the nearest large chunk of loose asphalt, which admittedly I had made just a little more loose, from the pavement. I flung it hard right at the rollerblader's front wheel.

She couldn't react quickly enough and bumped hard on the rock, falling headfirst and rolling when she hit the ground. Ken got there in time to step on the hand that held the syringe and crush it. The woman yelped a bit with his foot on her hand.

I got to his side while I looked around. Elroy had vanished into the evening, leaving not so much as a pheromone in his wake. It figured.

All we had, then, was the rollerblader. 'Let up off her hand,' I said to Ken. He looked a little disappointed but I reached down for her other arm and when he removed his stupid giant foot (the one that had probably just helped save me from another abduction) I pulled her to her feet by the arm that probably didn't hurt quite as much.

'Nice to meet you, Myra,' I said to her. 'Why don't we go someplace where we can talk?'

THIRTY-THREE

'I don't know anything,' Myra said.

'Oh, don't sell yourself short,' Ken told her. 'I'm sure you know *some* things.' That's Ken being witty.

We were sitting in a minuscule coffee shop three blocks from the park. I hadn't wanted to let Myra assess escape routes for too long during transit, but I also didn't want to be so near the scene of our little brouhaha (which had attracted a grand total of no interest from the gathered populace, other than an iPhone video of me throwing the rock in Myra's path, which would surface on YouTube later that night) that Elroy, wherever he'd slithered off to, would be able to find us and exact his revenge. Yeah, you read that right. Exact his revenge.

We'd taken the only booth in the place and Ken had sat to Myra's right, ensuring she couldn't slip away. She'd have an easier time sneaking around the Metropolitan Museum of Modern Art than my brother in a diner booth.

'You know who hired you and what your instructions were,' I said, ignoring my brother's hilarious comment. 'Let's start with those.'

'Do you think that's how this works?' Myra said, staring straight into my eyes despite her having an iced coffee on the table before her. I'd ordered another of those for myself and my brother had gotten a vanilla milkshake because Ken. 'You think you beat me in a fight so the only option I have is to tell you everything you want to know?'

'That's how it works in the movies,' Ken muttered. He's not so much for questioning and tends to let me handle anything that requires, you know, words.

We had managed to disarm Myra, who'd been equipped with two more filled syringes and a straight razor. Her hand wasn't broken but had a nasty bruise, so when I was patting her down (because there was no way I was going to let Ken do it) she hadn't offered much resistance. We'd found a cell phone, which

I'd pocketed, and a small wallet with two credit cards issued to 'Kristen Washington,' a made-up name if ever I'd read one. Ken had taken everything but the phone because he had actual pockets that you can fit things into. I want an explanation, fashion industry, even though I know it's about dudes wanting to see the curve of woman's hips in tight pants. I reminded myself to take on the patriarchy one of these days. Maybe I could get Mank to help me.

'That's *not* how it works in real life,' Myra snapped at Ken. 'If you're not going to kill me – and you're not – you have no leverage. So I can sit here and not answer you until you get tired of the whole thing and let me go.'

I needed to take control of the conversation. 'We know you hired Elroy to abduct me, and when the attempt this afternoon didn't work you decided to take matters into your own hands. That's actually enough.'

'But we're *not* going to let you go.' Ken was eyeing, of all things, the plate of French fries that the people at the table next to us had just received. There are times you have to wonder. 'We need to know some things. You know those things. That's how this *does* work. Because right now you can't call anyone, you know you can't beat us physically, and I can sit here blocking your path for days if I have to.'

Myra was not petty enough to point out that at some point he'd have to use the restroom, largely because she knew I'd take Ken's place and keep her in check just as efficiently. I had, after all, flung her into another person, whom we'd left bleeding and at the very least stunned in Washington Square Park.

'Elroy will be looking for me,' she said. 'He probably followed us here. He'll be getting me out because he knows how valuable I am and he can order up seventeen guys to fight you off if he wants to.'

I didn't sneer because that's just not me. I'm more a *Seriously?* blank-look sort of woman. And I used it on Myra right now. 'If Elroy could get seventeen guys capable of fighting us, why'd he send the two – no, *three* bozos – we beat the hell out of today? No, you're on your own, Myra, and frankly, I don't see why you're staying loyal to the people who hung you out to dry and failed in every attempt to do whatever it is you're trying to do. So why not answer those two simple questions: Who hired you and what were your instructions? Because otherwise we can walk you over to a police precinct where we have friends and wait for the YouTube video of you trying to sedate me to surface.'

She flattened out her mouth as she realized (incorrectly) that she had no way out. The fact was that we'd never have taken her to the police for fear that too much information about us would come out. Mank already wanted to have a serious talk with me and I hadn't even started to make up my answers yet. But we also aren't in the business of arresting people. We were in the business of finding birth parents. For other people. And identifying Caroline Seberg's killer. That was something of a side hustle at this point.

'Here's what I can tell you,' she said, staring at her iced coffee as if it were her father confessor. 'There are people I don't know who want you taken alive. I don't know what they're going to do with you once they get you. That's not my end of the deal.'

'What people?' I demanded. 'I'm tired of playing games. Who, exactly?'

Myra seemed to take a long time to think that over, but that was in my view. In her own mind it probably felt like a second. 'The main guy is named Bob,' she said. 'I didn't get a last name, but I saw him once. He's kind of short and has gray hair. No beard.'

'Does he wear a dark trench coat?' I asked.

Myra looked at me like I'd asked if Bob was a tentacled visitor from the planet Orbach. 'It's, like, a hundred degrees out,' she said after a moment.

So maybe The Voice hadn't been tailing me in front of Mank's precinct window. That was useful, even if I didn't know how right at this moment.

'OK.' Ken decided to take over because I was being insane. 'Bob is an older guy, not tall and he's in charge of the project to kidnap us?'

Myra shook her head. 'Oh, not you,' she said to Ken. She pointed in my direction. 'Just her.'

It took us a moment to absorb that. 'Just me?' I said. Granted, it wasn't my wittiest comeback but I didn't understand what I was being told. 'Why?'

She shrugged. 'I don't get that kind of information,' she said.

Ken, seeming insulted that the nefarious Bob didn't want to grab him, was recovering faster than me. 'So this guy Bob wants to kidnap my sister. How much was he paying you to do it?'

Myra looked up. 'I don't discuss that,' she answered.

Ken is very protective of me. Any threat will be met with his full fury and believe me, that's not something you want to receive. He spoke through clenched teeth. 'How. Much.'

Myra got the message. 'Three hundred.'

My eyes felt like they'd opened up about a foot. 'Three hundred dollars? All this for three hundred dollars? Were you and the Pips splitting it three ways, or was it a full three large apiece? Hell, I'll give you four hundred to leave me alone!' I didn't have the money in my purse but I started rummaging around in there for effect.

Ken was grinning and Myra, who probably had not grinned since she got a gold star in kindergarten, shook her head at me. 'No, you don't understand. They're paying three hundred *thousand* to bring you in.'

I sat back. 'Oh.'

'And this Bob guy,' Ken was amused but the whole full-fury thing was still on his agenda if necessary. 'He's been after my sister all this time? Like that's his full-time job?'

Myra bobbed her head a bit, *yeah, sort of.* 'Pretty much. Except he had to take a couple days off maybe a week and a half ago.'

'Why?' I said. 'Was there someone else he needed to kidnap?'

'No, from what I heard he had to go to London.'

Oh, wouldn't that just figure. 'Don't tell me,' I said. 'He went to an auction.'

'Yeah, of a ukulele. Can you believe it?'

THIRTY-FOUR

We 'dropped Myra off' at the 14th Street subway station and saw to it that she got on the 5 train and that she didn't get off before it left. Even if she decided to bolt at the next stop we still had enough time to head in the other direction and go home with no concerns that she might be able to pick up our trail. I mean, they knew where we lived but it was the principle of the thing. I guess.

If we had been really ruthless operatives, I suppose we would have seen to it that Myra was incapacitated somehow. We could have killed her, I guess, but that's so not what we do. Besides, murderers really shouldn't date cops. It's sort of a professional conflict of interest on both sides.

Neither one of us spoke for a while as we walked. There was a lot to process. I had a thousand loose ends and I'd never learned to crochet. On the one hand, I finally had the connection to use on my list that joined The Voice to Caroline Scberg's murder. But somehow gaining that information had just made the whole picture more cloudy, not less.

The problem was, the connection didn't make sense. Ken and me being the way we are had nothing to do with Caroline as far as I could tell. She was just the unlucky crooked auction dealer who had somehow crossed the wrong buyer and paid a really steep price for it. If she hadn't contacted the K&F Stein agency, she'd probably still be dead as far as I could tell.

But it seemed like someone was truly desperate for us to notice Caroline's murder and to investigate it. And it was looking more and more like that person was Augustus Bennett. Except that at five foot nine, Gus was only *fairly* short. Myra had been very clear about that: The Voice (Bob) was a smaller man. Could Gus be Bob?

Of course, maybe her idea of short and mine were two different things. I was dating a man whose gaze barely made it to my shoulders. And yet he was a really good kisser. Sometimes you just can't figure life.

My mind wasn't wandering so much as it was flitting from idea to idea and never landing on any of them, like a moth in search of a bright light to bother. Dad was dead. Probably. Aunt Margie would be home any minute and I'd have to tell her. The killer, if it was indeed Bob, had hit Caroline Seberg with a heavy candlestick. Caroline, back when she was Evelyn Bannister, was tall. If Bob was indeed as short as Myra suggested, would that have been an efficient way to knock her out? Would he have had to stand on something to reach?

Sometimes really strong heat makes my battery run out faster. I needed a charge. That was why we'd diverted our paths and not gone straight to Grand Central. I had to get back to the apartment and Ken was uncomfortable leaving me alone what with all the syringes floating around New York and Elroy still on the loose.

'None of it makes sense,' I said to Ken when we were about three blocks from the apartment. 'None of it adds up. It's just random facts that don't seem to relate to each other.'

My brother looked straight ahead as he walked. 'There's a guy who's following us and it's not Elroy,' he said.

I tried not to show any surprise. 'Is he wearing a dark trench coat?'

Ken bit his lip so as not to turn his head and sneer at me. 'It's ninety-five degrees. No.'

'What does he look like?' Two blocks. Should we veer off to avoid leading someone to our front door?

'I only got a couple of quick glimpses. Medium height, dark hair, mustache.' That wasn't awful for a couple of quick glimpses.

'Wearing?' I asked.

'Shorts and a polo. If he was wearing a woven belt and white New Balance shoes he'd be the model of a suburban dad.'

'You sure he's following us and not looking for a great frozen yogurt place?' I said.

'Stop.' Ken moved out of the flow of traffic and reached down to tie his shoe. 'He's all of a sudden really interested in that wig store. I think he's following us all right.'

I ventured a peek at the man. He was indeed in his fifties,

maybe. No paunch, which was refreshing. 'That's not a mustache. That's the shadow from the visor of his baseball cap,' I told Ken.

'Team?'

'Mets.'

'So, Long Island.' Ken stood up straight and we continued walking. I could only picture the man behind us picking up his pace again. 'Should we run for it?'

'He's a middle-aged suburban dad and we're two genetically perfect superbeings,' I hissed at him. 'I think we can take him. Should we divert or keep heading home? I need to plug in some time in the next ten minutes.'

'Keep heading home. It's quieter on our street.'

We turned the corner on to our street (I'm not telling you our address either) and actually slowed our pace as we approached the building. Ken didn't exactly lean over to whisper to me but made certain his voice was not audible from more than a couple of feet away. 'On my mark we turn and confront, before we get to our building. Yes?'

'Yes.' I was actually looking forward to it. Finally I could get some answers about what was going on and why. 'But you're going to have to do most of the confronting.'

'OK.' Ken walked a little more heavily, which for a guy his size makes a pretty noticeable noise. 'On three.' He meant steps. 'So one, two . . .'

We both stopped and turned at the same moment. Ken said, 'OK, buddy, what's the . . .'

But the man was gone.

There wasn't so much as a hint of him. Not a scent of after-shave, Ken informed me. Nothing.

'What the hell was that about?' My brother sounded just as frustrated as I felt.

'Worst intimidation tactic ever?' I attempted.

'Let's get inside. We have a remarkably inefficient air conditioner upstairs.'

We walked up the flights and unlocked the apartment door. Nobody had been home since dinner and we'd been foolish enough to turn off the air conditioning before we'd left for the meeting with Elroy. The place felt like it had been abandoned for seven years. I made a beeline for the air conditioner in the living-room window (it's actually attached by a hose to the window and stands on wheels because we have bars on our windows that won't allow for a unit to be installed) and turned it on.

I sat there on the sofa right next to the air conditioner for a moment. I needed a charge more than I'd realized, but something was nagging at me. 'The Voice is named Bob,' I said to Ken.

He flopped down on the easy chair, annoyed that he was farther away from the cool air than I was. Tough. 'I believe we've established that,' he said.

'We also believe that Augustus Bennett, in the guise of Gus the super, killed Caroline Seberg, in the guise of Evelyn Bannister,' I went on. It was for my benefit, not Ken's, that I was talking anyway. That was better because he was just going to be a brother and that wasn't what I needed right now. 'But we know Bob went to London for the auction.'

'Riding on a pony.' Ken sat back as the cool air reached him secondhand and closed his eyes. 'You should plug in.'

'Was there enough time for Gus to plan my abduction, take a break and go to London, and then come back and poison Caroline after bashing her on the head?'

'Sure,' Ken said. 'She made it back here in time to be bashed.'

'Caroline didn't *go* to London,' I reminded him. 'She was orchestrating the bidding online from her apartment, or one of her apartments, in New York. By the time we knew the auction had taken place, she was already dead. It's possible Bob made it back but he'd have left Sotheby's, gotten on a plane and gone straight to Caroline's to put on his Gus suit. Not to mention, Gus is not a small man. You saw him.'

'I saw him,' Ken's eyes remained closed.

'He wasn't small. Myra said Bob is a fairly short man. Either Bob didn't kill Caroline, or Gus isn't Bob.'

'I dunno . . . third base!' my brother said. He sounded groggier than I felt but I knew he'd charged up this very morning. He was just in a mood.

'Bob,' I said. 'Robert. Rob.' It made hideous sense. 'Kenny. Rob.'

'Rob who? And of what?' He amuses himself. It's half the game. Sometimes all the game.

'Rob Van Houten.' He'd been the one to tell me about Gus

Bennett. He'd given me the idea that Dad's name had been used for the anonymous bidder on the Gibson. My buddy Rob the billionaire had been playing me this whole time, and then – if I could get any sense of his height or lack thereof – had me kidnapped and strapped me to a hospital gurney.

Ken's eyes opened and he sat up. 'The rich guy?'

I nodded. 'The rich guy. Think about it. He's a collector of rare stringed instruments and he *told* me he wasn't interested in the Gibson. He *told* me Augustus Bennett was. He *told* me it wasn't worth one-point-two million and he *told* me the buyer had used one of Dad's names. I took him at his word because he was charming and wealthy and didn't seem to have any reason to lie. He was being helpful. But all that time . . .'

Ken was wide awake now. 'He was really Bob.'

'Yeah.'

'How tall is he?'

I considered all the research I'd done about Van Houten. 'I honestly have no idea.'

Ken shook his head. 'Wait. What possible motive could Rob Van Houten have to kill Caroline Seberg?'

'I don't know but it's got to have something to do with that uke. Kenny, you've got to go to Grand Central and find that package.'

'Now? Why?'

'Because it's a million degrees out and I need a charge so bad I can barely stand up,' I said, knowing not only that it was true (with the exception of my exaggerating the temperature by well over 999,900 degrees) but also that Ken couldn't argue with it. I had some private business to conduct while plugged in and didn't want him around to see me conduct it. 'Besides, I have to tell Aunt Margie about Dad when she gets home and I *know* you don't want to do that.'

'Fine.' He stood up and looked grumpy about having to go back outside, despite the fact that the AC had lowered the temperature in our apartment by maybe two degrees. 'Where's the ticket?'

'Stuck to the fridge with the magnet from the National Comedy Center,' I said. 'I promise I'll go the next time we need to claim a million-dollar ukulele.'

Ken was already in the kitchen fetching the ticket. 'Thanks a heap,' he said, and let the door slam behind him on the way out. He wasn't really mad but he wanted to use it for leverage at some later date.

I just sat there for a few minutes to try to stop being hot. But my brain wouldn't turn off. If Rob Van Houten really was the mysterious Bob he'd had Ken and me on his radar long before I'd called his number and gotten his incredibly polite assistant. He'd gotten wind of us and, being the kind of man I was now assuming he was, had done very thorough research on us. He might have had an inkling – in fact, considering what he'd said when I was strapped down, more than an inkling – about who and what we were and how we got to be this way. But he had to have us followed on the street to get to me and that meant he hadn't known where we lived.

Until today. The man who'd followed us here this evening could have been a Bob minion. Elroy had sent two men directly to my door, so he'd known where we were. Ken and I might have to move after all. I'd have to tell Aunt Margie so many things when she got home.

I needed more brainpower; that meant I had to charge right now.

So I stood up, which took more effort than I'd hoped, and walked into my bedroom. The charger was on wheels under my bed. Just reaching over to drag it out made me a little woozy; I hadn't realized how close I was to a dangerous power situation. It was good that I'd get to this right now. I plugged the charger into the wall.

My phone buzzed with a text and I glanced at it.

It was from Robert Van Houten.

I'm in town. Are you available?

The magnetic USB end of the charging cable just barely found its way into the port in my side. I felt the surge of a charge beginning and that relaxed me just a bit. But I was at least an hour from being fully charged. Should I set something up with Van Houten for then? Was that safe?

Not at the moment, I sent back. *Can we meet in a couple of hours?*

I lay back on the pillow. I was sweating. I had a window

air-conditioning unit in the bedroom because there were no bars on that window. Apparently my landlord didn't want anyone climbing in my living-room window but if they wanted to show up in my bedroom that wasn't an issue. For my landlord. The light tingle I get from charging was just starting to kick in.

Can't wait that long. Van Houten was in a hurry? Why? Had he already heard from Myra? *I'm right downstairs. Why don't you buzz me in?*

Holy shit. He knew where I lived. I cursed myself for going too long without a charge and then sending Ken away when it was clear someone was after us. Getting low on power makes my brain work slower too. I didn't even want to open my eyes, let alone sit up.

And that was the moment when all the power in my apartment went out.

THIRTY-FIVE

B arely able to raise my head from the pillow, I had to rely on the hired muscle in my agency. In other words, I immediately texted my brother.

He's here! Get home now!

Ken, fast as lightning in a crisis, texted back, *Who?*

I had to rally. Even if Ken *was* fast as lightning in a crisis, I'd probably have to deal with the darkness, the lack of cool air, and the possibly homicidal maniac who might very well have abducted me for study and was now hanging around somewhere in the vicinity of my front door. At least the lack of electricity would mean Van Houten couldn't pull the trick where you ring all the bells and hope someone buzzes you in. Maybe that would buy me some time.

Except then he texted me: *Never mind. Some1 came out 2 see what was going on with the lights and let me in. B right up.* My former friend and current foe was being cute with the texting while planning to . . . what? Surely not kill me. Myra had said they wanted me alive.

There was a rush of adrenaline involved with being in mortal danger so I could get myself out of bed and head toward the apartment door. Maybe I could lose myself on another floor. Did Van Houten know my apartment number? I had to assume he did, and was on his way even as we spoke. I could get down to Aunt Margie's apartment with a key I have because she's Aunt Margie. But what if he knew about Aunt Margie?

I informed my brother exactly who we were dealing with and he said he was on his way. I had no idea how far away Ken was so had no timetable on when he'd be back. In short, I was on my own.

Luckily there was a moon that night and we have windows. The apartment wasn't completely black. I made it to the door that led into the living room and opened it.

I was greeted with a flood of torches, as the British say.

Flashlights held by people wandering my hallway. A few were also carrying cutlery, for some reason. Either they'd been interrupted during dinner or they thought forks would be good defensive weapons. When the lights go out in New York City everybody looks for a good defensive weapon.

Mrs Mandorelli from 4-C walked by carrying a gardening trowel. It was bigger than a fork, I had to admit. She stopped when she saw me. 'Fran,' she said. 'You look terrible. Are you OK? It's just a brown out. You know ConEd.'

'I'm fine, Mrs Mandorelli. I just didn't get much sleep last night.' It was the default excuse when one of us needed a charge and was showing it. 'Where's everybody going?'

'Out, I guess. The air outside is hot, but at least there's a breeze once in a while. You coming?'

I desperately needed a place to roost. 'No, but are you going to be in your apartment? Could I just sit there for a little bit?'

Even in the dark (plus flashlights/torches) I could see her look at me like I'd suggested I move in with her permanently and raise my children there. 'I'm going out, Fran, sorry. But I promise you my apartment isn't any cooler or brighter than yours.'

Yeah. Thanks a heap, Mrs Mandorelli.

I didn't know any of the other people milling about, so I wished her well on her quest for less stultifying surroundings and watched them all shuffle down the stairs. At least that would slow someone trying to climb up to my floor.

Should I climb up to the roof? *Could* I climb up to the roof? Just standing now, adrenaline or no, was getting to be a chore. Where was that backup generator? If I could get a boost from that I might have a fighting chance. I figured the best bet was to head back into the apartment and look in the 'closet,' as my brother had so helpfully directed me.

It wasn't in the front closet, I discovered after locking all three of the locks on our door. That left the two bedroom closets and the small one in the bathroom, unless Ken had meant one of the kitchen cabinets, but why would the generator be there? My mind was definitely not operating at peak capacity.

I figured I'd know if it was in my closet so I dragged myself into Ken's bedroom while chewing on my lower lip just to keep myself feeling something other than fear. I'm not used to fear and it doesn't play well with me. My stomach was clenched. I was sweating, but there was this heat wave, see. Biting my lip gave me a sensation to concentrate on.

I'd just gotten the closet door open and was using my phone's flashlight app to assess the random socks strewn over the floor and the various sports equipment taking up space where a generator should be, and that was when the knocking started on our door.

'Fran?' That familiar jovial voice had a sinister edge to it now and I couldn't tell whether it was Van Houten's tone or my newfound viewpoint. I quickly decided it didn't matter.

I don't know why I hadn't thought of it before. I frantically texted Mank: *Someone's trying to break into my apartment.* All I had to do was wait behind my extremely locked door until the cops arrived.

'*Fran!*' Van Houten sounded more insistent. The knocking got louder. Even if I could find the generator now I wouldn't be able to charge enough to do much. I left Ken's bedroom mostly out of disgust and walked into the living room to await reinforcements.

Mank texted back: *What's the joke? We're dealing with a blackout here.*

The men in my life were not exactly reacting with the chivalrous heroism one might desire. *No joke! I need cops here!* That ought to be clear enough.

No answer right away. I figured the three locks could hold out at least until Ken made it back. Had he made it to the train? Were the subways out with the rest of the power?

I went into the kitchen, which was darker, and shone my flashlight around looking for a suitable weapon. I wanted something that wouldn't require me to get too close to Van Houten if it came to that. If I could reach him with, say, a knife, he could reach me with, say, a syringe and I couldn't count on my usual strength or speed feeling like this.

'Fran! It's me, Rob Van Houten!' No kidding, Rob. Why do you think I'm keeping the door locked?

More shaking of the doorknob as he must have tried to shoulder the door open, but this was a good New York City apartment door and those things are built to stand up to rampaging Visigoths. It would shake but it wouldn't open. Where the *hell* was Ken?

'Fran,' Van Houten's voice got softer, doing the we're-just-buddies thing again. 'I think you're going to want to let me in.'

That was the best he could do? 'Somehow I don't think so,' I said. 'I'm pretty sure you tried to kidnap me once and there's a decent chance you killed a client of mine. So don't count on getting inside this apartment.'

But he didn't answer. Instead there was a considerable shuffling sound and then I heard Aunt Margie, her voice strained, say, 'Don't let him in, Frannie. He doesn't know who he's dealing with.'

My stomach re-clenched itself and went stone cold.

'On the contrary, Fran,' Van Houten said through the door. 'I know *exactly* who I'm dealing with.'

'She didn't mean me,' I told him. 'She means if you even think about harming a hair on her head she can take you down in four different ways. She's just trying to decide on which one to use.'

I was full of shit, but I think I came across convincingly. Aunt Margie, while a tough reporter, couldn't punch her way out of a paper bag even if someone took the paper bag away. She did carry pepper spray on her keychain but I was betting Van Houten had relieved her of that.

'Let me in, Fran,' he said with an unearthly calm. 'You do want to see this lovely lady alive again, don't you?'

Aunt Margie tried to say something but this time she was muffled. Something was being put over, or into, her mouth.

He had me and he knew it. I walked over to the door and undid the three locks. The door swung open and I could barely see three dark figures enter my apartment because the entrance isn't one of the rooms whose window faced the moon that night. One of the figures was the general shape of Aunt Margie and her hands were being held behind her by a shape not much larger than she was. Myra had said Bob The Voice wasn't very tall and she hadn't been kidding.

The figure behind him, wearing a baseball cap (I couldn't see which team), was much taller and broader. The cap obscured his face. I was guessing that wasn't a bad thing.

'Now, Fran,' Van Houten said. 'Was that so hard to do?'

I wasn't about to answer that condescending question. I decided Bob, on top of everything else, was a misogynist. If I could bounce him and his bulky friend off a few walls, that would add to the pleasure. As it was I was lucky to stand in the center of my living room without leaning on the arm of the sofa for support. Although I was thinking about it.

'Are you OK?' I asked Aunt Margie.

Van Houten let go of her hands and she pulled a handkerchief out of her mouth. She looked at him. 'Classy,' she said. Then she turned her attention to me. 'I'm fine. You should have left us out there. He wasn't going to hurt me.'

'Oh no, that's not true,' Van Houten said. 'If you hadn't opened the door I definitely would have done your *aunt* here considerable harm. Now all *you* have to do, Fran, is come along quietly with my associate and myself and I won't be forced to prove it.'

What I wouldn't have done at that point for a USB plug and a couple of D batteries! 'I don't get it.' Stalling was an option. 'What does this have to do with a semi-rare ukulele that sold for over a million dollars? What interest do you have in me?'

Van Houten, if I was seeing him clearly (and I wasn't, although my pupils were adjusting to the darkness and my eyes are a bit more sensitive than most), looked surprised, of all things. His voice took on a quality of honest instruction. 'I am a collector of rare objects, Fran,' he said. 'You are possibly the rarest on the planet. But I have to be certain you're genuine.'

I was trying to summon adrenaline, which can help in short bursts, and was coming up with whatever hormone it is that is produced by disgust. 'So you bought a ukulele for over a million dollars and told me a fake name for the buyer to attract my attention?'

'I needed you to look for *me*,' he said. 'I couldn't find your home and your office was much too public a place. I needed to get you to come to me, after having heard rumors of such beings as you and your brother for years. So I asked my dear friend Evelyn Bannister to hire you.'

'You snatched me into a van from the street and my office was too public?'

He chose not to answer that one. So I attacked from another angle.

'You hired Caroline Seberg, under whatever name she was using at the time. Then once you attended the auction, way overpaid through Caroline for the only somewhat valuable ukulele so it wouldn't be traceable to you, and came back to New York, you killed her with strychnine. Why'd you do that when you'd just cracked her head?'

'She wasn't cooperating. She wanted another million dollars for the uke. That wasn't our agreement. As for the strychnine, well that was the plan and I never deviate from the plan.'

'Strychnine. Where'd you manage to get that?' I said. Aunt Margie was supposed to look terrified but she looked supremely pissed off. I could use that more efficiently than I could use my muscles at the moment.

'You've seen my lab, Fran. Do you think finding some strychnine would be a problem? Yes, Caroline was the conduit. But she had hired someone to steal the ukulele from a home in Maine because it was easy. It wasn't really valuable and there was no security around it. Then she took a commission on the listing *and* the sale. The case was in her apartment, but nothing else. But I never really cared about that silly instrument. I wanted you to look me up and mine is one of the first names you'd find if you Googled collectors of stringed instruments.'

'But you weren't at the apartment. The guy pretending to be Gus the super was.' If I kept him talking I could get all my answers. And keep him from hurting Aunt Margie.

'I'd left something there and he was supposed to retrieve it,' Van Houten said, seemingly proud of himself for being so clever. 'Unfortunately the idiot Elroy found for the job was unable to find the object.'

It clicked in my mind. 'The ukulele strings? Does that plastic wrapper have your fingerprints on it, Rob? Because I know where that is. Of course, I thought Gus the super was really Augustus Bennett, so I've made a few mistakes of my own.'

He looked sincerely amused. 'August Bennett? Oh, that would have been sublime. And when we get where we're going you can tell me about the strings and hand them over. But that's enough; you're just trying to distract me. I'm hoping I won't have to use the sedative this time. Just remember that Aunt Margie isn't as strong as you are.'

I knew something Van Houten didn't know, largely because my eyes *had* adjusted really well to the darkness (it was the heat and the lack of electric power that were getting me). I looked at Aunt Margie. 'You're pretty strong, aren't you?' I asked her.

'Strong enough,' she answered.

'I think Leonard here and I can withstand her if we have to, but we will use a great deal of force if necessary,' Van Houten said. 'Isn't that right, Leonard?'

The large man behind him, face hidden in the shadow of his cap, grunted. Then he picked up Van Houten from the back and flung him into the general area of our stove, where he landed in a sitting position and groaned.

'Leonard couldn't make it,' Ken said. 'I threw him down the basement stairs and stole his hat just before you came in. I guess you didn't see that with the streetlights out, huh, *Bob*?'

'Did you get the confession?' I asked.

Ken tapped his phone. 'Right here. He's going away for Caroline's murder and your kidnapping.'

Van Houten, eyes wide, struggled to his feet, raised a finger as if to make a profound point in the argument, and then ran for the apartment door, a move none of us was anticipating. But Ken and Aunt Margie could react quickly and were right behind him as he ran. I lumbered after them, my arms out in front of me to feel my way where it was especially dark.

Strikingly, Van Houten decided to run *up* the stairs toward the roof access, something we use on warmer nights (not as warm as this one) because there is a gas grill up there. Don't tell the building inspector. Van Houten climbed up the next two flights of stairs, Ken right behind him, Aunt Margie huffing a bit in third place and me rumbling up behind the bunch of them. They were barely visible from where I stood, and I was running out of gas in a hurry. After one flight I had lost them, but could hear their footsteps above me.

When I reached the door to the roof, now wide open, it was a surreal scene. You're never really prepared for New York without lights. I felt my way around, careful to avoid the perimeter of the roof, which was flat. But you could see the lights on in New Jersey, which didn't seem fair.

I made out the outlines of the three of them: Aunt Margie was farthest back, closest to me. I stumbled over to her and stopped. 'Careful,' she said.

Ken was about fifty feet away, standing with his shoulders back, resisting the impulse to try to reach Van Houten, who for reasons I couldn't begin to imagine was right on the ledge. And since he is Ken, he was making the issue all about himself.

'How come you took Fran but not me? Was it because I was too tough on the guy who tried to take me on the street?' he demanded.

'*What* guy on the street?' Van Houten said.

Ken looked even more livid. 'So I just wasn't good enough for you?'

I didn't think that was the way police negotiators operate but I'd have to ask Mank.

Mank! I hadn't gotten a text back. That did it. No more dates, even if he found an operating Thai restaurant.

'She can reproduce,' Van Houten answered.

Eww . . .

Ken took a step forward. 'Back off!' Van Houten said. 'I'm not going back to jail!'

Back to jail? 'You've been there before?' Ken said.

'None of your business.' For a friendly billionaire he was a strangely touchy guy. Must have been all the evil-genius-ing he'd been doing. 'Just back off and let me go and I'll leave the two of you alone.'

'No, you won't,' Ken said.

'No. I won't.' Van Houten nodded. Then he looked down as I saw flashing lights and a *blip!* of a police siren. Mank had come through after all. 'What's that?'

'The cops.' I was just strong enough to walk to Ken's side. 'Even if we let you go they'll get you, Rob. So walk on over here and let's try to figure this out.'

Van Houten nodded. I swear, he nodded and said, 'OK.'

And then he stepped off the roof. He didn't even scream on the way down.

THIRTY-SIX

'I have a *lot* of questions.' Aunt Margie was sitting at my bedside watching me charge. She'd located the portable generator (in the 'closet' Ken had mentioned, which was really the cabinet over the refrigerator in the kitchen that we never opened) just in time for ConEd to restore the power to our part of the city. So I was charging up finally and besides I now knew where the generator was stored. That was useful.

'I wish I had a lot of answers,' I told her. 'But there's something you need to know, Aunt Margie, and I'm sorry to be the one to tell you. My father is dead.'

'Dead!' Aunt Margie looked at me sharply.

'Yes. Apparently a car accident in France.'

The air conditioner in the window was humming and that was the only sound in the room for a long moment. Then Aunt Margie started to laugh.

Now, people process their grief in many different ways but I have to admit that was not what I would have expected. She laughed heartily until a couple of tears actually fell from her eyes. 'Oh Frannie,' she said when she could catch her breath. 'You really had me going there for a second. A car accident in France. Don't you recognize the pattern?'

'Well yeah, but a car accident *is* possible, isn't it? Dr Mansoor died in a car accident and we're certain of that.' I was gaining strength by the minute. The meter now read nineteen percent. I'd been really, dangerously, low.

'When they were packing to leave Brad told me I should tell you and Kenny they'd been killed in a car crash until you were ready for the truth,' she answered. 'He said that was the go-to explanation, and that if he had to, he'd use it again. I guess he got wind of this guy Van Houten sniffing around you two and he decided to send us a signal.' Everybody was sending us a signal all of a sudden.

It had taken a while to get to this point. I'd barely made it down the stairs before Mank came up to the apartment. Van Houten had, of course, been spotted plummeting off our building and the cops were dealing with it. I'd told Mank what I knew but not *all* I knew: That he was a tech billionaire with a fondness for stringed instruments, that Ken had a recording of him confessing to Caroline Seberg's murder and that when we'd cornered him he'd taken the wrong way out. All of that was true. The part about him wanting me to 'reproduce' in a laboratory I'd decided it was best to omit.

Mank had looked at me with at least as many questions in his eyes as Aunt Margie had in her mouth, but had taken my statement and gone on to deal with the, you should pardon the expression, fallout. He said he'd see me tomorrow and there were a lot of implications in those words.

'I'll bet my last dollar your dad isn't dead, and not your mom either,' Aunt Margie said. The cops were still questioning Ken, who had been the closest to Van Houten when he'd jumped, and who had the confession on his phone. That was going to take a while.

'I saw the death certificate,' I said, suddenly determined not to have hope.

'You want to see the one from the last time?' Aunt Margie's eyes actually twinkled. It might have had something to do with the tears from laughing.

I lay back on my pillow and shut my eyes, which felt wonderful. 'Can you give me a minute?' I asked her.

'Of course, sweetie.' Aunt Margie kissed me on the forehead like when I was six. 'You rest up. It's been a long day.'

'Long week.'

I heard her close the bedroom door and sat up, looking through my phone for the secure email address I'd gotten from Eve Kendall. I'd been working up the nerve to use it and decided that now was definitely the appropriate moment. Especially if Dad wasn't actually dead.

Dear Olivia, I typed. *This is your daughter Fran. Dr Kendall gave me your email but you shouldn't be angry at her. I've been hoping to talk to you for a really long time.* I went on at some length from there, but there are things I'm willing to tell you and things I'm not, and what's in that email falls into the latter category. I've gained a reputation in my field for being big and tough. I don't want to go back to just being big.

When I was done typing I let the pillow swallow me up and the next thing I knew it was about two hours later. My laptop was still on the bed and there was an email waiting there from the address I'd just used. I held my breath.

Oh, Frannie! You can't imagine how many times I've wished I could talk to you. Dad and I have been trying our best to stay away but the temptation has always been there. I'm heartsick that I didn't get to see you grow up. What you must have thought about me, abandoning you when you were such a little girl! I'm tearing up now just thinking about it. I'm glad to see from your email that apparently you don't hate us. That's been my biggest fear.

The second biggest was that you'd be discovered. We've heard rumors lately that someone had gotten information about you and Ken. We weren't able to do much about it but we've been busily keeping our ears open. Apparently this Van Houten man you mentioned was the only one who had any inkling. Where he got his information is a concern and we will try to find out.

Yes, my love, we. Your father is not dead. It's better for the moment that some people think he is, and so a certificate was issued and reports were logged in. But he's here, with me, and he was with you for some time this past week. You might have seen him in the street wearing a dark-colored trench coat. The man thinks he's James Bond. It wasn't until the temperature hit 95 that I convinced him shorts and a polo would do the trick. Seriously. He's incorrigible. And he just wanted to see you and Kenny for himself.

It's been so tempting to see you since we've been here in New York, the first time in decades. I visited your office a few days ago but the woman there – she seems very nice – said you weren't in (I think that's what she said) and I didn't have the courage to leave you a real message. I regret that.

I'm sorry you were put through so much, from the time we left until these past few days. But you were never in any real danger, I promise. I made sure Van Houten couldn't do you any harm. When I handed you back your cell phone at his lab I was so proud. You had found a way out of the predicament without my help. Substituting – we'll call it 'substituting' – for his assistant was worth it just for that. And when your dad left you at the apartment he saw Van Houten there. He's not a violent man but he does know how to dial 911.

I was sorry to hear about Aziz Mansoor and hoped to attend his funeral service in some sort of disguise but once we realized you and Ken were on a track toward Van Houten we were sidetracked. We visited Aziz's grave two days later. He was a nice man. You would have liked him.

It's time for me to sign off, Frannie. I'm glad you found this address; I don't know if I ever would have had the courage to contact you myself. Any connection with me or your dad could be dangerous. You should know that we're always aware of what you're doing (oh my, that sounds more ominous than it should!), we love you and we are very proud of you.

For the time being, it's probably best that you and I keep this line of communication to ourselves. If I tell Dad he's going to go into security mode and change all our email addresses, possibly sending money to Margie for you to move out of the apartment because he'll believe it's compromised. So I'm not going to tell him for now. I'll leave it up to you to decide if you should tell Kenny. I'd love for him to know we're OK but I don't know his nature as an adult. As a little boy he was impulsive. He might not know how to deal with that kind of information, your father might get wind of it and we'd be in the same situation. Like I said, you know him better than I do so I'll let that be your decision.

I promise you it will be much *sooner between messages next time. We love you both very much. And I think the work you're doing, to help people find their birth parents, is just wonderful. What lovely children we made. You make sure you two stay safe, now.*

I'll be watching.

Mom

I slept better that night than I had in weeks. Maybe years.

THIRTY-SEVEN

'It was the uke,' Ken said.

He does things like that – just brings up a topic out of the air with no segue or context. I think it's mostly for effect, but it's also because he's thinking about something and doesn't understand why you aren't too.

'What was the uke?' I'm always available if you need a straight line fed to you.

'The package at Grand Central. The thing from the key your pal Morris the cop sent along.'

'Miller.'

'Whatever. It was the uke. Want to see it?' Without waiting for an answer Ken got up from the breakfast door and briefly visited his bedroom, coming out with a package he'd finally picked up that morning that was exactly the size of a ukulele. 'Damned if I can figure out what's so special about the thing.'

He removed it carefully from the box, from which he had clearly torn off a good deal of wrapping. The instrument was small, as you'd expect, and had a brown wood for the body. The neck was a lighter tone with flowers painted on various frets. Painted on the lower half of the soundboard was the flower for which the uke was named, in red.

It looked, frankly, like a ukulele and wasn't exactly designed to help some poor high-school sophomore get to second base in the back seat of a Subaru. I laughed a little looking at it.

'A million two hundred thousand dollars,' I said in wonder. 'And once Caroline figured out that Van Houten was a homicidal lunatic she sent it to us, for all the good it did her.'

'You have to assume whoever inherits our pal Bob's estate will be somewhat, um, disappointed with what they can get back on this,' Ken said. He tried to play the uke but I got nervous just watching him pick it up and gently took it out of his hands. 'How do we figure out who gets it?'

'That's for his lawyers to sort out, but I think it should go back to the family in Portland, Maine if we can prove this is the one that was stolen from them,' I said. I put the uke back in the box, which had no case. It was probably a ukulele expert's nightmare to have it packed that way. 'Why do you think Van Houten asked her to steal a ukulele? Couldn't he have used something from his collection?'

I'll let you know right now that I had heeded my mother's advice and had not told Ken that I was in touch with her. If she thought he was impulsive at four she should see him now. I wouldn't have kept him from making some very public mistakes, perhaps in spaces like Instagram or Facebook where they never really get erased. There would be a time to let him know. This wasn't it.

'Everything the guy did was designed to get our attention, right until the moment he stepped off our roof,' my brother said. Like that was an image I *hadn't* been replaying in my head over and over. Could we have stopped Van Houten from jumping? *Should* we have? 'He was doing all he could to get us to find him.'

'Yeah,' I said. 'Well, we found him.' I stood up with no place to go. I mean, Rob Van Houten was an evil guy; there was no way around that conclusion. And his death, now that it had been universally reported, had drawn a great deal of attention. Mank and the NYPD were doing their best to deflect it from Ken and me but we still felt like we were under siege in the apartment and I still felt like maybe I could have saved his life. But for what? To spend it in prison? 'Did you find out anything about his previous stay in jail?' I asked Ken, knowing full well he'd have researched it overnight. Ken doesn't sleep when there's something on his mind. I had been drained of power and even after charging didn't feel like doing much.

'He got caught lying to the IRS eight years ago and was sentenced to eighteen months in a minimum-security prison for people who lie to the IRS,' Ken said. 'Got out in five.'

I shook my head. 'And that was what he couldn't bear to endure again?'

'I imagine the murder rap would have gotten him more than five months,' my brother pointed out. 'And in a nastier jail.'

Just to prove that he wasn't the only one who could research something (and to avoid telling him I'd emailed with Mom, which was burning a hole in my tongue) I said, 'I think I found Augustus Bennett, for what it's worth. He died a rather quiet death six months ago.' Ken gave me a look. 'Natural causes. It never made the papers because he wasn't using his own name, but the notice in a Central New Jersey paper had it listed correctly.'

'So he never had anything to do with the auction,' Ken said, stating the obvious.

'Just another lie my friend Rob told me,' I said. 'I so wanted to believe he was just a nice billionaire.'

'Nice Billionaire would make a great band name,' my brother said. It was time for me to leave.

Detective Richard Mankiewicz was seated behind his desk when I was allowed into his division squad room. He was on the landline and looked weary. I had a flash moment where I thought that he should plug in for a while to feel better. Sometimes I forget.

'There'll be a press briefing at three this afternoon,' he was saying. 'I can't tell you anything before that because frankly, everything I know has already been released.' He said a few words of dismissal and hung up the phone.

He regarded me closely. 'Want to get some lunch?' he asked.

'It's ten o'clock in the morning.'

'I've been up since seven a.m. yesterday,' Mank said. 'I could use some food.'

'Thai?' I suggested.

We ended up at a diner that was trying so hard to be a diner that it was really a parody of a diner. I didn't especially care since I was just having coffee and Mank didn't seem to notice as he tucked into a Reuben. My sense of smell was a little offended at this hour, but I decided my sense of smell should mind its own business.

'The press is wearing you out,' I told Mank just in case he hadn't noticed.

He chewed extensively and swallowed. 'No kidding. They're not asking that much about you but they want to talk to Ken.'

I closed my eyes at the thought and then looked at Mank. 'Try to avoid that if you can. The idea of my brother trying to dazzle a gang of reporters scares the living hell out of me.'

'I'll do what I can but you two should probably get a publicist to work with you on a temporary basis. It'll blow over in a few days, but they'll be a few rough days.' He took a sip from his Diet Coke. With a Reuben and fries. Men crack me up.

I recoiled at the thought of a publicist and then thought it over a little. 'Might not be a bad idea for a week or so. I'll see if we can afford it.'

'What, the valuable ukulele won't cover the expenses?' Mank asked. 'I hear it sold for over a million bucks.'

I felt my eyes narrow. 'How did you know about that?'

'I'm the NYPD. I know all.' He took another bite while I gave him a withering stare. 'OK. Miller called me, too. He thought the whole anonymous package thing smelled a little fishy and when we checked with the USPS we found that whoever mailed the package had insured it for five hundred thousand dollars and listed the contents as a rare ukulele. How many of those could there be in New York today? What are you going to do with it?'

'Give it back to the people it was stolen from. I don't want it.'

Mank, chewing, nodded his agreement. When he could, he said, 'Probably smart. That thing has bad juju.'

'Bad . . . juju?'

'Like us trying to find an open Thai restaurant in a city filled with them,' Mank noted. Then he studied the fries without actually eating one as a way of avoiding my eyes. 'Last time we talked, you know, before the billionaire took a nose dive off your roof, I said we needed to have a serious conversation.'

I'd prepared a very intricate and involved explanation of a lot of the things he was going to ask me about. I'd been preparing it, actually, for most of my life. How Ken and I came from a line of very strong, large people and how we'd trained all our lives to build up our bodies, how in our line of work it helped to be defensively capable and alert. It had never failed me as a cover story.

So I stayed silent until Mank looked up from his plate to

see my expression and I looked him directly in the eyes. Because, finally, he deserved it.

'OK, you're going to think this is the weirdest thing you've ever heard in your life, and you'll be right,' I said. 'Brace yourself.'

9 781448 312337